Queen of Hearts

Queen of Hearts

Dorian Sykes

www.urbanbooks.net

Urban Books, LLC
114 Norman Ave.
Amityville, NY 11701

ISBN 13: 978-1-64556-796-7
EBOOK ISBN: 978-1-64556-797-4

First Trade Paperback Printing May 2026
Printed in the United States of America

10 9 8 7 6 5 4 3 2 1

Distributed by Kensington Publishing Corp.
Submit Orders to:
Customer Service
400 Hahn Road
Westminster, MD 21157-4627
Phone: 1-800-733-3000
Fax: 1-800-659-2436

The authorized representative in the EU for product safety and compliance
Is eucomply OU, Parnu mnt 139b-14, Apt 123
Tallinn, Berlin 11317, hello@eucompliancepartner.com

Queen of Hearts

Dorian Sykes

Chapter 1

"Love don't live here, love don't live here anymore," Mecca sang while doing her morning exercises. She was grooving to Faith Evans. It was her theme song. Every morning she'd wake up at the crack of dawn and get her Jane Fonda on.

"Finished!" she said, out of breath. She had just completed her last set of squats, and they were indeed serving their purpose. Mecca was in perfect shape. She stood five foot seven with 140 pounds of ass and titties. Mecca was what niggas referred to as a red bone. Her hair was silky black and fell damn near to her behind. She was the total package.

Mecca stood in front of her workout mirror, looking at her calves and rear end. Satisfied that everything was at its best, she grabbed an awaiting towel and headed toward the bathroom. She showered while listening to Faith on repeat. After showering, she walked over to one of the two walk-in closets located in the master bedroom of her five-bedroom colonial.

Her home was located five minutes outside of Detroit, in Grosse Pointe. It was a bit of a suburb, and you had to have a few dollars to live out there. Her home was equipped with an in-ground swimming pool, an attached guesthouse, and a three-car garage.

Mecca and Matt, aka E-Way, had purchased the house some six months earlier after E-Way settled out of court for $2 million on a civil suit. One night while at a gas station, E-Way was approached from behind by two men wearing hooded sweaters and brandishing handguns. One of the men put his pistol to E-Way's head and told him not to make a scene and to get inside the back seat of his car. E-Way, realizing that the men wanted more than just money and that they were attempting to kidnap him, pushed the man back, giving himself enough time to run. The two gunmen fired several rounds at E-Way as he ran for his life. He managed to fire back a few rounds while still scrambling for safety. The Arab working the gas station locked the inside, leaving E-way to fend for himself. The two men finally retreated as a Detroit police car pulled into the scene. Without warning, the two white officers fired several rounds at E-Way as he stood at the gas station door with the gun still in hand. He was hit eight times and was placed in ICU. E-way stayed in the hospital for two months recovering from his wounds, while Mecca hired an attorney and filed suit against the Detroit Police Department for negligence and pain and suffering.

Mecca and E-Way had been boyfriend and girlfriend for five years. They had been kicking it since the eleventh grade. E-Way was your average dope boy. Prior to getting the settlement, he was getting a little money, but once he received the settlement check he began to live out his "Butch Jones" fantasies. He purchased their home, three late-model cars, jewelry for himself and Mecca, and enough dope to supply half of Detroit. He also gave Mecca some money to open up a salon. For the most part, E-Way was good people, not to mention an attractive brother. He stood at six foot three, at about 210 pounds, was dark skinned and bald, and had perfect white teeth and a swagger like no other.

Mecca browsed through the many shoes and clothes inside her walk-in closet. She selected an Apple Bottom outfit she recently bought, along with a pair of white stilettos to match. It was a shorts set, white with red piping, and it fit Mecca like a glove. She grabbed one of her Gucci handbags and walked over to her jewelry box. She decided to rock a pair of five-carat diamond stud earrings, a matching tennis bracelet, her white gold necklace, and her Rolex watch. She modeled in front of the mirror, inspecting every aspect. Satisfied with her pretty, Mecca walked into the bedroom and kissed E-Way goodbye. He was sound asleep from running the streets the night before.

It was off to the salon. Mecca dropped the top on her BMW 645 and enjoyed the morning sun as she drove down Houston Whittier. It was summertime, and that's exactly what was bumping from Mecca's sound system: Will Smith's "Summertime." She pulled into her parking spot at the salon and made her entrance. She was greeted with the usual phony "hey, how you doing's" from the assorted hating-ass low-budget bitches who were either getting their hair done or doing hair, with the exception of Benji.

"Where you going, Ms. Thang, to an audition for Luke's new video?" asked Benji as he examined Mecca from head to toe.

"You got jokes, huh?" laughed Mecca, not at all offended because she knew Benji was only playing.

Benji, whose real name was Benjamin, was a homosexual. Let him tell it, he was a woman trapped in a man's body. Mecca and Benji were best friends, had been since third grade. As far back as Mecca could remember, Benji had always been gay. As a child he was a bit different. He may have been gay, but he had always been a real mothafucka, which was why he and Mecca became best friends.

Both Benji and Mecca grew up poverty-stricken. Mecca was raised by her late grandmother, but she passed away when Mecca was 16. Life had always been rough for Mecca. Her grandmother would take her to the Salvation Army thrift store to buy hand-me-downs for school clothes. Mecca's mother, Yvette, was a crackhead, and Mecca's father, James, turned her mother out to the streets at the age of 15. As a result, they both became full-blown crackheads. Mecca would only see them when walking to and from school. They'd be at the corner store panhandling, and Yvette would often be trying to turn a trick.

By fifth grade, Benji began stealing from the local malls, trying to keep up with the Joneses. He tried turning Mecca out to stealing, but she wasn't good at it, so Benji, being the friend he was, kept Mecca laced with all the latest fads. Whatever Benji stole for himself, he made sure Mecca had it too. If it weren't for Benji, Mecca probably wouldn't have graduated because she hated going to school with the clothes her grandmother bought her.

When Mecca's grandmother passed away, she had nowhere to live. Her grandmother didn't have any life insurance, which left Mecca homeless. All her relatives had kids and problems of their own. To live with one of her aunts meant even worse conditions than living with her grandmother. It was Benji who copped an apartment along with a Nissan Maxima for the two to share. Benji turned his petty shoplifting into a hustle and started boosting. The boy was so cold. He'd take orders from customers before going to the mall. Benji's boosting paid for prom, senior trips, everything. Mecca felt like she owed Benji her life, so when E-Way received his settlement, she vowed to open a salon because Benji always wanted his own shop. He and Mecca were partners.

"Girl, you know I'm just being silly. Turn around and let me see the whole shit," Benji said as he stood twirling a pair of curlers. He was finishing up one of his early morning clients. It was Thursday, and every chickenhead with a balla as a boyfriend-slash-sponsor was getting ready for the weekend. By Sunday, they'd be in need of a fresh 'do.

Olivia, one of the shop's stylists, had said something smart under her breath as Mecca modeled her new fit for Benji and of course the haters.

"You likes?" she asked Benji, coming to a pose.

"You stay killin' shit. That's why you my girl. I'ma have to go snatch me one of them shits. Devin wouldn't mind seeing all this in one of those," said Benji, rubbing his girlish frame.

Everyone in the shop burst out laughing at the thought of Benji in an Apple Bottom outfit. Benji was hella funny. He was the life of the shop. He stood at five foot eight, was 165 pounds, had a caramel complexion and hazel contacts, and wore his hair in short perm-brushed waves. Benji was one of them dudes on first sight you knew was gay. Everything about him from his wiggle walk to his clothes said, "I'm gay."

"I'm sure he wouldn't," laughed Mecca.

Devin was Benji's current boyfriend. He was another one of them down-low, "I'm not gay" niggas. Who do they think they're fooling?

The shop was jam-packed as always. It would be that way on any given day from morning to closing, which sometimes was after ten o'clock depending on how much a bitch was spending. The shop was called Elite. Mecca and Benji chose the name in effort to eliminate the riff-raff, separate the ballas from the fakers. That way they could charge top-notch prices. As a business major and ghetto entrepreneur, Mecca knew how to appease the urban economy. Blacks tended to go for the most expensive shit they could find just to be able to say, "I paid X amount for this here." Mecca suffered from the same insecurities many other young blacks did. She had to have the best of everything.

Everyone inside the salon indeed felt they were elite, from the customers to its owners. The shop was located on the east side of Detroit on 7 Mile Road and Mackay Street. It was an old bank that was closed down because it kept getting robbed. The salon consisted of five booths, with four hair stylists and one barber. There was also a station near the entrance for a nail technician. The shop was very spacious and comfortable. In the waiting area sat two black leather sectional couches, two loveseats, and a few recliners. All the latest magazines filled the two coffee tables, along with a stack of DVDs for the forty-two-inch plasma mounted on the wall. The floor was white granite, giving it that marble look. Everything about the shop was elite.

Benji manned the first booth, and next to him was Olivia, a bad-ass mixed broad from the Buffalo Projects. She and Mecca were neck and neck as far as looks, but for some reason or another they couldn't stand each other. They kept it professional and remained cool on the strength of Benji. Olivia and Benji became friends while attending cosmetology school together.

Next to Olivia was Marie. She was a petite dark-skinned sista from Oak Park, Michigan. She grew up in the suburbs but also went to school with Benji and Olivia. Marie was quiet. She was always watching and soaking up game from the many gem-running whores at the shop. Benji would always tease her and tell her, "You're square as a pool table, girl, and twice as green." Marie earned her booth because she brought the suburban clientele to the shop, plus she was very creative. She created several new hairstyles that earned the shop slots in local hair magazines and hair shows.

Next to Marie was Tae, the old head of the shop. Tae was in her late fifties but looked no part of it. She had been doing hair since Diana Ross was with the Supremes. Tae was hella jazzy. She wore her hair cut short, and she stood a mere five foot four with a petite frame still intact. Tae was good people and was very knowledgeable in the hair field. Mecca and Benji rented Tae her booth because she was good for the money, and she brought the older clientele to the shop.

Pete was the shop's barber. He was the only other man who worked in the shop. He was a young brother from the west side, quiet, brown skinned, with a medium build, about five foot nine and 180 pounds. Pete landed his position at Elite for reasons not related to his craft. He, too, was a down-low brotha. He had met Benji at a gay bar and learned that Benji was part owner of the salon. To earn his position, he had to pay like he weighed, fucking and sucking Benji.

Across from Pete was Tory, the nail tech. Girl was always late, but she was tolerated because she was always on time with her booth rent. Plus, she kept everyone laughing. She'd cuss you out in a minute but while smiling. If your gear wasn't up to par, best believe Tory was gon' pull you up. She was one of the few real ones. She always spoke her mind no matter whose feelings were at stake. Tory was what you call funny built. She was all chest and no ass. She kept her attire on 1,000, and her hair and nails were always done. She stood five foot six, was 175 pounds and dark brown, and wore wire-frame Cartier glasses.

Mecca's nook was in the back room. She didn't do hair. She would go to the shop every morning just to have something to do.

"So what's the deal, Mecca?" asked Benji. He had just finished up his customer's hair and was waiting for the new shampoo girl, Veronica, to finish with his next head.

"Ain't much. Looking forward to tonight. We're still on, aren't we?" asked Mecca. Once a week, sometimes twice, the salon would have ladies' night out at the local male strip club called Henry's Palace.

"Babe, I'm going to have to pass. I already got some ass lined up. Devin is taking me over to Canada tonight."

"Sounds romantic," said Mecca, a bit disappointed.

"I guess it would be or-man-tic considering," laughed Tory.

Everyone caught the sly statement and began laughing. She was trying to be funny. Seeing as how Benji and Devin were both men, the evening would be "or-man-tic." Everyone laughed, with the exception of Benji. He was a little salty, so he shifted the spotlight.

"I know your undercover brotha ass ain't over there snickering and whatnot!" Benji snapped, looking directly at Pete.

Everyone ceased laughing and waited for Pete to reply to Benji's bold allegation. No one knew about Benji and Pete's fling, except Mecca, and she, too, was all ears waiting for Pete to respond.

"That's what I thought, snack butt. I knew you ain't have shit to say for real."

Pete had the shit face. He continued to cut the hair of the gentleman seated in his chair, pretending not to hear Benji, but Tory wasn't letting it go that easy.

"Say it ain't so, Pete," Tory said, then burst out laughing. "I knew you had a little sugar in yo' tank. Ya damn near pretty as me," she continued between laughs. She was riding Pete's ass like a professional comic. She couldn't even finish the young lady's nails she was laughing so hard, and she was in tears.

"All right, all right. Tory, that's enough. Y'all know Pete isn't gay. Isn't that right, Benji?" asked Mecca in an attempt to clean up the mess. She was looking at it from a business sense. She didn't want Pete to feel uncomfortable and quit. "Isn't that right, Benji?" Mecca said, repeating herself.

Reluctantly, Benji retracted his statement. "That's right. Pete's not gay. Although he does act like it sometimes."

"Um . . . hum. Don't try to clean that shit up now," said Tory.

"Girl, you know you's a mess," laughed Tae.

It was just another day at the shop, gossip on top of more gossip.

"A'ight, my man, good looking out," said the man whose hair Pete was cutting. He was examining his fresh cut. "What I owe you?" he asked, then stood up, handing Pete the mirror.

"Fifteen dollars," answered Pete.

All the women in the salon were gawking at the brother who was six foot one, 200 pounds, light brown, and well-groomed.

"Damn he's fine," one woman said as she looked over the *Essence* magazine she was reading. Marie was doing her hair.

"Huh, girl," Marie whispered.

Mecca was checking out the man's behind as he stood with his back to her. After paying Pete, the man looked in the mirror one last time. He was about to turn and leave but noticed Mecca staring at him. She immediately broke her stare and then reached for a magazine on the coffee table. She was sitting in one of the recliners. The guy smiled and then turned to face Pete.

"Ah, look, my name is Mario, man, and I was hoping you could cut my hair on the regular. No one has ever been able to get my line as straight as you got it."

"Anytime, man. Just stop through. Here's my card. I even do appointments," said Pete.

"A'ight, good looking," said Mario, taking the card and then heading for the door. "Y'all ladies have a nice day," he said, looking at Mecca in particular.

"Girl, did you see how that nigga was eyeing you, Mecca?" asked Benji after the door closed.

"I thought the nigga was looking at me for real, for real," said Olivia in a matter-of-fact tone of voice.

"I knew you were a bit cross-eyed," said Mecca.

"Ooh wee," Tory said, instigating as always.

"But anyhow, you hoes know what time of the month it is. That's right. It's the first. See me before ya leave and please have my cheese," said Mecca, and with that, it was off to her office. She sat at her Dell computer, surfing the internet, looking at handbags and shoes, while eating her favorite cheat food: soft batch chocolate chip cookies.

Chapter 2

Meanwhile, E-Way had made his way to his hood. He hated being at home. The only time he went home was at night to go to sleep. No sooner had Mecca left for the shop than he was up and at 'em. E-Way owned a bar on Mt. Elliott Street called Tippin' End. He bought it from old man Sal out of his settlement money. E-Way grew up in a historical mansion four houses down from the bar. He used to run numbers for old Sal as a young'un, and when Sal decided to retire from the streets, E-Way made him a proposition on the bar. Old man Sal not only sold E-Way the bar, but he also gave him his connect. Old man Sal had been dealing dope since the seventies and had never been caught. He was now in his mid-seventies and felt it was time to pass the torch.

Every morning, E-Way and his street team, who called themselves KFB (Known for Balling), would all meet up at the bar and break bread. KFB was a neighborhood clique E-Way and his best friend, Bubbles, started back in high school. Its members consisted of Kev, Chuck, Chuckie Bom's, Big Whitney, Bubbles, and E-Way. Together they were really known for balling. Everything was boss this, boss that. That's what they called themselves as individuals. They'd tell you in a minute, "I'm a boss, bitch, boss up!" That was their motto.

E-Way had invested in some studio equipment, which he put in the upstairs of the bar. He formed a record label called Floss-A-Lot, using the same members of KFB as artists. They put out several independent projects and soon became local celebrities. They had the entire city saying, "Boss up!" As with anything else, the haters and competitors came out mimicking. In this case the haters were known as Murkland Niggas. They were from the flip side of 7 Mile. They were in the same age bracket as E-Way and his boys, they all went to Pershing High School, and they had been feuding since then.

E-Way parked his Range Rover behind the assorted European whips that lined up in front of the bar. He entered the bar, which was empty on the ground floor. He walked upstairs to the studio to find Kev, Chuck, and Bubbles smoking blunts and recording their new song, "What Cha' You Is." Chuck, was the youngest of the bunch, but he was getting just as much money. He stood five foot six, weighed 150 pounds, shit black, wore a bald fade, and stayed fresh to death. He was in the sound booth getting ready to record the chorus. He was in mode, tipping his Cartier Buffalo frames and swinging his Floss-A-Lot chain from side to side. The whole clique had one.

"You ready?" asked Bubbles, working the switchboard.

"Yeah."

Real niggas don't count money, bitch, we weigh it
Got work for the low, got K's for hates
Pull up jump out stuntin', bitch, you know who I is
I'm a boss fo' sho'. I'm 'bout my dough

Chuck finished dropping the chorus. E-Way, Bubbles, and Kev were all bobbing to the beat as it played back.

"That shit nice," said E-Way as he rolled his first blunt of the day.

Big Whitney, Chuckie Bom's, and a little busto broad all came up to the studio.

"Who this?" asked Bubbles, referring to the young lady.

"Oh, she on the house. You want some head?" asked Big Whitney in boss mode.

"Hell yeah," answered Bubbles, taking the young lady into the back room.

"I got next!" hollered E-Way.

"A'ight, now that everybody's here, let's get to it. What you do last night, Kev?" asked E-Way, talking about how much money Kev's houses made.

Chuck and Chuckie Bom's gave E-Way a duffle bag with close to fifty grand in it.

"A'ight, I'm about to re-up. I should be straight this afternoon. Y'all can pick the shit up then," E-Way said. When E-Way got his lawsuit, he bought fifty kilos using the connect old man Sal plugged him with. E-way gave Big Whitney, Kev, Bubbles, Chuck, and Chuckie Bom's each two bricks. He did that just on the strength so everyone could get their money right. The deal was that they would cop from E-Way and he would give them the work for the low-low.

"Y'all niggas ready for the show tomorrow?" asked E-Way.

Their record label was sponsoring a concert at the State Theatre. They had B.G. from the Hot Boys as the headline, while they would be the opening act.

"Man, we gon' ball out. We gots to do this new track right here," said Kev.

Kev, Chuckie Bom's, and Big Whitney were the stars of the label. Bubbles, Chuck, and E-Way were more like features. E-Way couldn't rap a lick, but he would be on skits talking cash shit. They didn't expect to make it big time. They just wanted to be hood stars.

"Damn, what, you back there making love to the bitch?" snapped Chuck, looking at his watch.

Chuck and Chuckie Bom's were best friends, and they could pass for brothers. They both were dark brown skinned, about six feet, medium build. Big Whitney was every bit of 350 pounds. He stood about six two, with light brown skin and no neck. When he breathed, he always sounded like he was out of breath. Bubbles was about six one, dark skinned, with short, nappy hair. With bags under his eyes, he always looked like he was tired.

"Was the head right?" asked E-Way, talking to Bubbles as he entered the room sweating.

"One thousand." he answered, referring to the young lady's mouthpiece. They continued to work on songs, smoke weed, and talk boss shit. That was their daily routine: meet up at the bar, shill, and run trains on bustos.

It was nine o'clock, and Mecca had been at the shop all day making sure everyone paid their booth rent before leaving. She wasn't in a rush to leave because E-Way was never home, and Benji had canceled their ritual ladies' night out at Henry's Palace. Mecca was still in the back room surfing the internet when Marie came to grab her purse.

"Girl, it's after nine. What are you still doing here?" asked Marie. "I know you're hitting Henry's tonight."

"Benji canceled on me. He has a date with Devin," Mecca said with as much sarcasm as she could.

"Shit, Benji's ass don't make no party. You and I can go, plus I think Tae and Tory are supposed to be going too. Come on, it'll be fun."

"Let me finish up. Give me about ten minutes and I'll be ready," said Mecca. She waited for Marie to go back out front and called E-Way's cell phone.

"Hey, baby, where are you?" asked Mecca.

"At the studio. I'm about to open the bar in a minute."

"What time are you coming home?"

"Don't wait up."

"When are we going to spend some time together?"

"You know I'm trying to recoup some of this money. Look at all the shit we done bought. You know I'm on the grind."

Mecca couldn't complain because E-Way was putting out a lot of money, and he had been more than good to her.

"I promise we'll spend some time together this weekend."

"Okay. Be safe, and call me when you're on your way home," Mecca said, ending the conversation.

"You ready?" asked Mecca as she entered the front of the salon.

"Where y'all going?" asked Benji.

"Marie and I are going to hit Henry's."

"I want details, you hear me? Details." Benji was finishing up his last head.

Mecca and Marie took Mecca's car. They wanted to pull up in style. They had the top dropped, trying to enjoy the warm summer night. Mecca pulled into the parking lot of Henry's Palace to valet her car. They were eyed by the many women as they were escorted to the VIP seats, center stage. Mecca and Benji were regulars in Henry's. Marie had just started going, but she had become a regular lately. They ordered a bottle of Moët as they waited for the festivities to begin.

"I heard Mr. Marcus is supposed to be here tonight," Mecca said as she looked around the club and spotted Tae and Tory.

"That nigga got a horse dick," laughed Marie.

"His ass looks like a horse's, too," added Mecca, "but he sho' knows how to work that mothafucka."

"Amen, girl. You see how he be punishing them hoes in the pornos. He could beat this pussy up anytime he wants to," Marie said, taking a sip of bubbly.

"I can't wait until my baby comes out," said Mecca.

"Who?"

"Drew sexy ass," answered Mecca.

"That nigga is that deal. I bet he can fuck his ass off."

"Oh, can he," Mecca said, leaning her head back, thinking about their last episode.

"You and Drew? Oh, my God, when?"

"Three days ago."

"How long y'all been kicking it?"

"For a few months."

"You better be careful. You know E-Way's ass is crazy."

"Yeah, I know, but I got this."

Drew was Mecca's thang-thang, as she referred to him. She was getting from him what E-Way wasn't giving her: good dick. Mecca, in return, took extra care of Drew, spending E-Way's money doing it.

"Ahh," screamed every woman in the club as the lights in the club dimmed, and the show began. Four cock-strong brothas hit the stage wearing nothing but pairs of tight Speedos. They were gleaming from the lights and baby oil, which covered their bodies.

"Work that mothafucka, work that mothafucka," the women chanted. Those were the lyrics to the song playing. Mecca was bouncing to the beat, sipping her Moët while enjoying an eyeful. Marie was standing up, throwing fistfuls of dollar bills on stage.

One of the men jumped down from the stage and pushed Marie into her seat. He began bumping and grinding up against Marie, giving her an exclusive lap dance. He spun around and shook it up while Marie filled his drawers with bills. She was going crazy!

"Hand me my purse, girl," she said, reaching for more bills. "Work that mothafucka," she said, slapping the guy on his ass to the beat.

The club was going as crazy as any other night. Drew appeared on stage wearing his white thong Speedo and a cowboy hat. Drew stood six five, 225 pounds, all muscle, light skinned, green eyes, and deep brush waves. The nigga was a stallion. Women rushed the stage, launching money to Drew's feet while he put on a show. Mecca for the first time felt jealous, and she peeped her feeling. Drew finished up his set, then made his way over to Mecca and Marie's table.

"I see your fan club is in the building," said Mecca.

"Here you go. They was only enjoying the show. I know you enjoyed it," Drew said, grabbing Mecca's hand and rubbing his twenty-pack with it. Mecca smiled and started to feel better. She could feel Drew's fan club watching.

"How about I put on a private show for you after the club? You'd like that?"

"It's a date," Mecca said.

Drew kissed her hand, then excused himself.

"That nigga got game," said Marie in a rhythm.

They continued to enjoy themselves, ordering more Moët and watching the many fine brothas do their thing.

Mr. Marcus, the main event, had the club going crazy. He came out wearing some leopard-print Speedos. The boy had a third leg. The women rushed him so hard he had to remain on the stage or risk being hurt. Marie had spent over $500 in the short time they were there. She indeed had become a fanatic. She wanted to stay until closing, but Mecca was eager to leave so she could hook up with Drew. Mecca dropped Marie back off at the shop so she could get her car.

"A'ight, see you in the morning. I want details," Marie said, closing Mecca's car door. Mecca laughed at Marie as she staggered to her car.

Drew lived downtown on Woodward in some recently constructed condos. Mecca raced on the Davidson Expressway, looking at her watch. It was almost midnight. Mecca wanted to hurry up and fuck Drew so she could beat E-Way home. She had E-Way's schedule down to a science. She knew he wouldn't be home until at least three o'clock in the morning.

Drew answered the door wearing a similar pair of Speedos to what he wore at the club, with a silk robe exposing his fine physique. At the sight of Drew's abs, Mecca became moist.

"Are you going to just stand there or are you going to come in?" asked Drew, breaking Mecca from her zone.

"Huh, oh, yeah," she said, smiling, then giving Drew a passionate kiss. He shut the door while still handling Mecca. It was all business. No words were exchanged with the exception of moans. Mecca removed Drew's robe and began kissing him all over, starting with his chest, then stopping at his Johnson. She helped him out of his Speedo and began jacking his dick.

"Suck it," Drew said in a soft, seductive, and demanding voice.

Mecca was turned on by Drew's authoritative statement. She did as she was told, taking Drew into her mouth and sucking him to death.

Drew pulled Mecca up from her knees, then walked her over to the sofa. He undressed her and then laid her across the couch. He took her legs and wrapped them around his neck, mouthing her entire pussy. Mecca sighed in satisfaction while gripping and guiding Drew's head. Drew expertly ate Mecca up. She couldn't take it anymore and wanted to feel him inside her. Mecca pulled

Drew up for air. She was breathing hard and beginning to sweat.

"Fuck me," she said.

Drew pinned Mecca's legs to her shoulders and began punishing Mecca's pussy. He was deep stroking Mecca while she clawed his back. "Ah, oh, fuck me. Fuck me," screamed Mecca.

Drew turned her over, long stroking Mecca from the back as she looked back into Drew's eyes. Her soft yellow ass bounced against Drew's pelvis with every stroke.

Drew was putting in work. He sat back, pulling Mecca onto his dick, and cupped both ass cheeks, sliding her up and down until reaching his climax. Mecca continued to ride Drew until he went completely limp. She kept him inside her while kissing on his neck and ears in an attempt to get him back up. They went for round two and round three. Mecca gave Drew the nickname Sweat because he was known to sweat a bitch's perm out.

It was almost two o'clock, and E-Way had yet to call Mecca. She wanted to continue to lie up but couldn't chance it. If E-Way beat her home, all hell would break loose.

"I have to get ready to get out of here," Mecca said as she lay spread-eagle on the floor beside Drew.

"You can spend the night."

"You know I can't do that."

"And why is that?"

"Because I can't," Mecca said, reaching for her clothes. "I'll see you next week."

"You think you can wait that long?" asked Drew when he was standing at the front door letting Mecca out.

"I doubt it, but it'll be worth the wait."

Drew kissed Mecca on the forehead, then watched her walk to her car. She raced home feeling like a new woman. Drew had knocked the lining out of her ass, and her pussy was still vibrating. She pulled in the circular driveway of her house and was glad to see that she had beaten E-Way home. She raced inside, stripping her clothes at the door, then rushed to the bathroom. She took a quick shower, wrapped her hair up, and then was off to bed.

Chapter 3

It was eight o'clock in the morning. Mecca woke up to find E-Way curled up next to her as always. She smiled at the thought of her and Drew's episode the night before. She and E-Way hadn't had sex in almost two weeks. Things had become monotonous. With E-Way it was like, "Okay, give me some head, bend over, let me hit you from the back." He'd bust his nut, then roll over, but they endured the adversity on the strength of their history.

Mecca got up and washed her face, then headed down to the basement for her morning workout. She ran through her sets still thinking about Drew's sexy ass. She carried her thoughts into the shower, getting an early morning nut off. She picked out her outfit for the day, got dressed, and was out the door. On her way to the shop, she stopped at Burger King to grab some breakfast. While she was waiting for her order, Mario, the guy from the shop, entered. He was with a little girl who appeared to be his daughter. Mecca noticed him first but avoided eye contact because she didn't want to feel like she was staring. The little girl pointed up at the menu, telling her dad what she wanted.

Mario gave their order, then stepped aside, waiting for his food. He recognized Mecca as she stepped up to the counter to get her food. He wanted to say something but thought it'd be inappropriate while with his daughter. Mecca turned to leave and said, "You have a nice day," obviously flirting with the man.

"You too," Mario said with a smile, enjoying Mecca's backside as she walked out.

"Who was that, Daddy?" Mecca could hear the little girl asking as she exited.

She pulled in front of the salon and parked. It was another beautiful summer day. Mecca was wearing a scarf over her head from the night before. She was escorted to the back room by Benji as soon as she hit the door.

"Excuse me, I'll be right back," Benji said to the woman whose hair he was doing. Marie, not wanting to miss the details, also excused herself. No sooner had the back door closed than Benji began drilling Mecca.

"Dish, bitch, I want full details."

Marie had pulled up a seat and was leaning on her hands in anticipation. "Well, how was it?" asked Marie, growing impatient.

Mecca flopped down in her desk chair and began recalling and almost reliving the night's events with Drew. "That nigga fucked me for almost two hours. I woke up and was still thinking about him. I couldn't even concentrate on my workout."

"Did he eat it?" asked Marie.

"Did he," sighed Mecca. "It's like the first time every time we do it," Mecca continued.

"Don't let that nigga get your nose too far open," said Benji.

"I got this. He's just my li'l thang-thang."

"A'ight, now, I'm telling you, don't go falling in love."

With that they all filed back into the front. All eyes were on them as they entered the room.

"Who you got next, Benji? I need you to touch me up," said Mecca.

"If Connie's boot mouth ain't in here by the time I'm done with her, I'll get you next."

Tory came dragging her tail through the door, late as usual. She was wearing a pair of tinted Versace sunglasses instead of her wire frames. She had a hangover from the night before.

"Tory, you're late," Mecca said.

"Aren't I always? But the important thing is that I'm here now. Chop chop, let's get to work, shall we?" Tory said, laughing and trying to get Mecca to laugh also. "Lighten up, boss lady," Tory said, being sarcastic.

"You know what your problem is?" she continued without waiting for Mecca to respond. "You're always here and don't have a job."

"Girl, you crazy. Do my nails while I wait for Benji to finish up," said Mecca.

"Is E-Way and them still performing today at the State Theatre?" asked Tae. She was in her fifties but was hip to the new era. She stayed laced in all the latest designers and hung out with people half her age.

"Yeah, it's tonight. I believe they hit the stage at nine," answered Mecca. "Y'all gon' fall through?"

"I don't fuck with local niggas," said Olivia.

"That's funny. Could you remind me who it was you fuck with? 'Cause I ain't never seen no nigga up here for you," snapped Mecca. Every time Olivia tried to pop slick, Mecca cut her ass up, putting her back in her place.

"Ooh wee," Tory said, instigating as usual.

Mecca got her hair and nails done and hung around the shop until the concert was set to start.

E-Way and the rest of Floss-A-Lot were all backstage doing mic checks, trying to get ready for the show. E-Way peeked out into the crowd from behind the curtain and didn't see one empty seat. Kev, Chuck, Chuckie Bom's, Bubbles, and Big Whitney were smoking L's, and they stood in a circle passing blunts. They had four blunts going around. They were fresh to death, in crisp white tees that read "KFB," black Evisu jeans, and white-on-white Air Force Ones. They were iced out, each sporting an iced-out Floss-A-Lot chain.

"Y'all ready?" asked B.G. He was the headline for the night. He wanted to show them his support.

"Yeah, man," said Kev, popping his collar. He was on cloud nine.

"A'ight, good luck, Whoodie," said B.G. as Chuckie Bom's, Big Whitney, and Kev took the stage.

The crowd went crazy as their local hit, "It's Nothin'," began playing. E-Way, Chuck, and Bubbles served as hype men. They were popping bottles of Cristal and throwing twenties into the crowd. They performed a total of eight songs, ending their set with their new song, "What Cha' You Is."

Mecca, Benji, Tae, Tory, and Marie were all in the front row. They yelled in support as E-Way and the rest of them exited the stage.

"Come on, y'all," Mecca said as they all made their way backstage, flashing their passes at security. Mecca rushed over to E-Way, giving him a kiss. "Y'all were great, baby."

"Yeah, y'all did y'all thang," said Benji.

"Oh, my God, B.G.!" screamed Tae's old groupie ass. "Can I please take a picture with you?"

B.G. flicked up with Tae, Benji, Marie, and Mecca before heading onto the stage. Kev, Chuckie Bom's, and Big Whitney passed out CDs and posters from their promotional van. E-Way had bought a conversion van and had it wrapped with Floss-A-Lot records on it.

After B.G.'s performance, they all headed over to the River Rock for the after-party. Only major-league players were in the house, with the exception of a few groupies. Bottles of Cristal and Moët filled the table. E-way had gone all out for the night. After the party, everybody was to hit the hotel. Mecca, Benji, Tae, and Marie had a VIP booth. They laughed it up and enjoyed the free drinks and entertainment.

"Girl, do you know that this is the third time I've seen old boy in two days?" Mecca said as she nodded in the direction of Mario, the guy from the salon.

"His ass is too fine," said Tory.

No sooner had she said that than Mario turned around on his stool. He was seated at the bar with another gentleman. They both were wearing suits and loafers. He met eyes with Mecca, and this time she didn't break her stare. Mario excused himself, then walked over to Mecca's VIP booth.

"Excuse me, ladies, but I was hoping I could steal a few minutes with . . . your name is?" Mario said, looking down into Mecca's eyes.

"Mecca."

"I'm Mario. Nice to meet you. I would buy you ladies a drink, but they're apparently free tonight. Listen, I won't take up too much of your time. How'd you like to go to the Source Awards with me next week? I know we've just met, but I'd really appreciate your company. You can even bring your girls."

"First class or coach?" asked Tory.

"Mario Lambert? And what do I owe the pleasure to?" asked E-Way. He had spotted Mario at Mecca's booth and wanted to see what was up.

"Just enjoying the festivities. By the way, y'all did ya thang tonight. When are you going to sign with me?" asked Mario. He was a music producer. A real one. He had worked with some of everybody and was looking to bring the glory days back to Motown. He wanted to produce KFB among other groups because they had a unique sound.

"Man, we already signed," E-Way said.

"With whom?"

There was a brief pause, and then E-Way responded, "We on some independent shit."

"Do you know how much money you'd make if you went major? Millions. You've got my number, man. Think about it. As a matter of fact, give yourself a break from the streets and fly out to Miami with me to the Source Awards. It'll give you a chance to see how niggas are really eating. Plus, these lovely ladies will hopefully be joining us."

There was a loud ruckus at the front door, breaking E-Way's and everyone else's attention.

"It's time to go. These niggas about to act a donkey. It was nice meeting y'all," said Mario.

No sooner had he completed his sentence than gunshots rang out throughout the club. Mecca, Tae, Benji, Tory, and anybody else with some sense got down. Not E-Way. He ran in the direction of the shots, upping a .44-caliber Desert Eagle from his waist.

He made it to the door to find Big Whitney crying, rocking back and forth while holding Bubbles's lifeless body in his arms. Kev and Chuck were in the middle of the street, busting at the gunmen as they sped away in an Astro minivan. Kev and Chuck entered the vestibule of the club where Big Whitney clutched Bubbles, still sobbing. E-Way stood over Bubbles in shock. Gun in hand, he was unable to say or do anything as he watched his best friend lie dead. He refused to believe it and just knew Bubbles would get up. He had to! Kev walked over to E-Way and tried to get him to take a walk with him. E-Way was like a brick wall. He wouldn't budge. By this time, people were rushing the exit, running and screaming, trying to get the hell out of dodge.

Mecca, worried that something might have happened to E-Way, rushed toward the entrance to find him in a trance. "Baby, are you okay? Let's get out of here. Come on, let's go home," Mecca said, pulling E-Way by the arm.

Police sirens could be heard in the distance. They were approaching at a mile per second. E-way reluctantly followed Mecca, still looking back at his best friend.

"What happened?" asked Mecca as she and E-Way walked into their house. E-Way hadn't said one word the entire ride home. His cell phone was blowing up with calls from Kev and the rest of KFB, but E-Way didn't even hear his phone. He was zoned out.

"What happened, E? Who did it?" asked Mecca as she followed E-Way up to their bedroom and into his walk-in closet. Mecca kept pressing the issue.

E-Way had one thing on his mind. Murder! He changed his clothes, dressing in all black. He pulled up two floorboards, removing an AR-15 fully automatic and two extra clips.

"What are you going to do?" Mecca grabbed E-Way's arm as he attempted to walk out of the closet.

He spun around and slapped Mecca to the ground. "Bitch, this is all your fault!"

"What?" Mecca asked as she began crying. She was holding her face and scooting into a corner as E-Way inched toward her with death in his eyes.

"If yo' funky ass wasn't flirting in my face, I would have been at the door. And Bubbles would still be here!" yelled E-Way.

He reached down and grabbed Mecca by her hair and started punching her in the face. He hit her at least ten times. Mecca screamed at the top of her lungs. She couldn't believe this was actually happening. E-Way had never hit Mecca. He was going crazy. Mecca thought that he was going to kill her.

E-Way dragged Mecca into the bedroom. He picked her up and threw her onto the bed, then just stood there staring. He was out of breath. "I'll finish with yo' ass when I get back. Clean yo'self up," E-Way said, then turned to leave.

Mecca lay on the bed, sniffling and crying. E-Way had busted her nose and blackened both her eyes, and she was soaked in blood. She heard the front door close and E-Way's car start. She reached over, grabbing the house phone, and called Benji.

"He did what? I'm on my way," Benji said.

He raced over to Mecca's house and picked her up.

Chapter 4

E-Way and the rest of the KFB met at the studio. They were drinking and smoking weed, trying to cope with the loss of Bubbles. E-Way paced back and forth with a bottle of Hennessy. Kev, Big Whitney, Chuck, and Chuckie Bom's were all seated. They were listening to some of the tracks Bubbles had produced. E-Way, out of nowhere, threw the Hennessy bottle as hard as he could against the wall. Everybody looked up at E-Way, who was just standing in the center of the floor, looking up at the ceiling.

No one had seen who killed Bubbles. There was just a big commotion, and then gunshots were fired. Kev and Chuckie Bom's were able to let off a couple of rounds but were unable to identify the gunmen.

"So, who was it?" asked E-Way.

No one said a word.

"You mean to tell me that niggas just pulled up, dumped my man, and ain't nobody see shit?"

Again, no one said a word. E-Way continued to pace the floor while plotting his next move.

"This what we gon' do. First, we gon' put a reward up for info on whoever did this. We'll kill those bitches ourselves. Put the word out that it's a hun'd Gs for information. If that don't work, we'll just kill every nigga we think could have done it. What cha'll waiting on? Hit the streets and find out who did this," ordered E-Way.

It was six o'clock in the morning. None of them had been to sleep, and they had pulled an all-nighter. They all combed the streets, spreading the word and seeking information, but to no avail. E-way had to go and break the news to his grandmother. She had raised him and Bubbles. E-Way and Bubbles had been best friends since birth. Their fathers were best friends back in the day. They were both serving seven life sentences for a robbery gone bad. Bubbles's mom, Nancy, was found raped and shot execution style in a crackhouse when he was only 6 years old. Ms. Nelly, E-Way's grandmother, adopted Bubbles and raised him as one of her own. Ms. Nelly nearly had a stroke after learning of Bubbles's death. It killed E-Way to watch her endure the pain. His eyes began to well up, and he became furious all over again.

Meanwhile, Mecca had checked herself into the hospital. Her nose was broken, and her jaw was dislocated. Being high yellow, she bruised very easily. Her entire face was black and blue. She cried as she looked into the mirror in her hospital room's bathroom. Benji heard his friend crying and entered the bathroom, holding Mecca and trying to comfort her.

"It's going to be all right, baby. We'll get through this. We always do," he said.

"Look at me," sobbed Mecca.

"Son of a bitch," Benji said. He was pissed. No one fucked with Mecca and got away with it. Benji was very protective over Mecca. He saw her as his little sister.

The doctors ran a few more X-rays on Mecca, then released her, giving Benji strict orders to keep her in bed for at least one week. They wanted Mecca to come back and do a follow-up. Her jaw was wired. She sounded like Kanye West when his jaw was wired.

Benji took Mecca to his house. He lived in Southfield, Michigan, in a three-bedroom ranch. His house was immaculate. Of the three bedrooms, Benji used one as an office, one as his bedroom, and the third as a guest room. He settled Mecca into the guest room, then ran her a hot bath with Epsom salt so she could soak her wounds.

Benji was playing momma, waiting on Mecca hand and foot. He had called the shop and had Marie take her schedule. He didn't tell her that Mecca was jumped on. He didn't want it all out in the streets. Mecca was on a liquid diet, seeing as how her jaw was wired. Benji tried to get her to drink chicken broth and Ensure drinks, but Mecca just lay in bed crying all day. She didn't think her face would ever heal.

Four days had past, and Mecca hadn't budged except to use the bathroom and when Benji gave her a bath. Benji hadn't budged either. He had declined two dates with Devin. Benji was by Mecca's bedside twenty-four seven. Mecca's cell phone was turned off. Her voicemail was full with messages all from E-way.

He had a feeling where Mecca was but had never been to Benji's house. He went to the shop a few times, threatening folks, Marie and Tae in particular, to tell him where Benji lived. They couldn't tell him if they wanted to because Benji was very particular whom he let know where he laid his head. On E-Way's last visit to the shop, Olivia's hating ass slipped E-Way a piece of paper. It contained Benji's home address and Olivia's cell phone number.

Olivia got Benji's address by running his home number through information. Benji had been using his house phone to call the shop, and his number was left on the caller ID.

E-Way hadn't washed his ass or changed his clothes in four days. His appearance was that of a deranged mental patient. He chain-smoked blunts and reeked of alcohol. You could smell it coming out of his pores.

E-Way pulled up to the address scribbled on the piece of paper. He squinted at the house and was convinced it was indeed Benji's house because he recognized Benji's Benz sitting in the driveway. He cut the engine, then got out. He rang Benji's doorbell like a madman.

"Let me see who this is," Benji said, getting up from the loveseat in the guest room. He and Mecca were watching *What's Love Got to Do with It*.

Benji peeped out the peephole and became furious. He snatched the door open at the sight of E-Way.

"Where is she? I know she's in there. Move, let me in," said E-Way as he tried to move past Benji.

Benji wasn't budging.

"You hear me? I said move, you faggot-ass bitch."

Benji dropped his ass. He hit E-Way with a stiff right jab, landing a solid blow to E-Way's chin.

"You bitch. You hit me, you bitch," E-Way said as he lay on his backside, holding his jaw.

"Get cho' bitch ass up so I can knock yo' ass out again," Benji snapped as the man was coming out of him.

E-Way went to stand up, but Benji was on his ass like a dog in heat. He pushed E-Way back down, landing on top of him. Benji was beating the sleeves off E-Way. He was biting him and trying to dig his eyes out. Mecca heard the commotion and climbed out of bed. She ran outside and tried to pull Benji off E-Way but was unable. Benji's next-door neighbor had called the police at the start of the ruckus. Southfield police were dispatched and on the scene within minutes.

The police managed to pry Benji off E-Way, whose face was covered in blood. Benji tried his best to repeat what E-Way had done to Mecca on his ass.

“I’ma kill you, bitch!” E-Way yelled after the police pulled Benji off him.

Benji was still going. The police had to hit him with a Taser to calm him down. They arrested both Benji and E-Way. They took E-Way in on some petty warrants. He could bond out at the station after his fingerprints came back. Benji was arrested on minor assault charges. He would have to see a magistrate in the morning in order to get a bond. Mecca contacted a lawyer for Benji so he would have representation at his court hearing.

The next day, Benji appeared in court and was given a personal bond because he had never been arrested before. E-Way bonded out as soon as he was booked. He was out just in time to bury his best friend. All of KFB wore white tees bearing a smiling picture of Bubbles. E-Way sat in front of Sacred Heart Catholic Church, smoking blunt after blunt and drinking Hennessy while listening to 2Pac’s “How Long Will They Mourn Me?”

E-Way couldn’t bear seeing Bubbles in a casket, so he just sat in his car and waited for the funeral services to end. He felt he was still paying his last respects and that Bubbles would understand him not going in. After the services ended, everyone trailed Bubbles’s hearse to the cemetery. E-Way again remained in the car. Kev decided not to watch his friend get lowered into the ground either. He and E-Way sat in the car, smoking and passing the Henny back and forth, not saying a word. Bubbles was the life of KFB. He kept everyone on their toes. His loss was a blow to all of the KFB and then some. Bubbles had one daughter, Vanessa, who was 4 years old. As she walked into the cemetery with her mother, E-Way thought about how he was going to talk to her about her father being dead.

The remainder of KFB met at the bar, along with the rest of the family. E-Way excused himself and went up to the studio. He wanted to call Mecca, someone who knew him and could understand what he was going through. He sat at the mixing board with his cell phone in hand. He had tried calling Mecca's cell over ten times, but he kept getting her voicemail. He looked at the piece of paper with Benji's address on it, then turned it around and noticed Olivia's number.

E-Way dialed the number on the paper and sat back in his chair as the phone rang. Olivia picked up on the third ring.

"Hello, may I speak to Olivia?"

"This is she. Who is this?"

"This ole boy you met at Elite a few days ago. You gave me Benji's address with your number on the back of the paper."

"E-Way, right?"

"Yeah. Listen, are you busy right now?"

"I'm at the shop. I have two more heads. Why, what's up?"

"Shit, I was hoping we could hook up, go somewhere and chill."

"Is this the number you're going to be at?"

"Yeah, this my cell."

"Okay, yeah, we can do that. I'll call you in a little while. Give me enough time to finish up these two heads."

"That's a bet, in a minute."

Olivia and E-Way met downtown at the Renaissance Center. E-way suggested they meet there because there was a hotel located inside along with high-end retail shops. He booked a room overlooking the Detroit River.

Olivia and E-way wasted no time once inside the room. They began undressing each other at the door. Olivia knew why she was there: to get fucked and that was it. She wasn't really attracted to E-Way. In fact, she thought he was ugly. She just wanted what Mecca had, period!

Olivia wanted to leave a lasting impression, so she fell on her knees and blessed E-Way with some head. She sat in a seductive posture, barely holding E-way's dick with her French manicured hands. She mouthed him while looking up into his eyes like an innocent schoolgirl. E-Way clutched Olivia's long black silky hair, manhandling her head to his satisfaction. Olivia reminded E-Way so much of Mecca that he almost called her name. He caught himself as he began nutting in Olivia's mouth. She swallowed every last drop and continued to knock him off until she got him hard again.

They made their way into the bedroom. Olivia walked over to the balcony and slid the doors open. She stepped out onto the balcony ass naked. She motioned E-Way with her finger to join her. No one could see them because the room sat so high up. Olivia climbed on top of the table next to the railing. Her ass was hanging off the table as she sat in a doggie-style position. E-Way took the invitation, inserting his long, hard black dick in Olivia's pussy. She jerked and sighed as E-Way began fucking her brains out. Olivia moaned and squirmed while holding the railing of the balcony. The sun was out, and E-Way's black ass was dripping with sweat. He was about to nut, so he pulled out and forced himself into Olivia's tight yellow asshole. He wanted her to feel pain, the pain that he was feeling!

They continued to fuck all afternoon, and E-way hit Olivia in every possible position. Whenever he finally busted a nut, she'd suck him back hard. For Olivia, this was payback for every time Mecca shined on her. She didn't just want this to be a one-time thing. Olivia wanted to fuck E-way on the regular and possibly fuck up his thing with Mecca.

Chapter 5

Word had gotten back on who had killed Bubbles. A little nigga who was parked outside the club that night, trying to parking lot pimp because he wasn't on the A-list, supposedly had seen the whole thing. He pulled off after the gunshots ceased, but he had heard about the $100,000 that was up for grabs. He didn't know Bubbles or the rest of KFB personally, but he knew where the studio was at. He ran down what he had seen, to the best of his memory, to Kev, E-Way, Chuck, Big Whitney, and Chuckie Bom's. They were all sitting in the studio, hanging on the young man's words.

"Are you sure about this? Don't be lying, li'l nigga," E-Way advised, trying to read whether the nigga was telling the truth.

"I wouldn't make up no shit like that. I'm telling you it was DJ and Marcus."

DJ and Marcus were the head niggas of Murkland Niggas, KFB's archenemies.

"Who else did you tell about this?" asked E-Way.

"Nobody. I didn't even know who got killed until the word spread. That's when I heard about the reward."

"A'ight, then, li'l nigga, good looking out," E-Way said.

"What about the money?" asked li'l man. His name was Dave.

"Oh, Kev gon' take care of you," answered E-Way. E-Way nodded at Kev, who then stood up.

"Come on, li'l nigga, follow me," Kev said as he and li'l Dave walked downstairs into the bar.

"How did I do?" asked Dave.

"You did good. Almost too good," answered Kev as he pulled a .38 revolver from underneath his shirt.

Boom! Boom! Kev gave li'l Dave two face shots, then stood over him, emptying the remaining four shells into Dave's neck and stomach.

E-Way was upstairs orchestrating the move they were about to bring Murkland Niggas. Big Whitney, Chuck, Chuckie Bom's all listened intently to their parts.

"Big Whitney gon' drive while the rest of us jump out and air that bitch out. I don't give a fuck who's out there: kids, old folks, mommas, grandmommas. I don't give a fuck. You air they past out too!" E-Way concluded.

There was no time to waste. E-Way wanted immediate gratification. He was so amped that he wasn't on his square. He was acting out of emotion.

E-Way sent Kev to steal a van for the job. Kev was an expert at stealing cars. He used to come through the hood every morning in a different "stoly" as they called them. He would give everyone a ride to school, then continue to joyride until the police snatched him up.

Kev stole a triple black conversion van similar to their promotional van. He hit the horn three times as he pulled in front of the bar.

E-Way walked over to the window of the studio and peeked out. "That nigga still got it."

"Who that?" asked Chuck.

"Kev. He got the van. Y'all niggas ready?"

No one said anything. They all filed downstairs and out of the bar, hopping into the van. Kev had their latest CD playing as he punched it up Mt. Elliott. They were blowing blunts, trying to get their heads right. E-way was all business. He turned down the radio as he spotted

Marcus, DJ, and the rest of Murkland Niggas posted on the corner of Bloom and Emery.

"There them ho-ass niggas go right there," he said.

Everyone sat up in an attempt to get a visual.

"Kev, lay your seat back and just keep riding. Go around the corner so you and Whitney can switch seats," E-Way directed as he climbed into the back with everyone else.

It was broad daylight. Kids were playing on their front lawns with the water hose. Old folks sat on the porch, and the hoodlums lined the block trying to make a few sales.

"Whit, when you get to the corner, just stop," E-Way said from the back seat. He, Kev, Chuck, and Chuckie Bom's were clutching the door handles, waiting for the van to stop.

DJ noticed the van for the second time and asked Marcus, "Who this van keep circling the hood?"

"I don't know, probably the hook," answered Marcus.

Everyone's attention was now focused on the van as it inched toward the corner.

As soon as the van stopped, everyone on the corner took off running in different directions. E-Way, Kev, Chuck, and Chuckie Bom's hit the doors wearing black hoodie sweaters pulled down over their eyes. Each carried fully auto AR-15s. E-Way was focused on Marcus, who had cut through a vacant lot. E-Way gave chase while busting multiple rounds at Marcus. He struck Marcus in the back as he attempted to jump a privacy fence. The impact from the bullet sent Marcus flying over the fence, landing on his face in the alley.

E-Way leaped over the fence to find Marcus crawling and leaking badly. E-Way kicked Marcus in his side.

"Roll yo' bitch ass over!" ordered E-Way.

He continued to kick Marcus until he rolled over. He wanted Marcus to look him in the eyes and know who killed him. E-Way snatched his hoodie off his head and watched as Marcus's eyes widened. Before he could speak a word, E-Way aimed the rifle at his head and held the trigger back, emptying the clip. E-Way stood there, still not satisfied. If he could have, he would have killed him again. That's how fucked up he was over Bubbles's death.

The horn of the van broke E-Way from his trance. Big Whitney had spotted E-Way standing in the middle of the alley. E-Way turned and began running down the alley until reaching the van. Big Whitney peeled off, checking his rearview mirror until crossing 7 Mile to familiar ground.

"Did y'all get DJ's ass?" E-Way asked excitedly as he turned in his seat.

"You know I got that bitch," answered Kev, taking a hit from his blunt.

E-Way smiled and began to relax. Chuck and Chuckie Bom's had laid down a total of seven niggas, including Blood, Marcus's father.

E-Way was finally returning to his normal self. He had gotten the closure he wanted. Kev ditched the van while everyone else jumped into their cars and went their separate ways. E-Way rode in the direction of the salon as he called Mecca's cell phone. It went straight to her voicemail. He started to leave a message but didn't know what to say. He hung up and continued to drive toward the salon. He was hoping Mecca's car would be in its spot, but her spot was vacant. He continued riding down 7 Mile thinking of ways he could get Mecca back.

Meanwhile, Mecca was still at Benji's house. She had just had the wire removed from her jaw, and the color was beginning to return to her face. She and Benji were sitting at the kitchen table playing two-hand spades. Benji was winning as usual.

"You know you can stay here as long as you want to, Mecca," Benji said as he looked into Mecca's eyes. He could always tell when something was bothering Mecca because she would clam up, not saying too much.

"I know, but I'm not sure what I'm going to do. I'm not even sure what it is I want anymore, Benji."

"I'll tell you what I'd do. I'd leave his ass and find me a nigga who appreciates my ass."

"I know, but it's not that easy."

"Once a nigga starts putting his dick beaters on you, it'll never cease. He'll come apologizing with flowers and a card until next time. You my girl no matter what, and I got your back either way. I just don't want to see anything happen to yo' ass."

"Thank you, Benji."

"A'ight, girl, call me if you need anything. I'm about to go get me some dick."

"I'm good," laughed Mecca.

Deep down Mecca knew she wasn't good. A part of her hated E-Way for what he did, and the other part of her wanted to forgive and try to forget the episode. Mecca told herself she would give things one more try, and if E-Way ever put his hands on her again, it was over. She packed her clothes, cleaned the guest room, and then wrote Benji a short thank-you note. Mecca took a cab home, and she noticed E-Way's car parked in the driveway. It was a first. E-Way would usually be out running the streets. Mecca paid the driver, then lugged her bags through the front door.

E-Way heard the front door slam and jumped to his feet. He grabbed his pistol and crept toward the front room. Mecca had set all her bags down and started walking through the kitchen.

"E-Way, are you home?"

E-Way relaxed at the sound of Mecca's voice. He tucked his pistol away, then took a deep breath. He and Mecca ran into each other in the kitchen, and neither one of them said a word.

Mecca was reading E-Way's body language. *He looks sorry.*

E-Way didn't know what to say. He looked at Mecca's still-bruised face, and his eyes began to well up. He walked over to Mecca and took her into his arms. He rubbed her hair and kept telling her how sorry he was, and that it'd never happen again. Mecca believed every word E-Way said. She wanted things to work between them and was willing to try again. She felt a bit of a debt to E-Way like how she did with Benji. E-Way had been there for her at times when she wasn't there for herself.

"How was the funeral?" asked Mecca, breaking the silence. She was trying to lighten the mood.

"I didn't go. Well, I went, but I just couldn't go inside. I couldn't stand to see Bubbles in no damn casket."

"I'm sorry, baby. Are you okay?"

"I'm all right. I should be the one apologizing. Baby, I promise not to ever take things out on you again. Bubbles's death wasn't your fault. It was just his time to go."

"Are you hungry?"

"Nah, I'm good. I'm just glad you're back home. Come on, follow me," E-Way said, grabbing Mecca by the hand. He led her into the bathroom and began running a bath. He lit some scented candles, which surrounded the tub, then began undressing Mecca while kissing her. This was the first time in a long time E-Way had done something romantic. He turned on a slow jams CD. LSG was playing. He undressed himself, then climbed in the tub after Mecca.

E-Way bathed Mecca like a baby. He washed her feet, back, legs, arms, then gave her a deep massage all over, starting with her temples and working his way down to her feet.

"So, a bitch gotta get whooped to get some affection, huh?" laughed Mecca as she enjoyed the massage.

"Baby, you deserve it. You been deserved it, and I promise to start being more affectionate."

"Um hum. Just don't stop," Mecca said as she closed her eyes. She knew E-Way wasn't the romantic type, but she would take what she could get whenever she could get it.

Chapter 6

After about a week of E-Way playing Prince Charming, shit got old. He was missing the streets, and Mecca was missing the salon, and of course that was not to forget her thang-thang Drew. Her face was back to normal, and she couldn't wait to hit Henry's Palace with Benji. It was Thursday.

"I'm going back to work today," said Mecca as she and E-Way ate breakfast in their kitchen.

"You don't work."

"Yes, I do. I'm the manager at the salon, thank you very much."

"Oh, if you consider that working, go right ahead."

"Forget you," laughed Mecca.

"I was just joking. It's good to see you back in the swing of things," said E-Way. He was jumping for joy on the inside, because that meant he was free to do him. As soon as Mecca left for the shop, E-way was out the door.

E-Way met with old man Sal on his yacht. Every so often they would sit on the boat and play chess. Old man Sal would always talk during the games. He'd give E-Way advice about life and the game he was playing on the street. It was like old man Sal knew exactly what E-Way was going through or about to go through.

"Life is much like chess. There's no room for error. You need to tighten up your circle and try to step outside it so that you may watch everyone in it. Always remember that love don't love nobody. In the end, you're all you've got.

Checkmate," said old man Sal as he sat back in his chair and smiled.

E-Way was still trying to figure out how old man Sal made his last move. He had never beaten old man Sal in a game of chess, and as far as he knew, no one had.

E-Way wasn't there for the chess game. He was there to absorb the jewels old man Sal gave him. The game he possessed was priceless. He made you work for it though, always speaking in parables. It was food for thought. E-way would smoke a blunt after meeting with old man Sal and try to decipher all he had said. He had a few beers with old man Sal, then thanked him for the knowledge before leaving.

E-Way sat inside the studio listening to some tracks Kev and Chuck had put down. It wasn't the same without Bubbles. Everything just seemed dead. E-Way thought about what old man Sal had told him about tightening up his circle and stepping outside it. He began analyzing Kev, Chuck, Big Whitney, and Chuckie Bom's. He realized that they were all dead weight and that he was putting out more than he took in. E-Way asked himself an honest question: *would these niggas have done the same for me?* He couldn't honestly say that they would have.

Gunshots broke E-Way from his train of thought. He and everyone else hit the floor for cover as bullets shattered the windows in the studio. Fire could be smelled coming from downstairs. The gunmen set a fire using gasoline all around the bar. It was the remaining Murkland Niggas. They set fire to the bar so E-Way and the rest of KFB would have to exit into gunfire. E-Way had been in situations like this before and had used the same tactic in the past. He knew he couldn't exit the bar at that very second, and most importantly he knew not to panic.

E-Way crawled into the back room and retrieved a MAC-11 and an SKS. He tossed the SKS to Big Whitney, who was slouched down in front of the studio's rear picture window. They nodded at each other, then jumped to their feet. There were two men out back and two out front. E-Way cleared the broken glass from the frame of the front window with the butt of his gun, nearly getting hit in the face with a bullet.

Big Whitney and E-Way were able to get the men to retreat as they let off close to a hundred rounds apiece. Once the men pulled off, E-Way opened the fire escape door, and he and the rest of KFB filed down the stairs. Kev, Chuck, and Chuckie Bom's were all coughing from smoke inhalation. E-Way stood there watching his bar go up in flames. Kev tried to run back up the fire escape. He wanted to get all their masters, but Big Whitney grabbed him. The fire had spread badly, and there was no saving any part of the bar or studio.

The fire department arrived well after the entire building had burned to a crisp. E-Way flashed on the firemen as they sprayed the ash.

"You bitches ain't never on time. I bet if this was on the other side of 8 Mile, you mothafuckas would have been there at the drop of a hat!"

"You've got insurance, don't you, man?" asked one of the firemen. That only infuriated E-Way because he had just realized that he hadn't paid the insurance. The Detroit Police had arrived on the scene and wanted to ask some questions. E-Way wasn't too cooperative with the police or the fire marshal. The police ran a gunpowder residue test on all of them and arrested Big Whitney and E-Way. Kev, Chuck, and Chuckie Bom's were let go after the police took a brief statement.

E-Way and Big Whitney sat in the musty Eleventh Precinct, waiting to be seen by a detective, which sometimes took three days or longer.

E-Way called Mecca's cell phone. It had rung over a dozen times, then went to her voicemail.

"Where this bitch at?" E-Way said to himself. The turnkey had let him use the pay phone and was becoming impatient.

"I'ma try one more time," said E-Way as he dialed Mecca's cell again.

"Hello!" answered Mecca, screaming into the phone.

"Damn, why you hollering all in my ear? Where are you?"

"I'm at the bar with Benji. How come your calls say 'unavailable'?"

"'Cause I'm in jail."

"Jail, for what?"

"Nothing serious. Listen, I'll probably be in here for about three days until I see a detective. I don't have a bond, but just in case, call my lawyer and tell him to try to get me out on a writ in the morning."

"Anything else?"

"Yeah, some lames burned my damn bar down."

"I'm sorry, baby. I wish I could say something. That's too bad."

"Don't worry about it. Just handle that business, and I'll see you in the morning."

"Okay, baby, bye."

"Who was that? You know we don't be taking any calls on our time," Drew said as he gave Mecca an exclusive lap dance.

"That was my man."

"Who, E-Way's funky ass?" asked Benji. "What the fuck he want?"

"He's in jail. Someone burned his bar down."

"Good for his ass," said Benji.

"So does that mean I'll see you tonight?" asked Drew.

"Most definitely. I'll see you after the club."

"Girl, you got a fine piece of meat right there. You ain't sucking all that dick right, we need to do the watoosie tonight," said Benji as he watched Drew walk toward the locker room.

"And just what in the hell is the watoosie?"

"Me, you, and his fine ass. An orgy, girl."

"I think yo' ass done had one too many shots of Patrón."

"Well, can I at least watch?"

"Yo' ass is a freak," laughed Mecca.

"Forget you then. I might have to take him home," Benji said, as he grabbed a passing waiter by the arm. "And what's your name?"

The waiter jerked away as if he were offended by Benji coming on to him. He shot Benji a look of disgust, then kept on his way.

"You's a queer for real. You just ain't had the right one bring it out ya ass yet!" Benji shouted.

Mecca was in tears laughing at Benji. When he got faded, everything was a go with him.

"Fuck this, I'm about to go get me some dick. I'm drunk and I'm horny."

"Where you going?" asked Mecca as Benji stood up and grabbed his purse.

"Over Devin's. I'll see you tomorrow. I want—"

"I know, I know, details."

"That's right goddamn it, details," Benji said as he dug through his purse.

"Don't worry about it, Benji, I got the bill."

"A'ight, then you be safe."

"You too."

Mecca continued to laugh as she watched Benji stagger toward the entrance.

Time had slipped past Mecca. She had stayed the night at Drew's. She was awakened by the sound of free weights hitting the ground. Drew was in the next room running through his workout. Mecca rolled over and looked at the clock. It was almost noon. Her eyes bucked at the sight of the time as she remembered that she was supposed to call E-Way's lawyer. She scrambled for her clothes, looking desperately for her panties.

"Fuck it," she said as she slid into her jeans raw ass. She ran into the other room to let Drew know she was leaving. "How come you let me sleep so late?"

"You looked so peaceful. I didn't want to wake you."

"I'll see you later, okay?"

"Do we have time for a quickie?"

Mecca was tempted by his offer as she stared at Drew's sweaty chest and arms. She shook her head, snapping out of the daydream. "Later," she said, giving Drew a kiss before leaving.

She punched her BMW down Woodward Avenue as she scrolled through her phone. She called the office of John Glaser, E-Way's attorney. His secretary informed Mecca that Mr. Glaser had already been to see E-Way and that he got him out on a writ.

"Shit," Mecca said, then thanked the secretary. She raced home, hoping not to find E-Way there.

Her stomach dropped as she pulled into the driveway and saw E-Way's car parked in its spot. Parked at the curb was a Grosse Pointe squad car. Mecca noticed the police car but didn't think it was of much concern. She was trying to get her lie straight before going into the house. She looked into the mirror and straightened her hair, then sprayed some perfume on her pants. She took a deep breath, then exited the car. She entered the house through the front door to find E-Way standing in the living room with two white cops. The house was ransacked, and glass was everywhere. E-Way turned from the police and rushed over to Mecca.

"Baby, are you okay? I thought you were kidnapped."

"Kidnapped!" Mecca repeated, then caught herself. "I came home last night and found the house like this, and I got scared so I went over to Benji's for the night."

"It's going to be all right, baby," said E-Way as he hugged Mecca, then kissed her.

"Do you have any idea who could have done this?" asked one of the officers.

E-Way shook his head. He honestly didn't know. He had never shown anyone besides Bubbles where he lived.

The police dusted for fingerprints and made a report. "We'll be in touch with our findings," said the other officer, handing E-Way a card.

"That's it? A mothafucka breaks in my house, violates my space, and that's it? You'll be in touch. Shit, I could have stayed in Detroit. It ain't no safer out here than it is there. Just get the hell out," snapped E-Way as he ushered the two officers to the front door, slamming it behind them.

Nothing was missing from the house, not even Mecca's jewelry. The burglars were looking for something in particular. Whatever they were searching for it sure wasn't in the house. E-Way made sure never to keep dope where he laid his head, and the bulk of his money was stashed at his grandmother's house. He was surprised that nothing had been taken and wondered who was responsible. He tried to tell himself that maybe whoever did it didn't know it was his home, and maybe it was a random robbery. But nothing was taken. It wasn't adding up.

Mecca was relieved that she hadn't been busted for her episode with Drew. She hurried into the bathroom, locking the door behind her so she could shower. E-Way wasn't giving two shits about Mecca and her whereabouts. It seemed things couldn't possibly get any worse for E-Way, with the loss of Bubbles, the fire at the studio, him going to jail, and someone breaking into his house.

The house phone rang. It was E-way's uncle Toby. His grandmother had just been forced into the house at gunpoint by two masked men. They slapped her around and demanded that she show them where the drugs and money were. She pleaded for her life and swore on the blood of Jesus that she didn't know anything about drugs or money. The gunmen reluctantly left empty-handed, but not before beating ole Grams. They beat her into a coma. The next-door neighbor had witnessed the men force her inside.

E-Way couldn't stand hearing any more, so he slammed the phone down. His eyes welled up at the thought of his grandmother lying in the hospital and being attacked. He began hyperventilating as he went berserk, throwing the remainder of the unbroken glass artifacts. He ran upstairs and grabbed his AR-15, then was out the door. He called each member of KFB and told them to meet him at his grandmother's house.

He punched it down McNichols, running every light that caught him. He was listening to Pac's latest CD, *Thug Mansion,* and was feeling every word that came through the speakers. E-Way's eyes were bloodshot from the anger inside. *Someone had the balls to put their hands on Grams,* he thought as he floored the accelerator. By the time he pulled up, everyone from family to all of KFB were already there.

"Man, what happened, my nigga?" asked Kev as E-Way approached the front porch, where everyone was gathered.

"Nothing compared to what's finna happen." E-Way told them what happened, how his house had been broken into and his grandmother was beaten.

"You think them ho-ass Murkland bitches did this shit?" asked Chuckie Bom's.

"Who else could have done it? They the only mothafuckas we at war with," said Kev.

"Yeah, but how they know where you live?" asked Chuck.

"That's a good-ass question," E-Way said as he looked off into space. He thought about the possibility of the gunmen returning to his house and didn't want Mecca to experience what his grandmother had. E-Way called Mecca at home and told her to leave the house and go stay with Benji until he got things situated.

Kev went to steal another van. He was unable to find a conversion van this time, so he settled on a minivan. All of KFB climbed into the van, leaving their cars parked in front of E-Way's grandmother's house. Big Whitney, the designated driver, turned the corner of Bloom, and lo and behold, the remainder of Murkland Niggas stood on the very same corner where seven of their homies lost their lives. Teddy bears and empty liquor bottles surrounded the telephone pole on the corner of Bloom and Emery.

The men on the corner were like sitting ducks just waiting to be killed. It was a vicious game of cat and mouse. They called it beef. E-Way wasn't focused on the group of men standing on the corner. He instructed Big Whitney to stop halfway up the block. They pulled in front of a red brick ranch home and parked. The house was packed with people, little kids were running back and forth in the front yard, and two old men sat on the porch drinking and playing checkers. Silhouettes could be seen in the house through the front door. The house belonged to Marcus's mother and late father, Blood.

"Kill every mothafucka in this bitch!" ordered E-Way as he, Kev, Chuck, and Chuckie Bom's exited the van wearing hoodies and carrying assault rifles.

The two older gentlemen on the porch hadn't noticed the gang as they climbed the stairs to the porch. Kev blindsided the first gentleman, shooting him in his left temple. Before the second man could react, Kev flatlined him. E-Way, Chuck, and Chuckie Bom's rushed inside the house. There wasn't anyone in the front room. Five women sat at the kitchen table adjacent to the living room. They began screaming at the sight of the assault rifles.

"Which one of you bitches is Marcus's mother?" asked E-Way.

No one said anything. They just continued to scream at the top of their lungs. E-Way figured that one of them had to be his mother, so he shot and killed all of them. Chuck went upstairs and found Bootsy, Marcus's little brother, hiding under the bed. Chuck had seen his shoe sticking out of the side of the bed. He acted like he was going to leave, then fell to his knees, shooting underneath the bed and hitting Bootsy in the face.

After killing everyone inside the house, they all jumped into the van where Big Whitney sat waiting with the engine running. Kev shot into the crowd of men standing on the corner, hitting three people as they sped past. It was all-out war, and everything was fair game. E-Way knew that he'd have to move his grandmother once she was released from the hospital. The beef was too intense and really foolish because everyone knew where everyone's people stayed.

There were too many of them niggas to try to kill them all. The immediate members were dead, but Murkland was a hood thing, just like KFB but on a larger scale. Everyone was getting involved from young to old. That's how it was when they were in high school. Every time KFB fought Murkland they would always lose because grown-ass men would come up to Pershing and jump in it. Old man Sal had much respect among both generations because he had that dust. What he said went. He would always get word to Blood, Marco's father, to squash the beef.

It was a new day and age. He couldn't squash the beef if he wanted to. A nigga would slump his old ass if necessary. He got word to E-Way that they needed to meet. E-Way knew exactly what the old man wanted: another life lecture. He and E-Way met on his yacht for another game of chess.

"Have you not been listening to what I've been trying to instill in you?" asked old man Sal as he and E-Way played their first game.

E-Way knew not to answer. His job was to listen.

Old Sal continued, "Your chess game is a reflection of you. The way you move on the board is how you'll move in life. Right now, you're moving without thinking. You've started a war that you're not prepared to fight. Look at the bar, and I know you let the insurance lapse. Checkmate," said old Sal. He was less enthusiastic about the game than before.

"Look at me, Matt."

E-Way looked up from the chessboard like a little boy about to be chastised.

"Son, death is near. You need to consider leaving the city for a while. I hope that you've put some money away. Take a vacation. Have you ever been outside of Detroit?"

E-Way shook his head.

"That's a damn shame, son. The world is bigger than just the east side of Detroit. I'm going to get you a passport. I want you to see that the world has a lot more to offer."

E-Way, as always, thanked old man Sal for his advice and concern.

E-Way drove down Jefferson lost in thought. He couldn't stop thinking about what old Sal said. *"Death is near."*

Chapter 7

Mecca had been staying at Benji's house while E-Way tried to sort things out. She was going to go to work from Benji's. Like any other day, she did her morning exercises and was out the door. She had to go back inside the house because Benji had her car blocked.

"Benji, come move your car, boy. You've got me blocked in," said Mecca as she pushed the door open to Benji's room. He was in bed, balled up into a fetal position, crying.

"Did you hear me, Benji? How come you're not up?"

Benji didn't respond. He was still sniffling and crying. He had his back to Mecca. She had realized that Benji was crying. She climbed in bed and took out some Kleenex from the box on the nightstand.

"Is it Devin's funky ass? 'Cause I will fuck him straight up," said Mecca as she wiped Benji's tears, then handed him a few tissues. "Benji, talk to me. What's wrong?"

Benji tried to talk but wept harder in his attempt.

Mecca felt helpless. She wanted to be there for Benji for once and couldn't even support him properly because she didn't know what was bothering him. Benji was always the strong one. He'd be comforting Mecca after a breakup or if she was just depressed.

"Benji, please talk to me," Mecca begged as she began crying.

The sight of Mecca crying made Benji try to gain his composure. Benji sat up in bed and took a deep breath. "Mecca, I want to tell you something, but I want you to promise not to flip out."

"What is it?" Mecca asked, wiping her tears.

"Okay, Mecca, I have AIDS."

"What?" Mecca yelled. "Who gave you that shit, Devin?"

"I don't know," Benji cried.

"How long have you had it?"

Benji was crying his eyes out but was still trying to communicate with his friend. "The doctor said I've had it about three years, but I just found out about six months ago."

"How come you didn't say anything?"

"I refuse to believe it. Plus, I didn't want you worrying about me. This morning, I woke up and discovered these on my legs," Benji said, pulling the blanket off his legs and revealing several lesions. "The doctor said that I'm in the final stage."

"What's the final stage?"

"Full-blown AIDS."

"Isn't there something that they can do?"

"Not too much of nothing."

"Oh, Benji," cried Mecca as she took him into her arms. "We'll get through this. I'll be right here by your side, I promise. You hear me?"

"Yes," cried Benji.

Mecca continued to hold Benji in her arms as they cried their eyes out. Mecca couldn't imagine life without Benji. He was her inspiration.

Without Benji, the shop would fall to pieces. He was the backbone for a lot of people, not just Mecca. Benji was the type of person who always protected those around him and would do anything to see them happy, even if it was at his own expense.

He made up his mind that he wasn't going to be defeated by this. He told himself that he had AIDS and it didn't have him. Telling Mecca was a burden lifted from his shoulders. He just needed to share the news with someone.

"Come on," he said.

"Where we going?" asked Mecca.

"Where else? To the shop. We done cried, and now it's time to smile. People need their hair done, so let's make it."

Mecca smiled as Benji got ready for another day at the shop. He had to be the strongest person she had ever met. *That's the Benji I know.*

She picked out Benji's clothes while he took a quick shower. He dressed to perfection as always, with his signature necktie and ass-hugger slacks. He slapped some Gucci perfume on, checked his situation one last time in the mirror, and then was out the door.

"Why are you smiling so damn hard, girl?" asked Benji as he and Mecca rode in his car on their way to the shop.

"'Cause I absolutely love you."

"What did I tell you about love? It'll only get you down."

"Well, Benji, you better not let me down."

Benji just smiled as he grabbed Mecca's hand and kissed it. "Have I ever?"

"No."

"A'ight, then."

The shop was as jam-packed as any other day. Mecca and Benji were greeted with the phony "hey, how you doing's" and complimented on their attire, and then it was right to work. Benji was running behind. He had two heads waiting. He handled the situation expertly as he directed Veronica the shampoo girl to take the second woman while he washed his first appointment's hair.

"Mecca, there's someone in the back here to see you. She said that she's your mother," Tae informed her.

Mecca frowned, then stormed into the back room, which she deemed to be her office. She swung the door open to find her mother, Yvette, looking through some photos of a recent hair show. Her mother looked up and smiled at the sight of her. She put down the photos and walked over to Mecca, who was still standing in the doorway. Yvette attempted to hug Mecca, but she jerked away.

"What . . ." Mecca yelled, then caught herself. She closed the door, then finished her initial question. "What are you doing here, and what do you want, Yvette?" Mecca had always called her mom by her first name. She hated her and had minimum respect for her.

"I came to see about my little girl. Am I wrong for that?"

"Well, first of all, I'm more than all right. And as you can see, I'm no longer a little girl. But I forgot, you missed me growing up."

"Mecca, baby, I didn't come here to argue."

"So, why did you come? Because you're certainly not welcome."

Mecca was always short with Yvette. She'd say something hurtful, then watch as it took its effect. She watched her words crush Yvette's world. Not for one second was Mecca about to let her believe that she had the right to call herself a mother. Yvette stood there looking like the true crackhead she was, wearing a musty, yellowing tank top, a pair of ancient Guess shorts that had seen better days, and a pair of run-down Nike cross-trainers that now just said "Ike." Her hair was still its original length, the same as Mecca's, but it was matted to her skull from many days of not washing it.

"Mecca, I need some help. I'm tired of living like this. I want us to be a family again."

"We were never a family. Ya left me, remember? I wish you would do the same right now because you crowding my space."

"Your father is sick and in the hospital. They believe he has multiple sclerosis."

"That nigga ain't my father, and too bad for his ass. I hope he got insurance."

"Are you going to help me, Mecca? I would appreciate it very much."

"What do you want from me?"

"Help me enroll in a treatment center and help me through it. Please, baby girl!"

"I'm not no damn drug counselor. You don't need me for that."

"Well, I tried," Yvette said, throwing her hands up in the air.

Mecca became furious at Yvette's sly, slick little statement. "You tried? Tried what? You act like a mothafucka supposed to just drop what they're doing and focus on you because you woke up today and decided you want to stop smoking crack. You're a grown-ass woman. News flash, Yvette, you're not a little girl anymore. Talkin' about you tried. You need to try to get yo' ass up out of here and let folks get back to their work."

Mecca's mission had been accomplished. She had scourged Yvette's ass once again. Mecca watched as

Yvette dropped her head, then turned on her heels, heading for the door. Benji stopped Yvette at the entrance and slipped her a fifty.

"Make sure you put something in your stomach," whispered Benji.

Yvette smiled, then thanked Benji before leaving. Benji had always been nice to Yvette out of respect that she was Mecca's mom. He'd see Yvette at the gas station from time to time and would always drop some change on her. Mecca hated when Benji was nice to her. She wanted everyone to hate Yvette just as much as she did.

Benji entered the back room to find Mecca slumped down in her office chair, pouting.

"Are you okay, Mecca?"

"How the hell she gon' bring her tainted ass up in here? Talkin' about she tried, asking me for help."

Benji just let Mecca vent her emotions as he listened. Mecca hated Yvette because it was like looking in the mirror every time she saw her. That's how much they resembled each other. People would always tell Mecca how much she looked like her mother. Boy, she hated that. Yvette had never come into the shop before. She would usually catch Mecca on her way in. Mecca felt like Yvette was out of bounds bringing herself into her place of business.

Mecca calmed down, and Benji returned to his client. E-Way and Kev had entered the shop, and all eyes were directed in their direction. Benji caught the specific eye contact between Olivia and E-Way. He broke up their obvious flirting by clearing his throat and then gave E-Way a look of death.

E-Way laughed slightly, then asked, "Where Mecca at, in the back?"

Benji didn't answer.

"Yeah, she back there," answered Marie.

Kev scanned the shop and caught the eye of a young lady getting her nails done. He walked over to the nail station and tried spitting a li'l game at the girl, but she wasn't feeling him. She looked him up and down with a look that said, "You're dismissed." Kev stood there with the shit face. And Tory's silly ass didn't help matters.

"Country black, can't you see the woman ain't feeling you?" laughed Tory.

Everyone in the shop joined in on the laughter.

Kev had to save face, so he went into boss mode. "You old bad-body, bucket-head bitch. I fucked you already anyway."

"Bitch! Who you calling a bitch?" yelled Tory. She and the young lady were both waiting for Kev to answer.

"I mean both of y'all some bitches."

Tory jumped up and charged toward Kev, but Benji intervened in the nick of time. "Kev, you gon' have to wait outside," said Benji.

"What? You putting me out? I'm a boss. Bosses don't get put out. I'm leaving," Kev said as he mean mugged Tory.

"Get your Marvin the Martian ass out of here," snapped Tory.

"You just mad because I ain't tried to hollar at yo' funny-built ass. You's a Floss-A-Lot groupie bitch," said Kev as he exited the shop.

"Who was that?" asked the young lady getting her nails done.

"One of E-Way's flunkies. Nigga faking like he getting money. Fake-ass, local-rapping nigga," said Tory. She was in her feelings because for once someone had roasted her.

"You sound a little salty," Olivia said sarcastically.

"Hey, baby," E-Way said as he entered the back room to find Mecca working on the computer.

"What are you doing here?" Mecca asked, surprised.

"Here to get you." E-Way pulled two first-class tickets to Barbados out of his pocket, then handed them to Mecca.

"Barbados," Mecca said.

"That's right. I told you we would spend more time together. Our flight leaves in a few hours, so I need you to go home and pack a bag. We'll go shopping when the plane lands."

Mecca jumped to her feet, forgetting about what she had been doing on the computer. She grabbed her purse, kissed E-Way, and then raced out the door.

"Where you going? You grinning from ear to ear," said Benji.

"Bitch, I'm going to Barbados," answered Mecca, handing Benji the tickets.

E-Way had made his way back to the front. Olivia was mean mugging E-Way from head to toe. She had the shit face.

"'Bout time you stepped your game up," Benji said, rolling his eyes at E-Way. "A'ight, Miss Thang, send me a postcard," said Benji as Mecca and E-Way made their exit.

E-Way dropped Kev off, then headed home so he and Mecca could pack a few things. E-Way hadn't bothered to tell anyone, with the exception of old man Sal, that he was leaving. Kev and the rest of KFB were under the impression that E-Way was going to re-up tomorrow because they were all just about out of drugs. E-Way hadn't thought much about selling drugs. He just needed to get away for a minute and clear his head. The trip was scheduled for four days and five nights.

Mecca had the window seat, while E-Way lay across her lap like a baby. "Wake me up when the plane lands," he said.

Mecca enjoyed the view and compliments of first class. She sipped several glasses of Cristal and enjoyed two bite-sized steaks. Mecca had never been out of the country, and she felt like a little girl on a field trip. The only traveling she had ever done had been with Benji for hair shows. She had been to Chicago, Atlanta, Miami, Vegas, and a few other spots, but who hadn't? *It isn't every day a bitch goes to Barbados,* she told herself. Mecca kissed E-Way on his cheek, awakening him.

"We there already?" he asked.

"No, sleepyhead. I'm just happy and thankful, that's all."

E-Way smiled, then drifted back to sleep. Mecca had the best of both worlds, or so she thought. With E-Way, she had stability and comfort. And with Drew, she had companionship. Everything that E-Way lacked she found in Drew, and vice versa. Together she had the perfect man.

After two movies and about ten glasses of Cristal, the plane finally touched down in beautiful Barbados. Mecca absorbed every detail as the plane screeched to a stop at the Barbados airport. Beaches with white sand could be seen within walking distance.

E-Way and Mecca took a shuttle to the Four Seasons Hotel about two miles from the airport. Old man Sal had already booked them a suite overlooking the ocean. Old man Sal suggested E-Way go to Barbados. It was one of his favorite getaways. Since the seventies, old Sal had been a regular tourist, taking his young thangs there for a rendezvous.

Mecca raced over to the balcony of their suite and opened the sliding screens. She nearly lost her breath at the sight of the sparkling blue water. The tranquility of the place overwhelmed Mecca, and she was speechless. It was a much different scene from the hustle and bustle she was used to in Detroit. She walked out onto the balcony and took a deep breath, then exhaled with her eyes closed.

E-Way joined Mecca out on the balcony. He was carrying two champagne glasses and a bucket of chilled rosé.

"Aren't you just Mr. Romantic?" Mecca said, taking one of the glasses.

E-Way poured her and then himself a drink and gave a toast. "Here's to us," he said, downing his glass.

E-Way's toast gave Mecca mixed feelings. She was happy to be there with him and couldn't imagine herself being there with anyone other than E-Way. But when E-Way said, "To us," Mecca knew deep down that those were just words. She had begun to feel guilty about her late-night affairs with Drew. She tried to justify her dealings by telling herself that E-Way had cheated on her too, although she never caught him red-handed, but she knew.

Just enjoy the moment, Mecca told herself. She refilled her glass and began to relax.

E-Way ushered her over to a chaise longue next to the railing of the balcony. Mecca lay across the sofa, and E-Way took a seat at its end. He lifted Mecca's feet into his lap, then removed her heels. He began massaging Mecca's foot, starting with the arch.

"Ooh, ah," Mecca sighed in satisfaction.

E-Way applied just enough pressure to every inch of Mecca's feet.

After massaging Mecca's feet, E-Way lifted Mecca's sundress and removed her lace panties. He positioned himself between her legs, putting them on his shoulders. He spread the skirts of Mecca's pussy with both hands, then began licking her clit. Mecca closed her eyes and laid her head back, while gripping E-Way's ears. He started licking faster with each moan Mecca gave. As she began to climax, E-Way sucked down on her entire pussy, swallowing every ounce of nut. Mecca mashed E-Way's face in her pussy as she continued to climax. She jerked with every thrust. Her legs had locked around E-Way's neck she nutted so hard.

E-Way slid out of his shorts and boxers, then climbed on top of Mecca. He inserted his foot-long dick and began stroking Mecca while kissing her neck. E-Way took Mecca's legs and pressed them up against her shoulders so he could deep stroke her. He watched as his dick slid in and out of Mecca's pussy. His dick was soaking wet and gleaming from the juices of Mecca's pussy. She moaned while biting her bottom lip and looking E-Way in the eyes.

E-Way couldn't last another stroke. He busted off a fat nut on Mecca's stomach, then slid his half-limp dick back inside her. They both were breathing heavily. It had been a good minute since E-Way had laid pipe like that on Mecca.

"Get it back up," Mecca said as she sat up and began giving E-Way head. After getting him back up, she climbed on top of E-Way's dick and worked him out of another nut. They went at it all afternoon until the sun set. The beach had been deserted with the exception of a few lovebirds. Mecca had noticed and wanted to carry their escapade down to the beach. She grabbed E-Way by the hand and led him out of the hotel room down to the beach.

The stars seemed as if they were within arm's reach, that's how clear the sky was. And the water had an aroma of freshness. It was like a heated swimming pool. The water was still warm, and the fossils below sparkled like diamonds. Mecca removed her bathing suit and walked out into the water. She turned around and motioned E-Way to join her with one finger. E-Way dropped his swimming trunks and ran out into the water. He swooped Mecca into his arms and began kissing her.

They made love in the depths of the ocean and again on the warm white sand on the beach. For the most part, all they did was have sex, with the exception of Mecca shopping for souvenirs for Benji. Neither Mecca nor E-Way wanted to leave Barbados. They dreaded the routines that awaited them back in Detroit.

"Do we have to go back?" Mecca asked.

"I wish we didn't have to," E-Way answered as he packed his things. He honestly meant what he said. And he realized the truth of his words as he spoke them. He stopped packing his bag and flopped down on the end of the bed.

"What's wrong?" Mecca asked as she had also stopped packing her bag. She noticed that something had come over E-Way.

"I'm done," E-Way said.

"Done? Done with what?" asked Mecca.

"I'm done with all the shit I have waiting on me back in Detroit. I'm done with all the street fame, money, all that shit!" E-Way said, then threw his bag on the floor.

Mecca was standing there like, *okay, where is all this coming from?* E-Way put his face down in his hands and rubbed his temples. Mecca sat on the bed next to E-Way and put her arm around him. She didn't say anything. She was now lost in her own thoughts. If E-Way stopped hustling, how would she support her lavish lifestyle? What would they do? She began adding up how much money E-Way supposedly had saved, and it wasn't nearly enough to just up and quit. She began to think out loud.

"So, what are we going to do?" she asked.

E-Way hadn't yet thought about that, but he knew it was time for a change. "I don't know, but I'll figure something out. We'll be straight, whatever it is."

Mecca didn't feel much assurance. She knew E-Way to be a drug dealer and that was it. He had no other skills to her knowledge. She knew that selling dope wouldn't last forever and was in favor of a change. But money was needed to make that change. She told herself that E-Way was just talking, and once they were back in Detroit, he would be his normal drug-dealing self again.

Chapter 8

Back in Detroit, both Mecca's and E-Way's real lives awaited them. The shop was as jam-packed as any other day. Mecca sashayed through the door looking and feeling fabulous with her bronze tan. She stopped in the center of the salon and struck a pose.

"People, people. Do gather," she said as she dug into a bag full of souvenirs, then began passing them out. She handed Benji a gold necklace laced with pearls, and a matching tennis bracelet. She then handed Marie a beautiful seashell. She gave Tae an hourglass filled with white sand. Olivia stood there waiting for her gift.

Mecca looked down into the bag, then back up at Olivia. "All out of gifts. No, hold on," she said, then tossed Olivia a bottle of tanning lotion.

Olivia looked at the label and said, "Lotion."

"Yeah, you a little ashy. That ought to take care of it," Mecca said.

Everyone in the shop burst out laughing, and Olivia stood there with the shit face once again.

"People, people. Please excuse the accent."

"Damn, Mecca, you ain't bring a bitch nothin'?" asked Tory.

"My bad, Tory. You know you my girl. I tell you what, tonight let's hit Henry's Palace on me."

With that Tory was bought.

"What about me?" said Pete.

"Oh, you can come too."

"So, you got jokes."

Benji excused himself from his customer, then ushered Mecca into the back room. "Details, bitch." He pulled up a chair.

Mecca also pulled out a chair and flopped down. She was all smiles as she gave Benji the rundown.

"Well, you look like you got your swagger back," said Benji, awaiting more details.

"Yeah, I'm good. Except for one thing."

"What's that?"

"E-Way flipped out down there."

"He ain't put his hands on you again, did he?" Benji asked, cutting Mecca off.

"No, no."

"I was about to say, but go ahead, girl."

"He's talking about stopping hustling and everything. I think the nigga is having a midlife crisis. Nigga go out of the country and don't want to come back."

"That's a good thing, isn't it?" asked Benji.

"It is, but it isn't. We don't have enough money saved for him to just up and quit hustling. A bitch need Prada, Gucci, gators, and whatnot. He doesn't even have a backup plan."

"Do you?"

Truth be told, Mecca didn't have a backup plan either.

"Hell yeah, I'm gon' leave his ass if he don't tighten up."

"That's the ho I raised," Benji said, giving Mecca a high five.

"Has Yvette been in here while I was gone?"

"I haven't seen your mom since the last time you put her out."

"She is not my mom, and good. I hope she stays the hell out of here."

"Let me get back out here to my customer before that perm mess her hair up."

"You hitting Henry's tonight with me and Tory?"

"Yeah, I might let my presence be felt."

"A'ight, now," Mecca said, laughing at Benji as he rubbed his thighs.

Meanwhile, E-Way got up with Chuck and the rest of KFB. They met at the State Fair Lounge deep east. They were all flipping out on E-Way because they thought something had happened to him.

"Man, you just up and leave without telling anybody. I thought niggas got at you," said Big Whitney.

"Yeah, man, on my word we was going through there today if you didn't surface," added Kev.

Now that everyone saw that E-Way was all right, it was time to talk business. Chuck and Chuckie Bom's together handed E-Way a brown paper bag. Kev and Big Whitney did the same. E-Way had thought about not re-upping, but he had to at least two more times, he told himself, and he would have enough money to leave the game alone.

"You know how much money we missing right now?" asked Kev.

"A couple of my custos started going across the bridge. I'm gon' have to call and let 'em know I'm back on," said Chuckie Bom's.

E-Way usually would have been in on the conversation, but it just felt elementary. He had indeed made a conscious decision to change. The conversation was so boring. E-Way decided to end the meeting.

"Since we're all here, I might as well tell y'all now," E-Way said as everyone sat up at attention.

"What's the deal, my nigga?" asked Kev.

"After we finish the next two loads, I'm done," said E-Way.

"Done with what?" asked Big Whitney, dreading the answer.

"I'm done with the game. It's time to do something else."

"Like what?" asked Chuck.

"Man, you done lost your damn mind. Ever since Bubbles got killed, you been on some other shit. What about us?" asked Kev.

E-Way hadn't given much thought to the rest of KFB's well-being. Everyone was all ears waiting for E-Way's response. Kev, just like everyone else, figured E-Way had enough money to get out of the game already and felt he was going Hollywood.

"I'm going to turn y'all on to the plug so y'all can keep doing y'all. More than likely, it'll be Big Whitney who I introduce to the plug. The rest of y'all can get on through Whit."

It sounded logical and fair, and having said that, everyone started to relax. Kev tried to lighten the mood.

"So, yo' ass got aspirations, huh?" Kev asked jokingly.

Everyone joined in laughter.

"But for real though, you serious, E? I mean, you can always change your mind," said Big Whitney. He was lying through his teeth. On the inside he was screaming for joy that he would be turned on to the plug.

E-Way read through the bullshit and didn't acknowledge Whitney's question. He was thinking whether the plug would allow him to turn Whitney on. E-Way doubted it. But he had to at least try, seeing that he just gave them his word.

First things first, E-Way had to run things by old man Sal, seeing as he was the one who plugged him. E-Way excused himself from the group and headed out to the Detroit River, where old Sal's yacht was docked. Sure enough, old Sal was perched on the yacht in a lounge chair. He was entertaining four young ladies.

"Glad to see you in good spirits, Pops," E-Way said as he boarded the boat.

He always called old Sal Pops. He was the only father figure he ever knew. Old Sal got up to greet E-Way. He was wearing a pair of Polo shorts, no shirt, a pair of Polo deck shoes, and a captain's hat. He was a bit tipsy and was in a good mood.

"Y'all say hello to my son," old Sal said, talking to the young ladies. They all said hello, then carried on their conversation. They were all in bathing suits and heels. Old Sal had a "no clothes" rule for women while on his yacht, but it was a little windy, so he gave them a pass.

"Which one you want?" asked old Sal.

E-Way laughed at old Sal's boldness. "You's out of control," E-Way said, still laughing.

"I'm serious. If I tell them skanks to jump in that water, I bet they do it. Watch this," old Sal said, removing a bankroll large enough to choke a chicken from his pocket. "I got five thousand for the first one who can swim to that yacht and back, but you gotta do it naked," he said, pointing to a yacht docked about twenty yards away.

The four young ladies all looked at each other, then raced to take off their clothes. They jumped in the water like they were on the swim team. Old Sal laughed at the sight of them swimming nude for the currency.

"The power of a dollar, boy, I'll tell you," old Sal said as he took two beers out of the cooler, then handed E-Way one. "So how was the trip?"

"It was wonderful. I started not to come back."

"I knew you'd like it. What about Mecca? Did she enjoy it?"

"Yeah, I'm going to have to start traveling more often."

"Now you're thinking."

One of the young ladies climbed back into the yacht soaking wet, ass and titties everywhere. She wasn't fazed by her nudity. She was too geeked that she won the five grand.

"Here you go, baby," old Sal said, handing the girl fifty $100 bills. It was all one big game to old Sal. Five Gs was like five cents to him. He was still amazed how people would exploit themselves for a few bucks.

E-Way was contemplating how he would bring up the topic of leaving the game and turning Whitney on to the plug. Old Sal interrupted his thoughts.

"Boy, what's wrong? Why you off in space?"

"I need to talk to you about something."

Old Sal snapped his fingers and motioned for the young ladies to excuse themselves. "What's on your mind?"

"I want out," answered E-Way.

Old Sal took a long swig of his beer, then repeated E-Way's statement. "'I want out.' You sound like we part of the mob or something. Ain't nobody forcing you to sell dope. If you want out, quit."

"Seriously?" asked E-Way.

Old Sal got up to get another beer, then returned to his nook. "Let me tell you something. What one won't do, another one will. If you were to die or go to jail right now, you don't think that Subi would find someone to replace you? Thirty years ago, when I met Subi's father, Ali, he was already filthy rich. You know why? Because before me there was somebody else. The name of the game is get rich and quit before your ass is late. Shit, I think it's a good idea you get out. Run, nigga, run," laughed old Sal.

One down, one to go, E-Way told himself. "I knew you'd understand, Pops."

"Now we'll have more time to play chess and mess with these tenderonies."

"Just one more thing. I promised my crew I'd turn 'em on once I'm finished."

"Hell to the nah. Them niggas is crash dummies. Don't turn them on to shit. I mean it."

"But, Pops—"

"There's no life after but to hell with them lames. I told you they would be your downfall. When you leave the game, leave it altogether. I turned you on because I trained you. I knew you were going to make it. You can't save everybody, Matt. Do you see me hanging with a bunch of niggas? No, and I never have. It's not my style, and it ain't player like. Niggas always think you owe 'em something." Old Sal downed his beer, then slammed the can down on the table.

"Pops, I didn't mean to upset you."

"I'm not upset. I just want you to start moving like a seasoned vet. You know what your problem is? Your heart is too big. It's going to be the death of you. You watch and see." Old Sal had enough. He got up and walked into the cabin where the young ladies were, leaving E-Way out on the deck.

E-Way sipped his beer and watched the boats as they passed. He thought about what old Sal had said and his promise to his boys. Whatever Old Sal said usually went, so E-Way told himself that they would have to find their own connect. He wasn't about to go against old Sal's instructions. He was one of the two people who could tell E-Way something and he listened. He and his grandmother.

Mecca, Benji, Marie, and Tory all sat front row in their usual VIP booth at Henry's Palace. They were yacked up and acting donkey as the many fine brothas took to the stage.

"Work that mothafucka!" yelled Marie. She was standing up, throwing bills onto the stage. She had come all the way out of her shell. Mecca and Benji laughed and egged her on.

"Spend that money, girl," said Benji.

"That nigga got an elephant dick," Marie said as she took her seat.

They all high-fived and laughed at Marie's comment.

It was a typical night out at ole Henry's. Dick was everywhere, and the women were spending big dollars. It could be argued that women were more addicted to strip clubs than men. Reason being, women tended to get emotionally involved with someone in the club. They became possessive and reckless. A woman would take her man's, sometimes husband's, money and give it to one of them steroid-taking niggas. In Henry's, it was happening every day.

Mecca excused herself and went to the ladies' room. On her way back, she noticed Drew sitting with a woman near the back of the club. He wasn't on business, or so Mecca thought. He wasn't giving the woman a lap dance or trying to work her out of a dollar. He was extra close, obviously flirting with the woman. The bitch was busted to Mecca's standards. He could have at least been fucking with a dime. Drew hadn't notice Mecca standing over him. He was too busy kissing on ole girl's neck.

"Drew!" yelled Mecca.

Drew sat up a little but didn't acknowledge Mecca quite how she expected him to.

"I didn't know you were coming through tonight. How come you ain't call me?"

"I bet you didn't know," Mecca said, rolling her eyes at ole girl.

"Drew, I didn't know you were married," the woman said, shooting a look at Mecca.

"Bitch, you tryin' to get cute?" asked Mecca.

"Who you calling a bitch, bitch?"

The woman tried to stand up, but Mecca grabbed a half-full Corona and slapped her across the face with it.

Mecca climbed on top of the woman and beat the shit out of her.

"Girl, look! Ain't that Mecca over there?"

"Sho' is," Benji said, removing his shoes, then running to assist Mecca.

"Let me get the bitch," Benji said, pulling Mecca off the woman.

Marie and Tory also came to Mecca's aid. They all took turns stomping the woman and ragdolling her until the bouncers broke it up. It was common for this sort of thing to happen on any given night. Damn near every night there was some type of drama, whether it was two women fighting over one of the dancers or a husband out in the parking lot threatening to kill one of the dancers for messing around with his wife.

The bouncers tossed Mecca, Benji, Marie, and Tory out into the parking lot. The woman whose ass they beat had to be rushed to the emergency room. She suffered severe head trauma.

Drew disappeared off into the locker room once the madness popped off. He couldn't afford for the owner to know he was the nucleus of the matter, or he would be fined. It was made known to every dancer when they first started that it was forbidden to have relationships with customers.

Mecca was in a blind rage. She was upset that Drew had tried to play her, so she walked over to his brand-new Corvette and keyed her initials in the driver's door. That wasn't enough damage, she thought, so she went to her trunk and removed a tire iron. Benji, Marie, and Tory were already in the car. They were buzzing and hadn't really noticed Mecca's absence. They were replaying the ass whooping they had just put down. A Detroit police car pulled into the parking lot, breaking up their laughter and blowing their high. Benji realized that Mecca wasn't in the driver's seat and scanned the parking lot for her.

Mecca was standing on the roof of Drew's Corvette, hammering his windshield with the tire iron.

"What the fuck is wrong with this crazy bitch?" Benji said as he got out of the car and called Mecca's name.

It was too late. The police pulled in front of the car and flashed the light on Mecca. They got out and drew their weapons, ordering Mecca to get down. She complied and was cuffed, then was hauled off to jail.

Chapter 9

The next day, Mecca was released from jail. Drew had told the arresting officers he didn't wish to press charges, but they booked her anyway for public intoxication, disorderly conduct, and for basically wasting their time. Drew wasn't tripping about the car, because Mecca had paid the bulk of the money for it. And he figured he'd just have her pay to get it fixed. Mecca had to explain to E-Way why she spent the night in jail. She couldn't say that she spent the night at Benji's because Benji had run into E-Way at an all-night eatery, Coney Island. He asked where Mecca was at, and Benji told him that they went to the bar and got into it with some chicks and that Mecca had been arrested.

Benji picked Mecca up from the Tenth Precinct early in the morning. He briefed Mecca on what to tell E-Way so that their stories wouldn't contradict each other's, and then he dropped her off at home so she could get her situation together.

"What the fuck you get arrested for last night, and how come you didn't call me?" E-Way shouted as Mecca walked through the front door. E-Way had slept on the couch, nodding in and out all night waiting for the phone to ring.

"No 'are you all right, I was worried'? Just what the fuck I get arrested for?" Mecca said.

"Don't play with me, Mecca. Yo' ass was probably up there fighting over some nigga. Don't let me find out you been giving my money to one of them pretty-ass niggas. I'ma fuck you up." E-Way had hit the nail on the head. His words were so convicting Mecca had to hurry up and flip the script before her eyes and facial expression told on her.

"I'm not the one out here lying up," Mecca said. She knew if she switched the focus, E-Way would leave matters alone.

"Whatever, I'm not about to argue with yo' ass. I hope I made myself clear."

"Yes, Ike," Mecca said, trying to be sarcastic.

While Mecca took a shower, E-Way rummaged through her purse. He scrolled through her cell phone and wrote down every number and name. He wasn't the jealous type, but he was a man of pride. He needed to know if she was stepping out on him. *Why would she?* he asked himself. She had everything she wanted and then some. E-Way left the house and began dialing every number he had found in Mecca's phone. He recognized most of the names because Mecca didn't keep up with too many people. He called them anyway just in case Mecca had disguised the names.

All except one of the numbers was answered by a female. The name listed in the phone was Judy, and it was unfamiliar to E-Way. He had never met or heard Mecca speak of a Judy. The phone was answered on the second ring.

"Hello," answered the deep voice of a man.

E-Way sat up in his seat as he drove nowhere in particular. "Who this?" asked E-Way. "Is there a Judy there?"

There was a slight pause, and then the man said, "She ain't in right now. Who is this?"

E-Way pushed the END button, hanging up on the man. The voice on the other end belonged to Drew. He was too swift on his toes to allow E-Way to catch him up. There was no Judy, but Drew wasn't about to let the cat out of the bag. He wasn't sure whose husband or nigga was calling, but he knew the game.

E-Way could sense from the pause in the conversation that there was some shit in the game. He started to turn his car around to go beat the shit out of Mecca until she confessed, but he decided not to because he might kill her. E-Way turned onto 7 Mile Road, heading west. His mind continued to race. He needed the truth. He flipped open his phone and called Olivia. He figured he could easily pick her brain.

"Hello."

"Can I speak to Olivia?"

"Speaking," Olivia said as she rolled over in bed still half asleep. It was going on eight o'clock in the morning, and Olivia wasn't quite the morning type.

"Damn, did I catch you at a bad time?"

"Nah, I mean, it's only seven fifty a.m. By the way, who is this?"

"E-Way. You done forgot about a nigga already."

"I was beginning to think you forgot about me. You ain't never called me back."

"Well, look, I need to ask you something and I want you to be honest with me."

"What is it?" Olivia asked, sitting up to attention.

"Is Mecca fucking one of them niggas up at Henry's Palace?"

"To be honest, I don't know. I know that all the girls at the shop go at least once a week on Thursday. And the next morning that's all they be talking about. I don't go because I don't fuck with them like that."

"Yeah," E-Way said, lost in thought. "Well, listen, do me a favor. The next time they go . . . when you say, Thursday? Go with them and see what's what. Can you do that for me?" asked E-Way.

"I can't believe you. The only time you call me is to go spy on another bitch. You need to get with a bitch like me."

"Oh, yeah, and what can a bitch like you do for me?"

"A hellava lot more than what you're used to."

"Imagine that. But are you gon' do that for me, or do I have to hire a private eye?"

Olivia thought for a moment and decided to do it. Not because E-Way asked her to but because of her hate for Mecca. She would do almost anything to witness her downfall. "If I do, what's in it for me?"

"A hellava lot more than you're used to."

"When can I see you again?"

"Shit, where you at right now?"

"At home, still in bed."

"What you got on?" E-Way asked, trying to sound all seductive.

"Just a T-shirt," answered Olivia in a soft, little girl voice.

"Shit, give me yo' address and I'll be through there in a minute."

Mecca had finished showering and was getting ready to leave. She decided to treat herself to a day at the spa after spending the night in jail. As she gathered her belongings, she noticed that her purse had been probed. E-Way was careful to put everything back how he found it, but she could still tell that he had been in her purse. Nothing was missing, so she figured maybe he was just looking for numbers.

After leaving the spa, Mecca stopped by the shop to update Benji on the current events. She was greeted with sarcasm by none other than Tory. "What'up jail bird, I mean, Mecca?"

"Go ahead and laugh it up, if you must. But please do not forget to cough it up. Yeah, that's right, it's booth rent time," Mecca said, holding out her hand.

The laughter ceased as everyone pretended not to hear Mecca. She looked around the salon and didn't see Benji.

"Has anybody seen Benji?" she asked.

"Oh, yeah, he's in the back," answered Pete.

"See me before y'all leave," Mecca warned as she headed toward the back room.

She opened the door to find Benji comforting Yvette as she cried and wept. Mecca wasn't fazed by Yvette's apparent grief. She looked at Benji, then at Yvette, and asked, "What is she doing here? I thought I made myself clear when I said—"

"Mecca, now isn't the time," Benji said, cutting Mecca off.

"It really isn't. What does she want?"

"Mecca, it's your father. He passed away this morning in the hospital," Benji said.

"Okay, so why are you telling me?"

Benji jumped to his feet, grabbed Mecca by the arm, and rushed her into the bathroom. He slammed the door behind him and pinned Mecca up against the sink.

"Look, I know how you feel about your parents, I do. But you need to show some respect right now. That woman out there is your mother, and she needs you right now."

"Why are you always being so damn nice to her? Where was she at when I needed her all those years, huh?" Mecca said as she began crying.

"Mecca, this isn't about you right now. Sometimes in our lives we have to learn to forgive. Nobody's asking you to forget, just forgive," said Benji.

Mecca didn't want to forgive, and she damn sure couldn't forget all what she had been through as a result of her parents.

"I'ma let you cool down for a second. I'ma go check on your mother."

"Her name is Yvette," said Mecca in between tears.

"Chile, it's gon' be all right," Benji said, leaving the bathroom. He went back out into the area where Yvette was seated, but she was gone. The back door was open. Yvette overheard Mecca and Benji's conversation and decided it would be best if she left.

Mecca came out of the bathroom after gathering her composure. She found Benji locking the back door.

"How'd you get rid of her?" asked Mecca.

Benji turned to face Mecca, then said, "I didn't. She left while we were in the bathroom."

"Ain't nothing missing, is there?" Mecca asked as she looked around.

"I can't believe you," Benji said, shaking his head as he walked out front to tend to a customer.

Mecca didn't think twice about the death of her father or once again hurting Yvette's feelings. She flopped down in her office chair and scrolled through her cell phone, stopping on the name Judy. She pushed the CALL button and tapped her foot nervously as the phone rang.

"Hello," answered Drew on the third ring.

"Are you mad at me?" asked Mecca.

"Nah, it's only a car. But it was fucked up how you put me on blast at my job."

"I'm sorry. Can I make it up to you?"

"And how you gon' do that?"

"However you want me to. I need to see you."

"How bad?" asked Drew as he began to rub himself.

"Really bad," Mecca said as if she were getting fucked.

"Meet me at my house in twenty minutes."

"Okay," Mecca said, then hung up the phone.

Her pussy was soaked. She raced out of the shop, rolling her eyes at Benji on her way out.

"Bitch, I know you ain't just roll yo' eyes at me," Benji said.

Mecca didn't acknowledge him. She was on a mission.

She beat Drew to his condo and sat in the parking lot, waiting for him to pull up. He arrived shortly after, driving a Chevy Tahoe. It was a rental, just until his Vette got fixed.

Mecca and Drew wasted no time, and once inside they started going at it, tearing at each other's clothes in a rush to get naked. Drew swooped Mecca up, wrapping her legs around his waist, and slid her down onto his awaiting throbbing dick.

He stood in the living room facing a mirror mounted above the fireplace. He watched every stroke as Mecca's yellow ass bounced in rhythm. She dug her nails into Drew's back as she reached her first climax. Drew then laid Mecca down on the plush cream carpet and stroked her from the side while holding up one of her legs. He looked into Mecca's eyes and could tell that she was about to have her second orgasm.

"Wait for me, baby," Drew said as he sped up his stroke. Mecca couldn't wait. She was already there. She reached back and grabbed Drew's ass, pulling him into her.

"Ah," sighed Drew as they came in unison.

They lay across the carpet, both out of breath and feeling better than ever. Mecca began kissing on Drew's chest, then asked, "Did I make it up to you?"

"Yeah, you did that," Drew answered, still out of breath. Makeup sex had always been better than normal sex. Drew felt like he had punished Mecca for what she did to his car and felt as though he could forgive her. He laid down the law for future reference in case Mecca had begun to think he was soft and going for anything. She agreed to never put him on blast again at his place of business. That's all she wanted, to feel dominated and controlled. With Drew, she got to explore that side of herself. With E-Way, she pretty much had her way. All she had to do was put that pussy on him and she got her way. There were a number of reasons why Mecca was fooling around with Drew. The number one reason was the danger and excitement of it.

Chapter 10

E-Way had finished blowing Olivia's back out and was ready to hit the streets. She promised him that she would go to Henry's Palace on Thursday with Benji and Mecca and try to find out if Mecca was indeed messing with somebody. E-way dug into his pants pocket and pulled out a wad of money. He peeled off five $100 bills, then handed them to Olivia. She looked at the money in disgust, then asked, "What's this for?"

"Ah, that's just a little something. It's nothing."

"I hope you don't think you just paid me for some ass, because this pussy is priceless," Olivia said with an attitude.

"Calm down. It ain't even like that. I just wanted you to have it. Do some shopping or something. I told you, fucking with me was a lot more than you're used to. I'ma get up out of here though," E-Way said, heading for the front door.

"When am I going to see you again?" asked Olivia as she and E-Way stood with the door ajar.

"Just call me," E-Way answered, then leaned to kiss Olivia on the cheek.

She was feeling all special and victorious, seeing as how she was getting it in with Mecca's man. Her plan was to take E-Way from Mecca by all means. Even if it meant losing her friendship with Benji, she wanted E-Way that bad. At first her fling with E-way was just to get back at Mecca for always shining on her. But now that Olivia began to explore all the possibilities, her imagination was getting the best of her. Just like everyone else, she had a hidden agenda.

E-Way had met up with his connect, Subi. They always met at the Pic 'N' Save grocery store on 7 Mile and Van Dyke. It was one of the many fronts Subi and his family had so they could launder their dirty money. Subi was an Arab. He was the son of Ali, old man Sal's connect. When Ali passed away, Subi was made the head of the family and the head of all the family business. He spoke perfect English because he had been in America since the age of 6. He was the perfect businessman. Subi could do four to five things all at the same time and not miss a beat. Selling drugs and flipping money was in his blood.

E-Way parked his car near the docking area of the store, then walked around front. He strolled into the store as if he were a normal customer, walking through the meat section, then stopping at two stainless-steel swinging doors. He looked around to make sure no one was in sight, then entered the storage area. Subi's office was located upstairs. Glass windows surrounded his nook, which enabled him to see E-Way as he climbed the stairs. Subi was on the phone. He waved E-Way in, then immediately ended his conversation.

"E, baby, what's up, my nigga?" Subi asked, trying to sound hip, throwing his hands up in the air.

"What I tell you about that 'nigga' shit?" E-Way asked, taking a seat in one of the leather chairs that faced Subi's desk.

"That's your problem, you're too sensitive, baby. What you got for me?" asked Subi as he rubbed his greedy dick beaters together in anticipation.

"Two hundred and fifty Gs," E-Way answered as he dug down into his pants and tossed Subi a large bag of all $100 bills.

"Good. Come with me," said Subi as he tucked the money inside one of the desk drawers, then stood up. Subi led E-Way down into the freezer and entered another freezer, which contained nothing but drugs. Subi tossed E-Way a jar that contained 1,000 pills.

E-Way examined the jar, confused, then asked, "What the fuck you give me this for?"

"That's the new epidemic. You're holding the next crack."

E-Way took another look at the pills and then handed them back to Subi. "Well, that's not what I'm here to purchase. Why you always tryin' to pin your get-rich-quick schemes on me? Tryin' to use me as a guinea pig."

"You're paranoid, my friend. What I just handed you will have this city going crazy in a few months. You just watch what I tell you. This is called ecstasy. It's a combination of coke, heroin, and a bunch of shit. Your paranoia is going to cause you to miss out. Anyhow, help me with this crate," Subi said as he and E-Way hammered a crowbar into the top of the crate. After about seven blows, the wood cracked and left an opening large enough so Subi could stick his hand inside.

"Am I getting paid for this?" E-Way asked as he leaned over the crate out of breath. Subi held the crowbar while E-Way hammered.

"My friend, you're getting the best coke in all of Detroit, and at Southern prices. I'd say yes, you're getting paid," answered Subi as he began removing kilos from the crate and handing them to E-Way.

E-Way couldn't argue with what Subi said. The dope wasn't stepped on, and at $15,000 per kilo, he was making a killing. The dope Subi was giving him could be stepped on and almost turned into triple the amount. Each kilo was marked with a stamp with some Arabic writing. It was the Arab drug cartel's trademark. E-Way put the kilos inside of some brown paper bags, then placed them inside some of the plastic grocery bags bearing the store's name.

Subi saw E-Way to his car, then exited through the dock. "When will I see you, E?" asked Subi as he stood out on the dock with his hand underneath his shirt. He was clutching the butt of a semiautomatic .45.

E-Way tossed the kilos into the back seat and then turned toward Subi. "I should be done in a few weeks. I've got something to tell you also, but it can wait," E-Way said, then jumped into his car and backed out.

E-Way called Kev, Chuck, Big Whitney, and Chuckie Bom's and told them to meet him at Chuck's house. They all knew that E-Way had just copped, so they raced over to Chuck's to get their work. Chuck lived on Caldwell, a few streets over from E-Way's grandmother on Mt. Elliott. All the money Chuck was getting, and he still lived with his momma. He didn't know how to manage his money. He'd spend it as fast as he made it. Chuck, like most niggas, thought that he could sell drugs forever. E-Way copping was music to his ears because he was out of dope and money.

Kev, Chuck, Big Whitney, and Chuckie Bom's had all beaten E-Way to the house. He pulled up shortly after noticing all their cars parked out front. He grabbed the work, then got out, looking up and down the block in search of no one in particular. Chuck jumped to his feet and headed for the side door as he saw the shadow of someone on the side of the house through the basement window. He swung the door open before E-Way could do his coded knock.

"What's good, what's good?" E-Way asked, entering the basement. Kev and Chuckie Bom's were playing *John Madden* on PS2, while Big Whit rolled the already third blunt. They all stopped what they were doing and focused their attention on the bags E-Way was holding. E-Way walked over to the coffee table and dumped the kilos out. Everyone gathered around the table as E-Way began passing out everyone's rations.

"One more load and I'm done," E-Way said as everybody gathered their packages and headed for the door.

"Did you holla at the plug about me?" asked Big Whitney.

Everyone was waiting for E-Way to answer.

"Nah, not yet. I got you though."

"Do I know 'em? Who is it?" asked Big Whit.

"In due time. Let's get this shit pushed," E-Way said, changing the subject.

They all filed out of the basement, hopping into their cars and going their separate ways. E-Way decided to finally face his fear and go visit his grandmother. He had gotten word from his uncle that she had come out of her coma a few days ago. He stopped in the gift shop, bought a get well soon card, a teddy bear, and some flowers, then headed up to her room. E-Way became teary-eyed at the sight of his grandmother laid up in her hospital bed. Tubes ran through her nostrils and arms. She rested peacefully as if she were still in a coma.

E-Way gently closed the door behind him, then walked slowly to his grandmother's bedside. He set the flowers, card, and teddy bear on the nightstand, then stood over her. He rubbed her silky gray hair while looking down at her asleep. Her eyes opened, and she smiled at the sight of her boy, as she referred to E-Way.

"Momma, I didn't mean to wake you," E-Way said as he kissed her hand.

"It's okay. I was beginning to worry. I thought you weren't going to come see about me."

"Momma, you know how much I hate hospitals. Plus, I couldn't stand to see you in no coma."

"I'm okay, baby. It's going to take a lot more than two street punks to get me out the way. The Lord ain't gon' let it be."

"Momma, I'm sorry. This is all my fault. I know this has something to do with me."

"We can't cry over spilled milk. It's done, and now we must learn from it and move on. Shit, they asses lucky I ain't have my piece on me. Every time I got my shit, don't nothing ever happen. Soon as I slip, here comes trouble. Won't happen again, you can bet on that," Momma said, sitting up in bed.

"Well, you won't have to worry about a next time, because I'm done with that life. I want you to promise me you'll let me buy you a house once you're released from the hospital. I don't want you ever to experience nothing like this again."

"Boy, I'm not going anywhere. I'ma die in my leased house. You know how long that house has been in our family? Damn near fifty years. I'm sorry, but I can't." Momma was set in her ways. There was no way she was going to let E-Way move her out to some quiet suburb. She enjoyed the constant happenings of Detroit. There was always something going on. She felt like if she moved out into the suburbs, she'd die an early death from boredom.

E-Way knew not to press the issue. He changed the subject. "Do you remember anything specific about your attackers, Momma?"

"I remember the eyes of one of them. I've seen those eyes before. I just can't place it."

E-Way became furious as he visualized two men attacking his grandmother. It wasn't making sense though. Momma had never met Marcus or any other member of Murkland Niggas. How could she have recognized the eyes of one of the men?

"So now that you're leaving that life—and I'm, oh, so glad—what are you going to do?" asked Momma, breaking E-Way's train of thought.

"I haven't figured that part out yet, but there's a million and one other things I can do besides selling drugs."

"That's the spirit."

"I have an idea. For starters, when you're released from the hospital, why don't we open up a soul food joint? With your cooking and my business sense, we can't lose. What do you say?"

Momma smiled as she thought of the idea. It would be something else she could do, plus she loved to cook. "What will we call it?" she asked.

"How about Mom Dukes?" E-Way suggested.

"I like it," Momma said, widening her smile.

"A'ight, it's settled then. Mom Dukes it is." E-Way kissed Momma on the forehead.

Momma now had something else she could live for. Her entire life, she always lived for others, from taking care of her siblings to raising her kids and their kids. Of them all, E-Way had always been her favorite. As much as it hurt her to see him out in the streets, she always supported him. When E-Way was in grade school, he used to always get sent to the principal's office, he and Bubbles. The school would call Momma, and she'd have to go pick them up. Kev's, Chuck's, Chuckie Bom's's, and Big Whitney's mothers would be going upside their heads while E-Way and Bubbles were on their way to Mr. Kennedy's penny candy store. Momma never whooped them. She said, "Experience will teach 'em. Ain't no need to beat 'em."

E-Way sat at Momma's bedside for most of the day watching soaps and eating white mint chocolates, Momma's favorite. The doctor told E-Way that she would be released in a few more weeks and that she seemed to be recovering well. Momma drifted off to sleep after *All My Children* went off. E-Way sat next to the window in a recliner, looking out at the semi-busy traffic. The sun had begun to set, and the passing cars headlights were glaring. E-Way watched the lights as he thought about all he planned on doing. He felt revived in a sense. He didn't want to just open Mom Dukes Soul Food Restaurant. He wanted to challenge himself.

E-Way dug into the nightstand and retrieved a pen and a yellow sticky pad. He sat back in the recliner and wrote down a list of goals. Number one was to start Mom Dukes and franchise it. Number two was to rebuild his studio and pursue a career as a producer. This would be in memory of Bubbles. He used to teach E-Way everything he learned, and he wanted to be a real producer. Bubbles attended the Specs Howard School of Media Arts. Out of the group, he was the only one taking the music side seriously. Number three on E-Way's list was to marry Mecca and have some kids. But first he had to be certain she wasn't stepping out on him.

Chapter 11

Benji, being the true friend he was, took care of all the funeral arrangements for Mecca's father. Benji went to Cole's Funeral Home and paid for the casket, suit, barber, funeral service, and for the funeral home to pick the body up from the morgue. Benji went all out, renting a limo for Yvette and the little bit of family Mecca's father had. He was sending Mr. Tobias out in style. The hard part was getting Mecca to attend the funeral. Benji vowed he would get her to come, even if he had to tie her up and drag her there himself.

The loss of Mecca's father crushed Yvette and any ambition she had built up over the past few weeks to stop getting high. To cope with the grief, she went on a crack binge. Benji scoured the neighborhood in search of Yvette. He wanted to let her know that the funeral had been taken care of and that she had someone, if not everybody, in her corner.

Benji spotted Yvette coming out an abandoned house, which appeared to be a crackhouse. She was walking down the steps of the house with her fist closed tightly. She was high-stepping toward a battered Honda Civic awaiting her at the curb.

Benji pulled behind the Honda and jumped out, leaving his car running. He approached Yvette as she opened the passenger door. Benji could tell from Yvette's appearance that she had been getting high. Her eyes were bucked like they were fighting to bulge out of their sockets. She had a stench like no other. She was so gone she almost didn't recognize Benji.

"Benji, what are you doing over here?" she asked.

"I was looking for you. I came to let you know that the funeral has been arranged. It's set for Wednesday, and it'll be at Cole's."

"You didn't have to do that, Benji, but thank you." Yvette knew Benji had done all the arrangements because had Mecca done them, why wasn't she the one looking for her?

"I'd like to take you shopping so you can look nice for the funeral," Benji said.

"Chile, you've got a heart of gold. But I'll be all right." Yvette had one hand on the door and the other closed tightly, concealing her purchase.

The driver of the Honda, a four-foot tall Chinese guy, was growing impatient, so he hit the horn. Benji kneeled down and looked in the car, then moved Yvette to the side.

"Who the hell you blowing your horn at, Chinaman? Mess around and get whooped," Benji said.

The man looked around nervously but said nothing.

"What's that in your hand, Yvette?" asked Benji.

Yvette didn't answer, and she dropped her head in shame.

"Do you want some help, Yvette?"

"Yes," Yvette answered like a little girl.

"Then hand me that and let's go." Benji reached for Yvette's hand, which concealed four dime rocks. Benji took the rocks and slung them at the driver, then grabbed Yvette by the hand and led her to his car. He put Yvette in the passenger seat and sped away from the curb, leaving Chinaman bewildered.

"Thank you, Benji," Yvette managed to say. She had begun crying.

"Don't thank me yet. There's a long road ahead of you to recovery, but I'm going to help you, only if you help yourself. Deal?" asked Benji, sticking out his hand.

"Deal," Yvette said as she shook Benji's hand.

Benji drove out to his house so Yvette could take a bath. Lord knew she needed two of them. He changed her into some fresh clothes. They fit just right, seeing as how most of Benji's clothes were female clothes anyway. Benji curled Yvette's hair, sprayed some smell good on her, and applied a little foundation. After giving Yvette a Jenny Jones makeover, Benji took her shopping for something to wear to the funeral. Benji ended buying Yvette damn near an entire wardrobe. Every outfit Yvette tried on Benji tossed on the counter. It had been ages since Yvette had been to the mall shopping. The only shopping she did was shoplifting. She felt like a little girl in a candy store.

Benji didn't mind. He was getting his enjoyment, as usual, by making others happy. After leaving the mall they stopped at Red Lobster. Benji told Yvette to order whatever she wanted. Why did he do that? Yvette ordered and demolished a jumbo platter of shrimp and lobster tails. She ate like she was just released from a concentration camp. Benji checked his cell phone messages. He had his phone turned off on purpose. Mecca's name was listed as seven missed calls.

Benji remembered that he was supposed to do Mecca's hair, among several others'. *Oh, well, they'll get over it,* Benji thought, then closed his phone.

"You about ready?" asked Benji.

"Now where we going?" asked Yvette.

"Back to my house. I got the guest room all ready for you."

"Benji, I would hate to impose upon you. I can't," Yvette said, finishing her platter.

"I insist, and besides I need to keep you away from Detroit, at least until we can get you into a treatment center. I told you, you've got a long road ahead of you."

"Benji, I've been smoking crack since its debut. Do you really think I can shake this thing?"

"My mother used to always tell me that when you get sick and tired of being sick and tired, you'll quit. She was talking about me always getting in trouble. Yvette, I know you're tired, and yes, I believe you can quit. Question is, do you? Come on, let's get out of here."

Mecca was so worried about Benji. She drove out to his house to see if he was at home sick or something. She used her spare key to let herself in. She called Benji's name at the top of her lungs as she searched every room in the house. "Maybe he's over at Devin's, laid up," Mecca told herself. She wrote a note to Benji, telling him she had been over and to call once he got the message. She locked up, and Benji and Yvette pulled into the driveway.

Benji noticed Mecca first. She had her back turned, locking up the house. *Damn,* Benji thought.

"Is that my baby?" asked Yvette, leaning forward in the seat to see.

"Yeah, that's her," Benji said, killing the engine.

Mecca walked up to the driver's door and began fussing at Benji, telling him how worried she was. She stopped mid-sentence as Yvette emerged from the passenger side. Mecca looked as if she had seen a ghost. She didn't even acknowledge Yvette. She turned to Benji for an explanation. "What is she doing here?"

"We had to get everything set for the funeral."

"Here you go again. Benji, you ain't Superman! You can't save everybody."

"You really need to quit," Benji said, walking around to the trunk.

"Who's all this for?" asked Mecca in reference to all the bags.

"Never mind that. Grab a few bags and help me carry them inside," Benji ordered.

Mecca reluctantly helped carry the bags inside. Benji got Yvette settled in the guest room, then took Mecca in the basement for a scolding.

"I know what you're thinking, and I know you're upset. But once again, it's not about you."

"You got her living in your house. Is you crazy?"

"I know what I'm doing. Mecca, your mother needs a helping hand. She really wants to change, and I'm going to help her. After the funeral, she's going to check into a treatment center. We can't turn our back on her."

"We ain't got nothing to do with it. If you wanna run around playing Oprah and shit, be my guest. But don't expect for me to partake."

"Anyhow, the funeral is Wednesday. I expect to see you in attendance."

"Well, you can expect to be disappointed." She headed up the stairs. She didn't bother saying bye to Yvette. She just walked out, got into her car, and peeled off.

"She hates me, don't she?" Yvette said as Benji entered the guest room.

"Like all things, give it some time. She'll come around. Mecca is just being Mecca," Benji said, trying to assure Yvette of better days.

It wasn't so much Benji helping Yvette that was bothering Mecca. It was a mixture of feelings. Mecca, for one, felt like Yvette was taking the one true friend she had away from her. "What right did she have to impose herself, and why was Benji so damn nice to her?" Mecca asked herself as she drove like a madwoman, weaving in and out of traffic. “I wish she would just die and leave me the hell alone.”

Mecca began crying. All the feelings and memories of abandonment were starting to replay in Mecca’s head. That night she cried herself to sleep, asking God why her life was the way it was. What right did Yvette have?

Chapter 12

The morning of the funeral, Mecca lay in bed staring at the ceiling. Usually she would have been up, finished her workout, and been on her way to the shop. She didn't feel like doing anything. She had made her mind up that she would not be attending the funeral, regardless of Benji. E-Way was up and at 'em early. He emerged from his walk-in closet suited and booted.

Mecca looked on in amazement. "Where you on your way to, *GQ?*"

E-Way was standing in the mirror, checking his situation. He snapped his fingers, then pointed to himself in approval. "I'm going to pay my respects. You need to get up and do the same," E-Way said, turning to face Mecca.

"You barely even knew my father."

"That's just it. He's your father, and that's good enough for me. Now let's go. I want to get there early."

Mecca didn't budge. She didn't give a damn what E-Way was talking about. *Is everybody on Yvette's side?* Mecca became a little irritated.

The doorbell sounded. E-Way rushed downstairs to answer the door as if he had been expecting someone.

"Where is she?" asked Benji, pushing past E-Way. He decided to put their differences to the side and work with E-Way on getting Mecca to the funeral.

"She's upstairs in bed. Talking about she ain't going."

Benji looked at his watch, then stormed upstairs.

Mecca wasn't in shock to see Benji. She knew he'd be there any moment playing Superman.

"Girl, if you don't get yo' spoiled ass up!" Benji shouted, snatching the covers off Mecca.

"I'm not going."

"The hell you ain't," Benji said as he walked into Mecca's closet, snatching something for Mecca to wear. "Here, put this on," he said, tossing Mecca some of her clothes.

"You gon' just make me go, huh?"

"Yup, now let's go. Get cha' ass up, pull ya drawers out ya cat, and let's go," Benji slapping his hands together.

Mecca reluctantly got up and headed for the bathroom. She showered, then dragged herself to get dressed. Yvette was waiting downstairs in the living room. Mecca flipped out at the sight of her sitting on her sofa. E-Way had fixed her some coffee, and they were talking when Mecca and Benji entered the room.

"I can't believe you brought—"

"Mecca, now isn't the time," Benji said, putting his hand over Mecca's mouth, stopping her from talking.

"Hi, Mecca," Yvette said all cheery.

Benji nudged Mecca.

"Hello, Yvette," Mecca said all dry in return.

E-Way and Mecca trailed Benji to the funeral home. They were running late due to Mecca dragging her ass getting ready. As they entered the funeral home, the service had just gotten under way. A pastor from Word of Faith Church by the name of Keith Butler was starting the eulogy. Mecca and Yvette were ushered to the front along with Benji. Mecca noticed in attendance Tory, Tae, Pete, Marie, and even Olivia. They were all there to show their support, and more so because Benji made them go.

Mecca felt betrayed and thankful somehow all at the same time. No one else was in attendance. James, Mecca's father, didn't have family. He'd burned his bridges over the years, stealing from family members to support his high. Yvette was his only family. Pastor Keith

Butler said some kind words about James as if he knew him. He asked if anyone else would like to say something as well. Yvette tried to stand and say something but was unable. She couldn't gather herself enough to speak.

Mecca looked at her in disbelief. *She knows she's puttin' a ten on it. It ain't even that serious,* Mecca said to herself as she watched Yvette cry.

The services were rather quick. Benji had planned a gathering at his house afterward, but Mecca was too far in her feelings. She demanded that E-Way take her home. Once home, Mecca got into her car and pulled off. E-Way called her phone and asked where in the hell she was going.

"I just need to ride around and clear my head," Mecca said, then hung up on E-Way.

The next day everything seemed to be back to normal. Mecca was her usual self, up early and out the door. She arrived at the shop and was ready for another day of gossip and ladies' night out at Henry's Palace. Mecca held her head extra high as she entered the shop. She didn't want a bitch to see her down for one second. She was greeted by everyone, and then it was off to the back. Mecca was rather short with Benji, so he politely excused himself from his customer.

"Miss Thang, do you got something you want to get off your chest?" asked Benji as he entered the back room and closed the door.

"Why you ask that?" Mecca asked, turning from the computer to face Benji.

"'Cause you got your ass on your shoulders and whatnot. You need to let that shit go."

"I'm sorry, Benji, I know I've got some issues with my mother, and I plan on dealing with them as soon as the time is right. When I'm ready, not when she's ready."

"Well, I think that's a start. When you're ready, sit her down and ask her what's in your heart without being hurtful. Ask her why she chose the streets over you. Ask her all the questions you've wanted to ask for all these years. Once you get the closure you need, then you can maybe start forgiving."

"You sure know what to say. I think you missed your calling. You should have been a counselor or something." Mecca began to lighten up. She could never stay mad at Benji and vice versa.

"So are we on tonight for Henry's?" asked Benji.

"Most definitely. I need to see my boo."

"Guess who wants to come."

"Who?" asked Mecca, looking puzzled.

"Olivia. She been asking me for the past few days whether we were going."

"I knew that she would see the light, actin' like she all high and mighty and whatnot. Anyways, I'ma let you get back to your customer. I'ma finish looking at these purses," Mecca said as Benji turned to leave, and she went back to surfing the net.

Mecca was almost turned away at the door at Henry's Palace. One of the bouncers remembered her from the incident last week. Mecca called Drew outside, and he cleared it up with the bouncers and promised that she would behave. Olivia was all ears and eyes, watching Mecca's every move. She noted how Drew paid intent attention to Mecca over the other women, and how Mecca kept referring to him as her boo.

"What's his name, girl? That nigga is too fine," asked Olivia as Drew left their table to get ready for his set.

"Drew, Mecca's li'l thang-thang," Marie volunteered.

"What about Drew?" asked Mecca, overhearing the tail end of Marie's statement.

"Nothing. Olivia was just asking who he was," answered Marie.

"Bitch, calm down. Don't nobody want Drew's high yellow ass but you," Benji said, then downed his drink. "Where in the hell is that waiter? Now his ass is fine," he said, lightening the mood.

It was a typical night at Henry's. Olivia enjoyed herself more than she thought she would. She enjoyed several lap dances by about five different brothas. After just one night, she was looking forward to her next visit. She could see how Mecca could get caught up with one of the many dime pieces Henry's possessed. What woman couldn't?

Chapter 13

Olivia couldn't wait to relay her findings to E-Way. After leaving Henry's, she called him and ran down everything she had witnessed. She gave E-Way a description of Drew, his car, and the relationship he had with Mecca. E-Way became furious, and he slammed the phone down while Olivia ran down the details. He was at home pacing back and forth in the living room. He had been waiting for Olivia to call. Struck by the news, E-Way started devising his plan.

"Nah, that won't work," he told himself at the thought of killing Mecca and chopping her body up. "Too messy." E-Way continued contemplating. His focus was broken by the ring of his cell phone. *Speak of the devil.* It was none other than Mecca.

"Hey, baby, listen, I'm going to stay the night at Benji's. I'm too bent to drive home," Mecca said with a slur.

This bitch trying to play me so she can go lie up with muscle man. "Where you at? I'll come get you," E-Way said, trying to hold back his anger.

"I'm on my way to Benji's."

"Why couldn't he drop you off?"

"He's drunker than I am. The bar ain't too far from his house though. I'll call you once we make it home. E, did you hear me, baby?"

"Yeah, I heard you," E-Way said, lost in thought.

E-Way grabbed his car keys and was out the door as soon as he and Mecca ended their conversation.

He drove down 7 Mile, passing the salon. He noticed Mecca's car still parked in its spot. He jumped on the Southfield Expressway, punching it and coming up on 9 Mile and Greenfield. Within ten minutes he was pulling in front of Benji's. He called Mecca's cell phone while standing on the front porch. Mecca and Benji were in the kitchen recapping the night's events. Benji was at the stove cooking Mecca and himself breakfast food.

"That's probably Drew wondering why you left without saying good night," Benji said in reference to Mecca's incoming call.

The call came in as unavailable. E-Way had pushed *67 before calling. Usually, Mecca wouldn't answer, but with her being tipsy and the anticipation of it might being Drew, she answered. "Hello."

"Come open up the door," E-Way said.

"E-Way, where are you?" Mecca asked as she got up and headed toward the front door.

"I'm outside."

Mecca hung up the phone and let E-Way inside. "Boy, what are you doing here? I told you I was all right."

"Mecca, who is that?" Benji asked as he walked into the living room. "Um . . ." Benji said at the sight of E.

"Who was y'all expecting?" E-Way asked, catching both Mecca and Benji off guard.

"I wasn't expecting nobody. Benji was waiting on Devin to come over," Mecca said with an attitude.

"You ready?" asked E-Way.

"Benji, let me go. I will see you tomorrow," Mecca said, giving Benji a kiss goodbye.

"That nigga pussy whipped. He came and got that ass," Benji said jokingly as he let Mecca and E-Way out.

Mecca could sense that something was bothering E-Way. And it sure wasn't a lack of pussy, because when she tried to unbuckle his pants, he pushed her hands away.

"What's wrong with you?" Mecca asked.

"Who you trying to play, huh?" E-Way asked out of nowhere.

"Boy, I don't know what the fuck you tripping off of, but you need to leave it alone whatever it is."

"Do I look like one of these suckas out here?"

Mecca's eyes were bucked as she listened intently. She was just waiting for E-Way to say it.

"Who the hell is Drew?"

Damn, he said it. "I don't know no damn body named Drew."

"Bitch!" E-Way yelled, slapping the dog shit out of Mecca.

Mecca immediately began crying. She balled up with her hands protecting her face and her back to the passenger door. "You said you would never hit me again," she cried.

"Aw, bitch, that ain't nothin' compared to what I'm about to do to that ass," E-Way said as he pulled up to a red light.

Mecca knew he meant what he said. The jig was up. She had been caught. There was only one smart thing she could do. Run like hell!

She bolted for the door but was unable to get out. E-Way had put the child-proof protection on just in case she tried to run. He grabbed her neck and slammed her back in her seat.

"Where you think you going, bitch?" He manhandled Mecca.

The light turned green and E-Way punched it, looking in all directions for the cops. Mecca's life began flashing before her eyes. She had to come up with something and quick.

"E, baby, please let me explain," she pleaded.

"Explain? Explain what? Just a minute ago you ain't have shit to explain. 'I don't know no damn Drew.' Now you see that ass is hit like good weed, you wanna talk. Go ahead, I want to hear how you gon' try to come up out of this one."

"I do know a Drew."

"So, you lied to me? And what the fuck you mean, you do know a Drew? Like there's more than one Drew. You better quit playing on my intelligence."

"I know Drew. He's a dancer at Henry's."

"So, this nigga you've been giving all my damn money to, huh?"

"I haven't given Drew anything other than tips."

"So, you ain't gave the nigga no pussy?"

"Absolutely not. I only see him at the bar. E, I don't know who you're getting all this from, but it's bullshit. You know I would never cheat on you."

E-Way thought about the credibility of his source, Olivia. *She could be lying just to get in good with me, but then again why did Mecca lie when I first mentioned Drew?*

"If ain't nothin' going on between you and Drew, why you lie about it the first time?"

"'Cause I didn't want to upset you. I know you're a man of pride, and I didn't want you questioning yourself. Women go to these bars to enjoy themselves, just like men. That doesn't mean you have to be fooling around with someone there," Mecca said, working her magic.

Mecca knew that she had to enter the house on a good note or risk the chance of another beatdown. She reached for E-Way's belt buckle, and this time he didn't refuse her. She undid his shorts, then reached down into his boxers, pulling E-Way's dick out. Mecca sucked him like an infant sucking its mother's tit. E-Way began to relax as he let his seat back and gently held Mecca's head with his free hand. He was about to bust, but Mecca gripped the head of his dick, preventing him from ejaculating. She wanted to carry things into the bedroom.

E-Way fell for it as always. All Mecca had to do was put that priceless head on him and it was a wrap. They pulled into the driveway, Mecca still serving E-Way up. He was so focused on getting that nut off that he wasn't even thinking about why he was mad at Mecca and his original plan to fuck her up. Once inside the house, E-Way took off all his clothes, dropping them at the door. He stood in the living room jacking his dick as he watched Mecca undress.

She teased him with every article of clothing, taking her precious time. She knew that E-Way was ready to bust at any second. After she dropped her panties, Mecca walked over to E-Way, then pushed him down onto the sofa. She climbed onto his throbbing dick, dug her nails into his chest, and began riding him. She closed her eyes and leaned her head back, as E-Way slid her up and down violently on his dick. After only ten strokes, E-Way reached his climax. Mecca, wanting more, immediately got him back up by continuing to ride his limp dick.

Mecca kept E-Way busy until the sun came up. He slept like a baby, while Mecca was already up and out the door, on her way to the shop.

E-Way didn't wake up until one o'clock in the afternoon. He rolled over and patted Mecca's side of the bed, then opened his eyes, looking around the room. He looked at the clock on the nightstand, then rubbed his face, trying to gather himself. Last night's events began to replay themselves. E-Way smiled at the thought of Mecca and his episode, and then he frowned as he remembered what Olivia had told him. E-Way pulled the covers back, then rolled out of bed. He grabbed his cell phone and called Olivia.

"Hello," Olivia answered on the third ring. She was at the shop, standing right next to Benji.

"What's up? Listen, are you sure about everything you told me last night?" asked E-Way.

"I'm quite sure. Why would you ask that?"

"I just wanted to be certain. That's all."

"Well, I'm not one to be making things out to be more than they are. I know what I seen," Olivia said, copping an attitude. She was salty that Mecca hadn't gotten her ass whooped, and now E-Way was questioning her credibility.

"A'ight. You ain't gotta get all hostile. Look, I'ma get up with you later."

"Whatever," Olivia said, hanging up on E-Way.

"Dick problems?" Benji said as Olivia put her cell phone back in her purse.

"Forget you."

E-Way showered, then was out the door. He drove down to the river to holler at old man Sal.

"Do you ever go home?" E-Way asked as he climbed aboard the yacht. Old Sal was seated in his nook, sipping a Mississippi Mud beer.

"I gotta enjoy this weather while it's here. Couple of months and I'll be stuck in the ole house. What's up, son? You want a beer?"

"Yeah, why not?" E-Way said, taking a seat across from Sal.

Old Sal returned with a beer and the chessboard. E-Way dumped the pieces out and began setting them up.

"So, what's on your mind?" asked Sal as he made the first move.

"It's Mecca. I think she's cheating on me."

"That's to be expected." Sal took a swallow of his beer.

"What do you mean, that's to be expected?" E-Way asked with his face balled up.

"Focus on the game. What I mean is only a fool would believe his woman is faithful. Let me ask you a question. Are you faithful? I didn't think so," Sal said without letting E-Way answer. He continued, "So what makes you think a woman is faithful? No one man could ever possibly satisfy a woman. It's impossible. A woman is too needy. She needs at least four niggas to make up that one nigga who doesn't exist. She needs a money getter, which is you. She needs an intellect, a feminine nigga who's in touch with his feelings, a family man, and a host of other shit they be having on their little lists. You only fit one of the many. That's why I'm still a bachelor, because I know what's in a woman's nature. If you can't deal with her cheating, as you call it, then cut her ass loose." Old man Sal lined up for his next move. "Checkmate. Ole tender-dick-ass nigga. That's what's wrong with you young niggas."

That wasn't the advice E-Way was looking for, but it was real. Old Sal always gave it to him in the real, sometimes too real.

E-Way didn't want to break things off with Mecca, but he damn sure wasn't going to sit back and do nothing while she cheated on him. Question was, what was E-Way going to do?

He drove to the hospital, as today was the day Grams was supposed to be released. He wheeled her to the car, put her in the passenger seat, and then drove her home. The doctor ordered that she stay off her feet for at least two weeks.

Grams wasn't buying it though. As soon as she got home, it was off to the kitchen. She had to cook something. She felt like she had neglected the family: her oldest brother, her son, and three great-grandchildren who all lived with her. Grams had always put family before anything, including herself. E-Way tried to get her to do as the doctor said, but to no avail.

Grams was a town favorite. Everyone stopped by to see about her and of course taste some of her famous home-cooked cooking.

"Matt, have you looked at any building for the restaurant?" asked Grams as she served dinner, fixing everyone's plate.

"I saw a building on Moenart and 7 Mile next to Dot and Etta's. It looks like a good location. I wrote the Realtor's number down. I'm going to see what their latest offer is, then make a bid."

"While I was in the hospital, I made up a menu of all the dishes I would serve. My friend Ms. Mae could do the desserts. And a couple other ladies from the church can help cook and take orders," Grams said.

"Sounds like a plan, Momma," E-Way said in between bites.

Grams had everything figured out to the last detail. Mom Dukes would sure be a smash hit, but what would E-Way do?

After leaving Momma's, E-Way drove out to the cemetery. He was just now accepting the fact that Bubbles had passed away. He got the plot number from Momma and told her he was about to visit Bubbles's gravesite.

E-Way walked slowly as he approached Bubbles's tombstone. He fell to his knees and started crying as he read the inscription and saw the photo on the tombstone. For a good while, E-Way didn't say anything. He couldn't. Deep down he felt responsible for Bubbles's death. He felt like he was supposed to be there. He was supposed to be the one lying six feet under.

"I'm sorry, Bubbles," he kept saying over and over again. "I'm sorry.

"Man, I'm leaving the streets alone. I wish you were still here with me, my nigga. We could leave them together. Out of all of us, you was the only one who had a vision.

I'm starting to see your vision, and you can live through me. The studio got burned down, but I'ma rebuild it and get things back going. Man, I miss you, my nigga. Things ain't been the same for me lately. Grams got out of the hospital. She a'ight though. Them clowns who did this to you, we took care of that. I just wish I'd been there, man. I'm sorry." E-Way leaned on Bubbles's tombstone and continued to cry his eyes out.

Chapter 14

Benji dragged Mecca downtown to the Cass Corridor, by far one of the grimiest parts of Detroit. It was the headquarters for every heroin addict and supplier. They were on their way to visit Yvette at Harbor Light halfway house. It was sponsored by the Salvation Army. Benji helped Yvette enroll after the funeral.

"Why we have to come down here?" asked Mecca as she looked at all the junkies outside the building.

"For support. Now come on and remember to be nice," Benji answered as he cut the engine.

Mecca followed Benji up to the entrance, clutching her purse with one hand inside on her pepper Mace. They were finally buzzed in and ushered to the cafeteria, where they waited for Yvette. She had just finished a twelve-step class when Benji and Mecca arrived. She was told by her guidance counselor that she had some visitors. Yvette entered the semi-crowded cafeteria looking like new money, wearing one of the many outfits Benji bought her.

Benji stood up to greet Yvette, and he put his hands over his mouth in astonishment. Yvette stopped and struck a pose as Mecca often did when feeling herself.

"Oh, my God. Yvette, you are killing that getup," Benji said as he spun Yvette around. "Mecca, isn't she looking good?" asked Benji.

"She looks a'ight," Mecca said, trying not to give Yvette too much credit. As bad as Mecca hated to admit it, she couldn't deny it. She had never in her life seen her mom look that good except in pictures from back in the day.

"So, what brings y'all down here?" asked Yvette as she took a seat next to Mecca.

"We came to check up on you and make sure everything was okay. Are you all right? Do you need anything?" asked Benji.

"Nah, I'm okay, but thank you. It's good to see you, Mecca. Thanks for coming."

"Um hum," said Mecca.

Benji kicked her under the table and bucked his eyes. "So, Yvette, have you been looking for employment?" asked Benji, trying to keep the conversation going.

"Yeah, I been looking, but ain't nobody hiring no forty-five-year-old ex-crackhead with no credentials."

"What are you going to do when you're released from the program?"

"I really don't know, baby."

"In the meantime, you could help us out around the shop," suggested Benji.

Mecca kicked Benji in his shin and bucked her eyes.

"What will I do?" asked Yvette.

"We're always in need of an extra shampoo girl and a receptionist. What do you say?"

"I don't know. What do you think, Mecca baby?"

Mecca balled her face up and didn't answer at first, then thought about the conversation she had with Benji a couple of days ago. "It doesn't sound like a bad idea, I guess."

Benji smiled, then said, "Well, it's settled."

Yvette was so excited that Mecca had finally let her guard down a bit. Mecca felt a little better. Seeing Yvette all dolled up and sincerely trying to change her life made her want to begin anew. They all sat around talking fashion and about Henry's Palace. Benji promised that he would take Yvette to Henry's on her first home pass. They chatted until visiting hours ended, and neither Mecca or

Yvette wanted the visit to end. Mecca looked at her watch and was shocked how much time had slipped away.

They stood and said their goodbyes. Yvette hugged and thanked Benji for all he had done and then reached to hug Mecca. Mecca didn't refuse her, but she was stuck not knowing what to do.

"Thank you, Mecca. I hope to see you again soon," Yvette said while hugging Mecca.

Mecca had to hold back the tears that formed in her eyes. Yvette provided the hug that only a mother possessed. Mecca had never been hugged like that before. She felt like there was nothing in the world that could harm her.

She took a deep breath, then reached up and hugged Yvette back. Not wanting to seem weak and show her emotions, Mecca ended the hug.

"I'll see you later. And it's good to see you're doing well for yourself. Keep it up," Mecca said as she and Benji made their exit.

"I'm so proud of you for giving your mom a chance. She really needed that," Benji said as he and Mecca drove to the salon.

"Yeah, well, she got one chance to fuck up and I'm done with her ass," Mecca said.

She was having mixed emotions about Yvette. A part of her still wanted to hate Yvette, and the other part wanted to bury the hatchet.

"Girl, I saw how you were trembling when Yvette hugged you. It's okay. You can let down your guard. Remember, try to forgive her."

Mecca was hearing Benji and wanted to forgive Yvette so bad, but her heart and emotions made it hard to. She wanted to hate Yvette for the rest of her life.

Chapter 15

After leaving the cemetery, E-Way went to holler at Subi at the grocery store. Subi had told him to meet him there because his package was ready. E-Way strolled through the entrance of the store as usual as if he were a customer. He headed toward the meat section, stopping at the two stainless-steel doors, then looking around before entering. Subi was in his office on the phone, delegating orders to his younger brother, Abdullah, who ran one of their car lots. Subi slammed the phone down as E-Way entered.

"E, baby, what's up, my nigga?"

"Here you go with that 'nigga' shit. You got my shit ready, man?" asked E-Way, standing in front of Subi's desk.

"Take a seat," Subi said, motioning E-Way to a chair. "Now what is it that you wanted to tell me? The last time I seen you, you said we needed to talk," Subi continued.

"After this, my good friend, I'm done."

"If it's the coke or the prices, you know I'm a fair guy. I'm willing to bend a little."

"Nah, nah. I mean that I'm done with the business altogether. It's a wrap."

"I would hate to see you go. Can I ask you why you're leaving the business?"

"It's time to do something else. I'm getting out before it's too late."

"E, it would be a slap in the face if the family were to find out you were still in the business."

"So, what the fuck you calling me, a liar?" E-Way said as he sat up in his chair.

"Not at all. I'm just saying that if you wish to get back in the business, do business with those who've proved loyal, that's all."

"Yeah, whatever. Where my goods at? I got shit to do," E-Way said as he stood. E-Way felt like Subi had threatened him on the sly and then tried to clean it up while still getting his point across.

"Well, follow me," Subi said as he led the way down to the freezer. He counted out fifty kilos, then handed them to E-Way to place in brown paper bags. E-Way, in turn, gave Subi a duffle bag full of currency.

"Remember, my boy, if you change your mind, holler at me." Subi let E-Way out through the back docking area.

E-Way didn't even acknowledge Subi. He loaded the kilos into the hatch of his Range Rover and then pulled out of the parking lot. He flipped open his phone and began calling all of KFB.

Within minutes, everyone pulled in front of Chuck's mother's house. They all filed into the basement and got their respective shares.

"This is it, the last of the Mohicans," E-Way said after he finished passing out everyone's ration. He flopped down on the loveseat, grabbed a Swiss Sweet off the coffee table, and began rolling a blunt.

"When you gon' turn me on to the plug?" asked Big Whitney. Everyone's attention was on E-Way. He hadn't prepared for the question. He licked his blunt seal, then flicked the flame of a lighter across the blunt to dry it.

"Well, what the plug say?" asked Kev, growing impatient.

"He ain't trying to meet nobody," E-Way said, then lit his L and took a long pull.

"Fuck you mean, he ain't trying to meet nobody? Like we some ole oddball-ass niggas or something. So, what the fuck we gon' do? Are you gon' continue to cop for us?" asked Kev.

"If I do that, I might as well stay in the game. I told y'all I'm done," E-Way said, then took another pull from his L.

"Who is the nigga?" asked Chuck.

"I can't tell you that."

"You on some old secret squirrel shit. 'I can't tell you that,'" Kev said, mocking E.

"So basically fuck us is what you saying?" asked Big Whitney.

"What, nigga?" E-Way asked all defensive.

"I knew that nigga wasn't gon' turn us on the plug," said Kev.

"I don't even think you hollered at the plug for real, for real," Chuckie Bom's added.

Everybody was ganging up on E-Way. He couldn't believe what he was hearing. *These ungrateful-ass bitches.* "I raised you niggas from pups to mutts, and now you got fleas and wanna bite," E-Way said, standing.

"Nigga, you already rich. You got yours, and now you like fuck us," said Kev.

"Who put two bricks in yo' hand? I put two bricks in all y'all hands and told y'all to blow up. It ain't my fault if you fucked over all the money you made. I'm done," E-Way said as he headed for the door.

"That's fucked up, E," Big Whitney said as E-Way exited the basement.

E-Way threw his hands in the air and kept it moving. The rest of KFB remained in the basement, each man feeling betrayed.

"I told y'all we should have hog-tied his ass. Either him or that bitch. He'll come of that dust for that ho," Kev said.

"Shit, it ain't too late," added Big Whitney. He was in his feelings about E-Way not plugging him in with the connect.

"Ole ho-ass niggas," E-Way said to himself as he drove toward the Detroit River. He was steaming as he thought of Kev and the rest of his crew jumping ship on him. It was like they were only fucking with him because of the money. E-Way knew that was a lie. He had grown up with all of them. They were best friends. *The money can't be that serious,* he thought as he pulled into the dock.

Old man Sal wasn't in sight as E-Way boarded the yacht. "Pops, are you here?" E-Way asked as he turned the door handle leading to the cabin area. Old man Sal was lying across the sectional couch as if he were sleeping. Channel 7 News was watching him, so to speak. Empty beer cans lined the coffee table, and the stench of weed filled the cabin. E-Way walked over to Sal and shook his leg in an attempt to wake him. Old Sal's leg was as stiff as a board.

E-Way's stomach dropped to the pits of its depth. From having seen and dealt with death in the past, E-Way knew that Sal was gone. He closed Sal's eyes, then kissed him on the forehead.

"Why now, Pops?" he asked, taking a seat across from Sal. "I did it. I'm done with the game. As you say, 'checkmate.' You were right as always. Niggas always think you owe 'em something. I kind of fell out with my guys about not plugging them. Oh, well. What am I going to do without you? First Bubbles, now you. You was like my dad. You raised me up from a young'un, and I thank you for all that you've done. If it weren't for you schooling me, I would have been dead a long time ago. I just wish you could see me get out the game and be a success at something else. Damn, Pops," E-Way said, putting his face in his hands, trying to hold back the tears.

It was Sal's time to go. He was old as dirt and had done everything under the sun at least twice. He had lived his life, and it was a long one. E-Way knew it was Sal's time. He just didn't want to accept it. He needed Sal. *But that's life. You gain one thing and lose two.*

E-Way walked into the deck and grabbed a beer, then went back inside the cabin. He continued to talk to Sal's dead corpse. *Can things get any worse?* E-Way thought as he stared at Sal's lifeless body.

Chapter 16

Since seeing Yvette, Mecca couldn't stop thinking about seeing her again so she could ask her all the questions that had been bothering her for so long. Mecca sat in her office in front of the computer lost in thought, daydreaming about the past and future. Her thoughts were interrupted by the ringing of her cell phone. The call came in as unavailable. She was hesitant to answer but reluctantly did.

"Hello."

"Mecca, baby, how are you?" asked Yvette.

Mecca was caught off guard. She recognized the voice, but thought, *how did she get my cell number? That damn Benji.*

"I'm all right," Mecca answered, not knowing what to really say.

"I hope I didn't catch you at a bad time."

"Nah, it's okay. What's up?"

"Well, my guidance counselor is giving me a four-hour furlough so I can get my birth certificate and social security card. I have to get those in order to obtain my driver's license."

"Yvette, you don't have those?"

"Nope. I haven't had a copy of my birth certificate in probably twenty years, and I have never had my license. I was hoping you could take me if you're not too busy."

Shit, the bus is running. "I guess I can take you. When does your furlough start?"

"Just as soon as you can get here. My time starts from the moment I sign the logbook."

"Give me about twenty minutes."

"Thank you so much."

"Um hum," Mecca said before hanging up the phone.

"Where you off to, Ms. Thang?" asked Benji as Mecca headed for the front door.

"Thanks to you, Yvette has my cell number. She called and asked for me to play taxi for the day so she can get her license."

"I'm so proud of you. Let me know how things go," said Benji.

Mecca just rolled her eyes and stormed out of the shop like a spoiled little brat. As she pulled in front of the dilapidated halfway house, Mecca started regretting agreeing to drive Yvette around. Dopefiends decorated the exterior of the building. They leaned forward in an attempt to see who was pushing the shiny BMW. Mecca tucked her purse underneath her seat after removing her pepper Mace and then exited the car.

"Say, Red, can you spare a few dollars?" asked one of the musty fiends as Mecca headed for the entrance. She didn't bother answering. She knew better than to engage in conversation and risk being robbed.

The desk guard buzzed her in and handed her a log to sign. After she signed the log, the guard continued to eat his lunch, Popeyes chicken. Mecca was standing in the small lobby for a few minutes, then grew impatient.

"Aren't you going to let them know I'm down here waiting?" Mecca snapped.

The guard smacked his chops, then licked his fingers before picking up his desk phone. "And who is it you're here to see?" he asked.

"Yvette Tobias," Mecca said with an attitude.

"She'll be down in a minute," the guard said after hanging up the phone. He went back to attacking his lunch. Mecca mean mugged his fat ass while she waited.

Within minutes Yvette emerged looking like a beach bunny, wearing a shorts set Benji bought for her. "He ain't giving you a hard time, is he?" Yvette asked in reference to the guard as she entered the lobby.

"Not as hard a time as he's giving that damn chicken," Mecca answered.

"You's a mess, girl. You better be nice to my daughter, Marion."

"That's your daughter? Damn, y'all look like twins," said the guard.

"You ready, Yvette?" asked Mecca. She wasn't trying to hear nothing about how much she resembled Yvette.

"Yeah. I'll see you in a few, Marion," Yvette said as she and Mecca made an exit. "His fat ass is always trying to holla. I'll be nice because he's in charge of the log. He can easily make my furlough for ten hours if he wanted to. Is this your car, baby? This damn thing is sharp," Yvette said as they approached Mecca's BMW.

"Yeah," Mecca answered as she rushed to unlock the doors.

Yvette rubbed the dashboard and the butter-soft interior with approval. "Just like yo' momma. You got expensive taste," Yvette said as she tried to get settled in her seat.

There was an awkward silence. Mecca didn't know what to say. She was just focused on not being rude. Once out of the Cass Corridor, Mecca let the top down. She needed the breeze to lighten the mood a little. Yvette watched in amazement as the hardtop folded back and disappeared into the trunk.

"So, Mecca, when was the last time you visited Momma?" Yvette asked, trying to make a meaningful conversation.

"It's been a while. I really need to go and see her and put some flowers on her grave."

"Maybe one day soon we'll be able to do that together. I haven't visited my mom's grave in God knows how long."

"I'd like that. So, how's your treatment classes coming along?" Mecca asked, trying to change the touchy subject about her grandmother.

"I have two more weeks until graduation. Let me tell you, I haven't felt this good about myself in years. My guidance counselor wanted me to take a job as an assistant, but I told her about me working at the shop. She's all for it. She says it'll give us a chance to build up our relationship. I've got so much to learn about you, Mecca. I know I wasn't there for you when you were growing up. But I don't want to miss another day of your life. I'm not going to pretend like the past isn't real and not acknowledge it. But, baby, it is what it is: the past. I want you to know that I'm proud of you, for what it's worth. You've made something of yourself and you're going places. Do you think we can start over?" Yvette asked.

Mecca was caught off guard. Yvette just spilled her guts out of nowhere as if she'd been thinking about this for a long time. Yvette waited patiently for Mecca to answer.

"Let me ask you a question," Mecca said.

"Anything," Yvette said, turning to face Mecca completely.

"What made you leave me? I mean, was the streets that much more important than me? Do you know all I've been through growing up without you? Do you know how many times I was raped as a child, and me thinking that it was normal all the things I was subjected to? Do you know how many nights I went to bed hungry and cold? Do you have any idea?" Mecca asked as she began crying.

Yvette looked at Mecca and felt helpless. She wanted to comfort Mecca but didn't know how.

"Why did you leave me?" Mecca cried.

"I was a foolish little girl when I had you. I wasn't ready to be a mother. I was afraid that I would fail you. Baby, please forgive me. I didn't know you been through all those horrible things," Yvette said as she also started crying. She grabbed Mecca's hand, then kissed it. "Baby, you remind me of myself in more than one way. I was raped and abandoned as a child too. To hear you say that you were raped and went to bed hungry brings back ill memories. I never meant for you to go through what I did."

"How do I know you won't up and leave me again? How do I know you're really done using drugs and running the streets?"

"Baby, I assure you that my intentions are good. It's a daily battle, and we can only take it one day at a time. I need you now more than ever. Don't be like me and turn your back on me. You're better than me, and I really need your support."

Mecca pulled in front of the social security office and parked. She and Yvette both were in the visor mirrors trying to gather their pretty.

"You coming in?" asked Yvette.

"Nah, I'ma wait in the car."

"A'ight, I'll be just one moment," Yvette said, as she exited the car and entered the office.

Mecca felt a hell of a lot better after venting her emotions. She didn't quite get the answers she was looking for out of Yvette, and in fact she felt guilty for some reason. She didn't know about Yvette's upbringing, being raped and abused as a child. Mecca tried to sympathize with Yvette's situation and her reasons for leaving her.

Mecca was deep in thought when Yvette opened the passenger door and got in. "Are you okay, Mecca? You look like you're in outer space."

"Yeah, I was just thinking, that's all."

"Well, one more stop. Get this damn birth certificate and next week I'll apply for my license. I may have to borrow your car for my driver's test."

"We'll see," Mecca said, pulling away from the curb.

After picking up the birth certificate, Mecca dropped Yvette back off at the halfway house. The sun was beginning to set, and she wanted to get as far away as possible from the Cass Corridor before dark struck. Yvette was making small talk once they pulled in front of Harbor Light.

"So, are you coming to my graduation?"

"I'll be there along with Benji, of course."

"Thank you for everything. Let me get in here before these folks go to tripping. I'll call you later to see if you made it in safe."

"A'ight, see you later, Yvette," Mecca said as she watched Yvette walk to the door before pulling away from the curb.

It was ladies' night out, and Mecca was in much need of seeing Drew. She met Benji and Marie at Henry's. Also in attendance was none other than Olivia's hating ass. She was there for one reason, and one reason only. To bust Mecca by all means.

Chapter 17

"Hello," answered E-Way. He was in the middle of closing the deal on the building for the restaurant.

"I've got something for you."

"Who is this?"

"You got that many hoes? It's Olivia."

"Oh, what's up? What you got for me?"

"I'd rather show you in person. Where are you?"

"It'll have to be tomorrow or something. I'm in the middle of something right now. Just tell me what it is."

"It can wait," Olivia said with an attitude.

"A'ight, then I'ma hit you up later."

Olivia hung up without saying bye. She was salty because E-Way didn't drop what he was doing to see what it was she had for him.

E-Way and his attorney finished signing all the necessary documents. He handed the Realtor a check, and in return the Realtor handed him the keys to the building. He stood in the dusty, unlit building, smiling as he envisioned customers coming and going.

After leaving the building, E-Way went to break the news to Grams. She had some news of her own to break to him. She handed him a large manila envelope as he entered the house.

The envelope was addressed to him from a law firm. E-way looked at the envelope in a state of confusion. "What's this?" he asked.

"I don't know. The mailman dropped it off earlier. It seems very important. Open it," said Grams as she and E-Way walked over to the sofa and took a seat.

E-Way read the contents of the envelope in disbelief. His eyes raced through the sentences. Grams could tell it was something exclusive by E-Way's body language.

"What is it, baby?"

"It's old Sal's will. He has named me as his sole beneficiary," E-Way said, handing Grams the will. E-Way stood up and began pacing the living room floor. Old Sal had left him $12 million cash, several rental properties, his yacht, and his estate. E-Way knew Sal had money, but he never put an exact amount on it.

"Baby, what are you going to do with all this money?" Grams asked after finishing reading the will.

"For starters I'ma send Pops out in style." E-Way handed Grams the keys and deed to the building. Her face lit up as she read the deed. She gave E-Way a big hug, then kissed him on the forehead.

"Let me go call Ms. Mae," Grams said as she ran into the kitchen and grabbed the phone.

E-Way smiled to himself at the sight of Grams being happy. His smile turned to a frown at the thought of Sal's passing. He grabbed the will off the coffee table and left out the front door.

It was ten o'clock in the morning. E-way wanted to share the good news with Mecca, so he drove up to the salon. He was mean mugged by Olivia as he entered the shop. Benji noticed the eye contact between the two and interrupted them.

"Mecca is in the back," Benji said, emphasizing Mecca's name.

"Thank you, Nicholas," E-Way said, trying to be funny as he headed toward the back room.

Mecca was at the computer and on the phone talking to Drew when E-Way walked into the room. Mecca's stomach dropped at the sight of E-Way. She quickly ended her conversation with Drew.

"Let me call you back," she said, hanging up on Drew. "Baby, what are you doing here?" she asked as she jumped to her feet. Her palms were sweaty, and she turned pale as if she had seen a ghost.

"I came to check on you. I don't need no invitation for that, do I?" E-Way said as he gave Mecca a kiss.

"Of course not. I'm just surprised to see you, that's all. What's this?" Mecca asked, pointing at the manila envelope in E-Way's hand.

"You might want to take a seat for this," E-Way said as he handed Mecca the will.

Mecca opened the envelope and began reading the will. She stopped at the $12 million. She jumped up into E-Way's arms, all excited. "Oh, my God. Did you call these people yet?"

"Nah, I just got it a few minutes ago. I'ma do that in a little while. I got some other good news. I just closed on the building for the restaurant. Everything's coming together."

"I can't believe old Sal left you everything. He didn't have a family?"

"I was the only family he had."

Chapter 18

E-Way hadn't seen or heard from Kev, Chuck, Big Whitney, or Chuckie Bom's since they fell out. He wasn't surprised to see them in attendance at Sal's funeral. Damn near the entire east side of Detroit packed the pews of Word of Faith Church. Those who weren't on the approved list of guests watched the service from a monitor posted outside the church. Old Sal was a legend. People from all over came to show their respect.

E-Way and Mecca sat in the front row. They were deemed to be Sal's family along with all Sal's young skeezers he sponsored and laid up with from time to time. They were all hoping to be named in Sal's will. Little did they know E-Way had already collected what would be issued from Sal's estate. E-Way looked at each of them with his face screwed up. *Shiesty-ass bitches.*

Several people gave eulogies about Sal and talked about how they met him and what a good-hearted man he was. E-way didn't give a eulogy. He wanted the services to end as soon as possible. He felt like for the most part everyone there had a hidden agenda, with the exception of a few people. E-Way thought that Sal didn't even fuck with these niggas like that.

After the services everyone tailed Sal's hearse to the burial site, and then everyone met at the State Fair Lounge for the reception.

E-Way was rather reserved. He and Mecca sat tucked off in a corner sipping Rémy Martin VSOP. Everyone knew how close Sal was to E-Way, so they stopped by his table to give sympathy and condolences. Kev and the rest of KFB approached E-Way and Mecca's table. E-Way told Mecca to excuse herself so he could holler at his men for a second.

"I'll be over here if you need me," Mecca said, then kissed E-Way on the cheek before getting up.

They all took a seat facing E-Way, who still hadn't said a word to any of them.

"E, man, I'm sorry about old Sal. I know how close y'all were," Big Whitney said, breaking the ice. Everyone else offered their sympathy as well.

"Thank y'all for coming. What y'all niggas been up to?" E-Way asked.

"Same ole two-step for real, for real. Niggas trying to find a connect with some decent prices."

E-Way tolerated the conversation because he missed his niggas, but he wasn't trying to hear nothing about no drugs. His mind was on higher stakes, and he just wished that his crew would see his vision and dare to dream big outside the streets. Here old Sal was dead and E-way was mourning, and all these niggas could think about was themselves. They kept hinting about getting plugged. E-Way felt as though that was the only reason they were there.

Mario, the music producer and the guy Mecca had run into at the salon and after-party, approached E-Way's table. He, too, knew Sal before making it big in the music industry. Mario used to promote events. That was his relationship with Sal. He used to promote gatherings at Sal's bar and other star-studded events.

"E-Way, man, I'm sorry about the loss of Sal. If there's anything I can do, don't hesitate to ask," Mario said.

"I'm good, but thanks anyway."

"I see you got your crew with you. I ain't heard nothing from y'all lately. What, y'all not rapping no more?"

The question hadn't really been pondered since the death of Bubbles.

"Yeah, we still doing us. I'm about to rebuild the bar and studio. Just with the loss of Bubbles, shit got kinda stagnated," E-Way answered.

"I still want to do something with y'all. Y'all definitely got what it takes. Whenever y'all ready, let me know."

"I'ma get up with you."

"A'ight, y'all be smooth," Mario said as he excused himself.

"Man, fuck that fake-ass Berry Gordy nigga. I'm trying to get this paper how I know how. Later for that rap shit," Kev said as Mario left the table.

"Man, I'm getting ready to get up out of here. Y'all niggas get up with me," E-Way said as he stood.

All of them looked like they wanted to ask him about the connect, but they didn't.

"A'ight, we'll get up with you probably tomorrow or something," Big Whitney said.

E-Way thanked everyone for coming as he and Mecca exited the lounge.

"Ain't no question," added Chuck as he downed a double shot of Henny.

"Come on, let's get the fuck up outta here," said Kev.

The next day, Yvette was to graduate from her twelve-step program. Mecca brought E-Way along with Benji to show Yvette some support. It was set up like an actual graduation, minus the cap and gown. Yvette opened up the ceremony with a song by Whitney Houston. She sang it as if she wrote it. Mecca watched on in amazement. She had no idea Yvette could blow like that. E-Way was even more blown away by Yvette's performance. He had just found his first artist, he thought as everyone stood, giving Yvette a standing ovation.

"Yvette, I didn't know you had vocals like that," Mecca said excitedly as she met Yvette at the end of the stage.

"Have you ever thought about recording anything?" asked E-Way.

"Not really."

"Well, listen, I would like to sign you to a recording contract. With your voice and image, you're guaranteed to sell. You've got a story to tell," said E-Way.

"You sound pretty convinced," Yvette said.

"Just give it a chance. What do you have to lose?"

"Go for it, Yvette," Benji said, trying to encourage her.

"Yeah, Ma. I mean, Yvette," said Mecca, catching herself. She had slipped up and called Yvette Ma.

Yvette smiled at the thought of Mecca calling her Ma. "Let's do it," she said.

Chapter 19

E-Way couldn't sleep for nothing. He just knew he had discovered the next big thang in R&B. He called Mario and told him about Yvette. Mario told him to bring her by the studio so she could put together a demo of about five songs.

Yvette was living with Mecca and E-Way until she was stable enough to get her own spot. E-Way interrupted Mecca and Yvette's conversation. They were seated in the kitchen, looking at some furniture for their new house. Mecca and E-Way were to move into old Sal's estate after everything was settled.

"I hate to break up y'all Martha Stewart Home Shopping Network session and whatnot, but, Yvette, I need for you to throw something on and take a ride with me," E-Way said.

"Where you taking her this early in the morning?" asked Mecca, looking up from the catalog.

"To the studio. Mario wants you to put together a demo."

"Who you think you is, Puffy or Jermaine Dupri or something?" joked Mecca.

"What time do we have to be there?" asked Yvette.

"As soon as possible," answered E-Way, looking at his watch, then clapping his hands together. "Let's go, let's go," he said like a professional manager.

"Can I come?" asked Mecca.

"Yeah, but don't be all in the way."

Yvette recorded five songs that Mario himself had written. He only had to run the melody of each song one time, along with the instrumental for Yvette. After playing the track, Mario sat at the mixing board, counting the prospective figures he was about to pocket. There was no doubt in his mind that Yvette was a born undiscovered star. The demo came out better than he expected. Mecca, E-Way, Mario, and a few other industry folks filled the studio. They all gave Yvette her just dues as she exited the sound booth. Mario was trying to sign her to his record label.

"Slow down there, Suge Knight. She's signed to me. I just want you to produce her," said E-Way.

"Fifty-fifty split," said Mario.

"I said produce, not rape!" said E-Way.

"Sixty-forty."

E-Way shook his head no.

"Seventy-thirty, my final offer."

"Deal," E-Way said, extending his hand.

He and Mario made a verbal agreement with just a handshake.

"I'll have my lawyer draw the papers up. Baby, you are about to be a star," Mario insisted.

"I'ma be your stylist. Can't have you out here looking skeptical," said Mecca.

Yvette was just so overwhelmed. She didn't care one way or the other, and as long as Mecca was happy, she was content.

After leaving the studio, Mecca took Yvette out to celebrate. What better place to celebrate than Henry's Palace? Mecca called Benji and told him to meet them there.

It was early in the day, so the bar was rather naked as far as customers. Mecca, Benji, and Yvette didn't mind because that meant more dicks for them. Yvette grinned from ear to ear at all the young stallions as they took to the stage doing their sets.

"So, this is Henry's Palace," said Yvette as she looked around. "How long has this place been here?" she asked.

"Not long enough," said Benji.

"Mecca, who are you looking for? You keep turning around as if someone is following us," said Yvette.

"She waiting on her thang-thang Drew," said Benji, teasing Mecca.

"Who is Drew?" asked Yvette.

"Just the finest nigga to ever walk the face of this earth. I wonder why he isn't here," Mecca said as she continued to scan the bar in search of Drew.

"You better be careful not to get caught up with this Drew," said Yvette.

"I keep telling her," said Benji.

Mecca wasn't hearing them. She grabbed her cell phone and called Drew to see where he was at.

Drew was pulling into the parking lot of Henry's as his cell phone rang. Mecca met him at the entrance of the bar as if they were a serious couple. Benji pointed in Drew's direction, showing Yvette what it was Mecca was tripping off.

"Bay is fine," Yvette said in approval as Mecca and Drew approached the table.

Mecca introduced Drew to Yvette. Drew couldn't believe Yvette was Mecca's mother.

"This is your mother?" he asked in disbelief.

"Chico DeBarge, when are you going on stage?" Benji joked.

"I don't go on until late night. You know, I'm like a headline. They always save the best for last," Drew shot back.

"Well, can I get an exclusive show?" Mecca said, rubbing on Drew stomach.

"Come on, follow me. It was nice meeting you, ma'am," Drew said as he led Mecca toward the rear of the bar. She looked back at Benji and Yvette smiling as she trailed Drew.

"Details," yelled Benji.

E-Way met Olivia in downtown Detroit at the Marriott Hotel. He had booked a room and was upstairs waiting on Olivia. He left a key to the room at the front desk for Olivia to retrieve upon arriving at the hotel. Olivia entered the hotel room to find E-way lying across the sofa in the living room area. She was still acting stank because E-Way hadn't dropped what he was doing earlier to see what she had for him. E-Way got up and attempted to touch Olivia, but she jerked away.

"If I had known you were gon' be acting shifty, I would've stayed home," E-Way said.

"Whatever, here," Olivia said, handing E-Way her cell phone.

E-Way looked at the phone all confused. "Why you give me this?" he asked.

"There's some pictures on there."

E-Way scrolled through several photos of Mecca hugged up with Drew at Henry's. He was unfazed until he stopped on the last photo. It was a picture of Mecca kissing Drew goodbye in the parking lot. Drew was gripping Mecca's ass with a yard of tongue down her throat. E-Way turned the cell phone off, then asked, "Can I keep this?"

"For how long?"

"I'll bring it right back," E-Way said, heading for the door.

"Where are you going?" asked Olivia.

"I'ma call you," E-Way said as he exited the room, leaving Olivia standing there looking and feeling stupid.

E-Way wasn't in the mood for what Olivia had in mind. She thought that after she gave him the pictures, E-Way would leave Mecca. Olivia stood in the hotel room feeling used. E-Way left the hotel and drove to Henry's Palace. He wanted to holler at Drew and see just how involved he was with Mecca. E-Way noticed Mecca's BMW parked in the lot as he pulled in, and parked next to her car was Benji's Benz.

E-Way valet parked his truck, then entered the bar. He noticed Benji and Yvette seated center stage, both receiving lap dances. E-way stormed toward their table. Benji's eyes bucked at the sight of him.

"Where Mecca at?" E-Way demanded.

"E-Way, what are you doing here?" asked Benji.

Mecca and Drew came walking up flirting. Mecca stopped dead in her tracks as she met eyes with E-Way. Benji, Yvette, Mecca, and Drew all looked as if they had seen a ghost.

"This how you gon' play me?" E-Way said.

"Baby, I told you that we just come here for leisure," Mecca tried to explain.

"You just gon' go to the grave with yo' shit, huh?" E-Way said, then tossed Mecca Olivia's cell phone and walked out.

Mecca wanted to go after E-Way, but she knew not to, or risk the chance of a beatdown.

"That's yo' nigga?" asked Drew as he watched E-Way leave.

Mecca stood there dumbfounded. She didn't know what to do.

"Girl, you better go after him," said Yvette.

"Yeah, you should go see about your man," suggested Drew.

By the time Mecca made it out to the parking lot, E-Way was already in traffic. She tried calling his cell, but E-Way kept ignoring her.

"What the hell he give me this phone for?" Mecca asked herself as she walked back inside the bar. She scrolled through the phone and discovered that the phone belonged to Olivia.

"What the fuck he doing with Olivia's phone?" asked Mecca as she handed the phone to Benji for his inspection.

"Look at this," Benji said as he showed Mecca the pictures of her and Drew.

"I'ma kill that bitch," Mecca said.

Chapter 20

Mecca stayed out as late as possible. She dreaded going home and having to face E-Way. Yvette tried coaching her, telling her to be honest and let the chips fall where they may. Mecca trembled as she stuck her house key in the door and turned the knob.

"I'll be downstairs if you need me," Yvette said before heading to her room in the basement.

Mecca found E-Way in their bedroom watching TV. He lay in bed staring at the television, not comprehending what it was he was watching. Mecca entered the room not saying a word. She walked over to a chair at her vanity and took a seat. E-Way hadn't acknowledged her presence. He continued to stare out in space. There was no sense in trying to carry on the lie. It was over. E-Way had busted her.

"E-Way, can we talk?" asked Mecca.

"What is there to talk about? It is what it is. You been lying to me all this time. Sucking that nigga's dick, then coming home and kissing me like nothing happened."

"I don't love him. I love you."

"And that's supposed to make everything all right? You don't love him?" E-Way said.

"What about you? How did you get Olivia's cell phone?"

"Like I said, it is what it is. You was doing you, and I was doing me. We was living a lie."

"So, what now?" asked Mecca.

"Ain't no sense in stopping now. Continue to do you. I'm not saying that I'm done fucking with you or that I don't love you anymore, because I do. It's just hard to stomach. I don't know where we'll go from here."

Mecca didn't say anything. There was nothing that could be said. They both knew, or subconsciously knew, about the infidelity. They knew each other was doing their own thing on the side, but now that it was out in the open, it seemed as if they couldn't move on.

Mecca crawled in bed next to E-Way with her back to him. She was thinking about how bad she wished she had never gotten caught up with Drew. E-Way was reflecting on what old Sal told him about women, and it being in their nature to cheat.

The next morning Mecca awoke lying next to E-Way. The both of them had slept in their clothes. E-Way was sound asleep. Mecca pulled his shoes off, then covered him with the comforter. She kissed E-Way on the forehead, then headed toward the bathroom to get ready for another day at the shop.

"How did things go last night?" asked Yvette as Mecca entered the kitchen. Yvette was seated at the counter drinking tea and doing a crossword puzzle when Mecca entered the kitchen.

"I really don't know. I think he understood for the most part. He didn't give me the feeling it was over. What I got is we have an unspoken agreement for each of us to do our thing but consider the other's feelings."

"That reminds me of your father's and my early relationship. After so long that's just how it is. That doesn't mean you lose love for the person you're with. It's hard to explain, but trust and believe I know where you're coming from."

Mecca said goodbye to Yvette and was off to the shop. She wore a pair of sweats, some Air Force Ones, and a

T-shirt. She had her hair pulled back into a ponytail, and she was ready. She entered the shop, all eyes turning toward her. Benji was doing a customer's hair when Mecca entered the shop. He hadn't said a word to Olivia about what she had done. Benji wanted to let Mecca handle the situation. All morning, however, Olivia had been acting shifty. She knew that ass was hit from the look in Mecca's eyes as she stopped in front of her chair.

"I need to see you in the back, Olivia," Mecca said.

"As soon as I finish with this head," Olivia said nervously.

"Now!" yelled Mecca as she started for the back.

Olivia excused herself from her customer. She grabbed her purse and bolted for the front door, but Benji jumped in front of her and pointed toward the back room. Everyone in the shop was looking on like, "What the hell is going on?" No one knew about Olivia's episode with E-Way and her taking pictures of Mecca and Drew.

"Benji, please let me explain," Olivia pleaded.

"You's the worst kind of bitch—a jealous bitch," Benji said.

Mecca returned to the front of the shop. She grabbed Olivia by the hair and dragged her into the back.

"Beat that bitch ass," Tory said, instigating the matter. "I never liked that creepy bitch no way," she continued.

Tae played peacemaker. She pulled Mecca off Olivia and held Mecca until Olivia made a safe exit.

"Don't come back, bitch," Benji said as Olivia hightailed it out of the shop with a well-whooped ass. Mecca pulled a plug of hair out of Olivia's scalp and busted her nose. She didn't get her how she wanted to. If it weren't for Tae, Olivia would have gotten a far worse ass whooping. The only reason Mecca stopped was because of the respect she had for Tae.

After the shop settled down, Mecca sat at her desk thinking about Drew. She wanted to dismiss him but was too far gone to do so. After being busted it just felt wrong all of a sudden. Mecca decided to fall back on Drew for as long as she could and deal with him on an as-needed basis. That would be whenever she needed to release some stress or just go somewhere outside the norm and let her hair down. This was her way of rationalizing the situation.

Meanwhile, E-Way had met with old Sal's attorney, so that old Sal's will could be released. His attorney handed E-Way the keys to old Sal's estate, all the deeds to the investment properties, and then he did a wire transfer for the $12 million from Sal's account to E-Way's bank. E-Way left the attorney's office feeling like a new man. With $12 million behind him, he could damn near do anything businesswise. On his way back into the city he stopped at an exotic car lot, and a four-door cocaine white Bentley caught his eye. It was parked on the showroom floor.

E-Way went almost unnoticed as he entered the dealership. The salesman didn't bother approaching him because he didn't come off as the type to possess the $320,000 listed on the bill of sale in the window of the Bentley E-Way was gawking at.

E-Way tried the driver-side door in attempt to get in, but the doors were locked. He looked around, then motioned for a salesman. The sales rep reluctantly came over. He was a middle-aged white man with salt-and-pepper hair, very clean-cut. He wore an Italian-cut blue power suit and Italian-cut loafers.

"How may I assist you, sir?" he asked.

"I want to test drive this," E-Way said.

The man laughed silently with his mouth open as he looked up at the ceiling. "I'm sorry, but we usually don't test drive here. Our customers usually buy the cars first. They've been driving that particular brand for a while and know what to expect," said the salesman in an attempt to shoot E-Way down.

"Well, *sir,*" E-Way said, mocking the sales rep, "before I spend three hundred and twenty grand, I would like to test drive this damn car. I don't care to hear what you usually do. Where's the manager?"

Again, the man silently laughed, looked up at the ceiling, then looked back at E-Way.

"We don't carry the term 'manager' here, sir. We all are co-owners," the man said, pointing around at the assorted white faces. "However, if you insist on test driving, I will draw the keys, but we must first check your credentials."

"Credentials?" E-Way repeated.

"Yes, bank account, stocks, bonds, et cetera. We must. It's protocol."

E-Way reached in his pocket and handed the man a piece of paper with his account number where old Sal's attorney just had the money wired to. E-Way then handed him his driver's license.

"Very well. I will be right back," said the man, leaving E-Way to finish dreaming about the Bentley. The sales rep walked over to his office and typed the account number into his computer. His eyes bucked at the dollars that came across the screen. He looked out the window of his office at E-Way, then back at the computer screen. He tapped the monitor of the computer, then sprinted out of his office, grabbing the keys. His entire attitude had changed.

"If you don't like this color, we can order whatever color you desire. Same for the interior and rims," said the sales rep as he and E-Way took the car for a quick test drive.

"Nah, I'll take this one," E-Way said as they pulled back into the dealership.

"Excellent choice. Just let me draw up the papers, and I can have you on your way," the rep said, racing into his office.

After all the paperwork was handled, E-Way was allowed to drive off in his shiny new Bentley. His truck was to be delivered to his house by towing service, courtesy of the dealership. E-Way called Kev to see where everybody was at. He wanted to stunt and show off his Bentley. All of KFB were at Chuck's momma's house in the basement, smoking blunts and playing PlayStation 2. E-Way called inside once he pulled in front of the house and told everyone to come outside.

"Who the fuck this nigga think he is?" said Kev, hanging up the phone.

"Who was that?" asked Chuck.

"E-Way. He talking about all us come outside."

"He in front of the house?" asked Big Whit.

"I guess."

They all got up and headed outside through the side door. E-Way had all the windows down so that his sounds could be heard. He was leaning up against the car with his arms folded like a boss when Kev, Chuck, Big Whit, and Chuckie Bom's walked up. They all looked at the car in awe.

"This how you doing it now?" asked Chuck.

"All you know. Nigga gotta treat his self every now and again," E-Way said, going into boss mode.

"Let me take this mothafucker around the corner," said Big Whitney.

"Shit, let's ride out," E-Way said.

"I gotta handle some business. I'm gon' get up with y'all niggas later," said Chuck.

"A'ight then," E-Way said as he, Kev, Big Whit, and Chuckie Bom's piled into the Bentley.

Big Whitney drove while E-Way rode shotgun, and Kev and Chuckie Bom's were seated in the back.

"It's enough wood in this bitch to start a fire," Kev said as he climbed in.

"Roll up the windows so we can catch a cloud," said Chuckie Bom's.

They rode downtown to Belle Isle, circling the island three times before leaving. They drove around River Rouge Park and Chandler Park. By the time the sun went down, they had been through every part of Detroit from east to west and back. Not wanting the night to end, Big Whitney suggested they hit a strip club called Pretty Woman. They pulled up like bosses, valet parked the car, and entered the club like hood stars.

E-Way paid for a booth in VIP, and within minutes they were swarmed by a pack of young ladies offering lap dances.

"Bar on me tonight," E-Way said, informing the shot girl.

"Damn, big timer, what you do, sign with Cash Money records?" asked Big Whit.

"Yeah, you around here pulling up in Bentleys and buying out the bar, so what's good?" asked Kev.

E-Way hadn't told them about old Sal leaving him a fortune, nor did he have any plans of telling them. Kev, Chuckie Bom's, and Big Whitney were left to assume what they had already expected, that E-Way had gotten right and said fuck them. Their imaginations were getting the best of them. That was what happened when niggas started trying to count your money.

"Y'all niggas worried about the wrong thing," E-Way said as he enjoyed the lap dance of two dancers.

Kev couldn't even enjoy himself. He was too focused on E-Way. From the corner of the booth, he mean mugged E-Way as he plotted his downfall. It was like the two young ladies who were draped over him didn't exist. Chuckie Bom's and Big Whit were in a similar mood. E-Way excused himself to use the bathroom. After he left the booth, Kev leaned over and told Big Whit, who was seated next to him, "Man, we gon' do that shit tonight!"

"Tonight?" asked Big Whitney.

"Tonight. Soon as we leave this bitch."

Chapter 21

E-Way returned to the booth where Kev, Chuckie Bom's, and Big Whitney were seated. They continued to pop bottles and enjoy lap dances until the club closed. E-Way paid the bar tab and exchanged numbers with one of the dancers, promising to get up with her in the near future. He was buzzing good from all the bubbly and shots of liquor. He exited the bar to find Big Whitney, Kev, and Chuckie Bom's already in the car. He walked around to the passenger side and got in after hollering at a few groupies in the parking lot.

Big Whitney pulled out of the parking lot and turned onto a side street leading back to the hood. It was just past two o'clock in the morning. They had been hanging since early in the afternoon, and E-Way was ready to call it a night. He flipped open his cell phone and scrolled down to Mecca's name. As the phone began ringing, Chuckie Bom's, who was seated behind E-Way, reached forward, choking E-Way from behind. He had him in a full nelson wrestling move, cutting off E-Way's windpipe. Big Whitney reached over from the driver's seat and frisked E-Way's waistband, removing E-Way's pistol. E-Way tussled as much as he could but was caught off guard. He tried to slide down in his seat so he could come out of Chuckie Bom's chokehold.

"Why are y'all doing this?" E-Way managed to ask. His life was flashing before his eyes. The lack of oxygen caused him to pass out. His body went limp as he slumped over and ceased resisting.

"Hello? E-baby, are you okay?" asked Mecca. E-Way's cell was still on. It was on the floor between his legs.

Big Whitney reached down between E-Way's legs and grabbed his cell phone.

"Hello?" Mecca said over and over until the phone went dead.

Big Whitney hung up on her, then turned the phone completely off. They pulled in front of Chuck's mother's house, where all their cars were parked. Kev sprinted inside to grab Chuck and some rope so they could tie E-Way up. Kev and Chuck returned to the car carrying a large brown box and an industrial-sized extension cord instead of the rope.

E-Way began to regain his senses but was still dazed and unable to move. Kev opened the passenger door and snatched E-Way out onto the curb. The street was completely dark. No one was out at this hour. E-Way was left to fend for himself. His only prayer in the world was that a police car would happen to ride past and save him. He knew the odds of that were slim to none because of the streetlights being shot out and the recent violence against police.

Kev and Big Whitney rolled E-Way over onto his back and began tying him up using the extension cord. E-Way lay there with his eyes open, staring at the stars. He couldn't believe what was taking place. All he could think about was what old Sal told him. *"Death is near."*

"This how y'all gon' do me?" E-Way said.

"Nigga, we gon' give yo' bitch ass one chance, and one chance only, to make a call and get some money. We tired of playing with yo' ass," Kev said as he finished tying E-Way up.

What the fuck is he talking about them being tired of playing with me? E-Way asked himself, then grew angry at the thought.

"So, it was y'all who broke into my house?" E-Way asked, but no one said anything. It was all starting to make sense. No wonder nothing was taken. "You bitch-ass niggas. Which one of you niggas put y'all hands on my grandmother?" E-Way yelled as he tried to sit up but was unable.

"As much as we'd love to take a trip down memory lane with you, we can't. What you gon' do?" asked Kev, looking down at E-Way.

Big Whitney called Mecca back using E-Way's cell phone. Once Mecca answered, Big Whitney bent down and put the phone to E-Way's ear.

"Hello," said Mecca.

"Man, tell her to put together a million dollars and have it ready immediately," instructed Big Whitney while holding the phone to E-Way's ear.

"E-Way, are you there?" Mecca said.

"Baby, listen, I love you. I just want you to know that."

"What's wrong?" Mecca asked, sensing something was wrong from E-Way's voice and speech.

"These bitch niggas got me. Don't give these niggas nothing. It's Kev—"

The phone went dead before E-Way could finish his statement. Big Whitney hung up on Mecca.

"Hello? Hello?" Mecca said over and over again. She tried calling back, but the voicemail picked up.

"Baby, what's wrong?" Yvette asked, sitting across from Mecca at the kitchen table.

Mecca had begun crying. "They got E-Way."

Big Whitney reached down and snatched E-Way to his feet. "Bitch, you gon' die tonight."

Big Whitney instructed Chuckie Bom's to open the trunk to E-Way's Bentley. Together Big Whitney and Chuck picked E-Way up and put him in the trunk of his car.

"What we gon' do with his ass?" asked Kev as they all stood at the rear of the car looking down at E-Way.

"Y'all niggas is the worst bitch-made niggas I've ever met," E-Way said as he began crying. He had accepted the fact that he was about to die. That wasn't why he was crying. He was fuming because he would have given his life for these very niggas, and now this.

Big Whitney, who was obviously in charge of the conspiracy, didn't answer Kev's question. He closed the trunk and told Kev and Chuck to follow him. Big Whitney jumped into E-Way's Bentley and pulled away from the curb. He led Kev and Chuck to the old studio and bar site. He pulled into the back of the bar, which was still burned to a crisp. Kev and Chuck pulled in next to Big Whitney and parked. They all exited the cars, then walked around to the trunk where E-Way was.

E-Way had already made his peace with God and was wishing that whatever these bitch niggas were about to do, they'd hurry up and do it. He could hear them talking near the trunk, and he knew that they had come to a stop but didn't know exactly where.

"Kev, grab that box out the back seat," ordered Big Whitney.

Kev returned to the rear of the car carrying the brown box that Chuck had come out of the house with earlier. Big Whit popped the trunk. E-Way hadn't budged. He squinted from the beaming lights that filled the parking lot from light poles.

"You ready to die, nigga?" asked Kev, looking down into E-Way's eyes.

"Nigga, fuck you nothin'-ass niggas!" E-Way yelled. Those were his last words.

Kev shot him a total of seven times in the face and head using a .40-caliber gun and emptied the remaining four rounds into E-Way's torso. Big Whitney, satisfied that

E-Way was dead, opened the brown box and poured its contents inside the trunk. The box contained white mice, which Chuck used to feed his pet snakes. The mice would literally eat E-Way's dead body or at least enough of it where he would be unidentifiable.

Kev closed the trunk, then helped Big Whitney clean the door handles and interior of any fingerprints. They jumped in the car with Chuck, leaving E-Way in the parking lot of the bar. Big Whitney took E-Way's cell phone and threw it out the window onto 7 Mile Road as they rode back to Chuck's house. They all filed into Chuck's basement and smoked blunts as if nothing had happened. Even if E-Way had given them the million dollars they were seeking, they still would have killed him out of envy.

Chapter 22

Mecca sat in the front room on the couch, staring at the front door all night, hoping that any moment E-Way would walk through the door. She refused to believe the worst. *E-Way is too strong to let some niggas just kidnap him,* Mecca tried to assure herself. She just knew that E-Way would come out of the situation. She sat there at the front door until the sun came up. Still no word from E-Way, Mecca called his grandmother and told her all what had happened. Old Grams nearly died after learning of E-Way's disappearance.

Yvette accompanied Mecca to the police station to file a missing person's report. Mecca left the station feeling like, "That's it." The detective put the report on top of a stack of other papers and went back to work.

Mecca and Yvette combed the east side of Detroit in search of E-Way's Range Rover. E-Way hadn't told Mecca yet that he had traded his truck in on his Bentley. Mecca subconsciously drove past the bar and turned on Robinwood, the side street leading toward the rear of the bar. She stopped in the middle of the street at the sight of the Bentley.

Mecca wondered whose car that was parked at the rear of the bar but didn't investigate the matter. She pulled off and headed toward the salon. She and Yvette were to meet Mario at the studio in a few hours for rehearsal, then later at St. Andrews for a showcase. Mario had some label executives who wanted to hear Yvette perform the five-track demo live. Mecca and Yvette had hair appointments with Benji. They wanted to get all dolled up for the evening.

"Hey, y'all," Yvette said as she and Mecca entered the shop.

"Y'all look so cute together. Y'all been hanging tough lately," Benji said. He was finishing up his first head of the day.

"What's wrong with you, Ms. Thang?" Benji said, referring to Mecca, who hadn't said one word.

She had flopped down into one of the leather recliners, let it back, and looked up at the ceiling. Mecca didn't answer. She was lost in her own world.

"What's wrong with that child?" Benji asked Yvette.

"It's E-Way. He's missing."

"Missing? Like 'didn't come home last night' missing?"

Yvette shook her head. Benji excused himself from his customer and took Yvette in the back to get the low-down. They returned shortly after. Benji, being optimistic as always, assured Mecca that E-Way would turn up.

"I believe that he's all right," said Benji.

As bad as Mecca wanted to believe that, she knew E-Way was dead. She could just feel it in her soul. She began blaming herself. *If I hadn't been cheating, he would have been at home with me.*

Benji went on and did Yvette's hair. Mecca passed. She didn't have the patience to sit in the chair. Benji wished Yvette good luck for tonight and said he would be in attendance.

"It's gon' be all right. Call me later, all right?" Benji said as Mecca and Yvette exited the shop.

"Okay," Mecca said in a low tone of voice.

Mecca and Yvette met Mario at his studio off Woodward Avenue and the Davidson Expressway. He was waiting on the ground floor for them as they pulled into the parking lot of the high rise.

"Where's E-Way?" asked Mario as he let Yvette and Mecca inside.

"We don't know," answered Yvette, not wanting to give him any details.

"Is he not answering his phone?"

"I keep getting his voicemail," said Mecca.

"Well, we're just doing a sound check and rehearsal. He doesn't necessarily have to be here for that," Mario said, ushering Yvette and Mecca onto an awaiting elevator.

Once inside the studio, Mario went straight to work, putting Yvette in the sound booth. Mario couldn't help but notice that Mecca was a bit distant. She sat in a chair near the entrance, looking off into space.

"Are you okay?" asked Mario, breaking Mecca's train of thought.

"Huh? Yeah, I'm all right," answered Mecca.

"You sure?" asked Mario, looking into Mecca's eyes, not at all convinced.

"How'd I do?" asked Yvette as she came out of the sound booth.

"You sounded wonderful. You do that tonight and you're well on your way," said Mario.

Yvette smiled at the overwhelming thought of having a recording contract and all the possibilities. Mario couldn't take his eyes off Mecca. He was genuinely concerned about her and could sense that something was indeed bothering her.

"Have you ladies eaten breakfast yet?" he asked, looking at his watch.

"No," answered Yvette.

"Let me treat y'all to breakfast. How does Denny's sound?"

"Sure, we'd love to," Yvette answered for both of them.

"Good, just let me wrap things up and I'll be ready in a few minutes," said Mario.

Yvette walked over to where Mecca was seated. Mecca looked so depressed, and Yvette felt sorry for her. "Baby, it's going to be all right. Come on, Mario is going to take us to breakfast," Yvette said, grabbing Mecca by the hand, helping her to her feet.

"Y'all ready?" Mario asked.

"Yeah, let's go," answered Yvette.

Mecca and Yvette followed Mario to Denny's out in the suburbs of Eastpointe, Michigan. During the entire drive, Mario stayed looking in his rearview mirror at Mecca. She hadn't noticed. She was too lost in thought. They pulled into the parking lot of Denny's and parked side by side. They were escorted to a booth by a waiter and handed menus.

"Um, this looks good," said Yvette as she looked at the picture of a steak, egg, and cheese special in her menu.

"What's that?" asked Mario, leaning over to see the picture. "It does look good, doesn't it? That's what I'm going to order," said Mario, then set his menu down.

"Me too," said Yvette as she continued to browse through the menu.

"What about you, Mecca? What are you going to have?"

Mecca hadn't touched her menu. She was seated across from Mario, and Yvette was seated next to Mario.

"I'm really not that hungry," she answered.

"Come on now, you've got to put something on your stomach," Mario said as he seductively looked Mecca in the eyes. Even without her hair being done and in the jogging outfit she wore, her beauty couldn't be downplayed. Mario had wanted Mecca the first time he laid eyes on her at the salon.

"Are we ready to order?" asked the waitress as she approached the booth.

"Um, yeah. Let us have three steak, egg, and cheese specials," answered Mario.

"And to drink?"

"Three large orange juices."

"Very well. Your food will be ready shortly," said the waitress, then grabbed the menus and disappeared to fill their orders.

Their food arrived shortly after the waitress left to fill their orders. Yvette and Mario dug into their plates while Mecca picked over her food.

"Are you always this down?" asked Mario. He figured Mecca would take offense to his statement and maybe offer a reason why she was so depressed.

Mecca didn't bite the bait. She just looked up at Mario and shot him a look that said, "Nigga, I wish you'd quit asking all these damn questions."

"My baby's kind of going through something right now," said Yvette.

"Top secret, or is there something I can help with?"

"Top secret," answered Yvette as she took a forkful of steak and eggs into her mouth.

There was no doubt that Mario wanted Mecca and not just a piece of her. Yvette could sense his intentions with Mecca as well.

"I think Mario likes you," she told Mecca after leaving Denny's as they drove toward E-Way's grandmother's house.

"That's nice," Mecca replied to Yvette's assumption. She found Mario attractive, but now wasn't the time. She must find out whether E-Way was alive. For the first time in a long time, she hadn't thought about Drew and Henry's Palace.

Mecca pulled into the driveway of E-Way's grandmother's house. She was hoping to see E-Way's Range Rover parked in the driveway, but her heart sank as she pulled in. Mecca didn't really care too much for Grams. Not because she was a bad person or treated her funny.

Mecca just felt uncomfortable around her and the rest of E-Way's family. That's just how she was. The only people she could truly let her guard down around were Benji, E-way, Drew, and now Yvette.

Grams had seen Mecca pull into the driveway and got up to meet her visitor at the door.

"Whose house is this?" asked Yvette.

"E-Way's grandmother's. Come on, let's go inside for a while," Mecca said as she opened the door and got out.

Yvette followed Mecca up the staircase to the historical mansion. Grams, recognizing Mecca, swung the door open and invited them in. "Mecca, baby, come on in," she said.

"Momma, I'd like to introduce you to my mother, Yvette. Yvette, this is Momma, E-Way's grandmother," Mecca said as they all stood in the living room.

"Nice to meet you," Momma and Yvette said at the same time.

"Y'all come on in and have a seat." Momma motioned Mecca and Yvette toward the sofa. "Can I get y'all something to drink?"

"No, thank you," answered Mecca.

"A'ight then. Now tell me when was the last time you heard from Matt?" asked Momma as she took a seat on the edge of a love seat.

"Yesterday morning before I went to work. He called me and said that some people had him, and then the phone went dead. I haven't heard back from him since."

"That boy told me he was done with that life," said Momma as her eyes began welling up.

"He did get out, at least to my knowledge."

"So, who would want to harm E-Way if he wasn't in that life anymore?" asked Yvette.

"Probably the same niggas who beat me into a coma and broke into you all's home," suggested Momma. "I think it's those bastards he's been running with and calling his friends."

Nothing or no one was to be overlooked in connection to E-Way's sudden disappearance. All the enemies from past and present were to be taken into account. Mecca wasn't concerned with solving a mystery. She just wanted E-Way to surface alive and unharmed.

She and Yvette kept Momma company and tried to comfort her. Momma called all around town in search of her boy. She called Chuck's mother and told her to ask Chuck if he'd seen E-Way. No one had heard from nor seen E-Way since the last time Mecca had seen him. Momma, like Mecca, refused to believe the worst until she saw it.

Chapter 23

It was getting late, and Yvette had to get home so she could get ready for her showcase. Mecca and Yvette said goodbye to Momma and promised to call if they heard from E-Way. Momma promised to do the same as she let them out and watched them walk to their car.

The entire drive home Mecca was praying that E-Way's truck would be in its usual spot and he would meet her at the front door. Again she was disappointed as she and Yvette pulled into the circular driveway. Once inside the house, Mecca checked the answering service. There were no new messages with the exception of Benji and Mario. She didn't even bother listening to the entire messages. She went to the next message to discover that was it.

Mecca reluctantly climbed the stairs leading to her master bedroom. She entered the room and walked over to her closet. She browsed through her enormous wardrobe, grabbing at basically anything that was black. That's how she felt on the inside: black, like her world had come crashing down and there was nothing she could do but accept it. She took a cold shower and cried her eyes out while standing under the water. Yvette had to bang on the bathroom door to get her out of the shower.

"Mecca, we're going to be late," Yvette said, looking at her watch.

Mecca turned the water off and grabbed her towel, then began drying her soggy skin. She quickly dressed, combed her hair, and was ready to go. Seeing Mecca depressed made Yvette want to forget going to the showcase.

"Baby, are you okay?" asked Yvette as she and Mecca drove in silence.

"He's not coming home, is he?" asked Mecca.

Yvette didn't know what to say, so she reached over and grabbed Mecca's hand. "I'm praying he turns up safely, baby."

Mecca damn near jumped through the roof of her Beemer at the sound of her cell phone ringing. She fumbled with her purse until retrieving it. "Hello!" she yelled into the receiver excitedly.

"Damn, girl, why you hollering all in my ear?"

It was Benji. He wanted directions to the hotel where Yvette's showcase was set to take place.

"I'm sorry, Benji," Mecca said, returning to her state of depression. She was hoping that it was E-Way on the phone.

Benji could hear the depression in Mecca's voice. "You still haven't heard from E-Way?" asked Benji.

"No."

"Well, I'm sure he'll turn up soon," Benji said, trying to sound convincing.

"Yeah, hold on for a second," Mecca said, then clicked over. It was Mario. He wanted to make sure she and Yvette were on their way to the hotel. He was already there.

Mecca clicked back over and gave Benji directions, and within minutes she and Benji both were pulling into the parking lot of the Courtyard Hotel. Benji parked a few spots over from Mecca and Yvette. He approached them as they were just getting out of the car. He wore a pair of black slacks that hugged his girlish frame, a silk shirt, more like a blouse, and a pair of Prada shoes.

"Aren't you dress to impress," Yvette said, commenting on Benji's attire.

"I mean, I do try," Benji said, striking a gay pose, then burst out laughing. "Nah, seriously though, you're absolutely killing the shit tonight, Yvette. I'm so proud of you."

Mecca was just standing there feeling alienated.

"Come on, we gon' be late," said Yvette.

Once inside the hotel, they were escorted to the ballroom by Mario, who was waiting in the lobby. He showed Mecca and Benji to their table, which was center stage. After settling them in, he disappeared into the back, taking Yvette with him.

"Yvette, you look terrific," he said, turning Yvette around in a circle. "Are you ready?"

"I think so. I'm a little nervous though."

"Just be yourself and everything will be all right. Wait a minute, where's E-Way?"

"No one has heard from him. That's why Mecca has been down. We're worried that he may have been kidnapped."

"Kidnapped?" repeated Mario. "I thought he was done with the streets."

"We haven't given up yet. Hopefully he'll turn up in one piece."

"That's too bad," Mario said sincerely as he looked from behind the curtain at the growing crowd and Mecca.

"Well, you're almost set to go on. Do your thang," Mario said, giving Yvette a kiss on the cheek, then leaving her to herself so she could gather her thoughts before taking the stage.

Yvette paced back and forth, rehearsing the lyrics to the first song she was to perform. Her train of thought was broken by the calling of her name. Mario introduced her as Yvette Tobias.

"Please welcome to the stage, ladies and gentlemen, the lovely Ms. Yvette Tobias."

Yvette closed her eyes and said a short prayer, then took the stage. She broke off into the first song on her demo, blowing like a seasoned vet. Watching Yvette perform was like being at an actual concert. Her voice was so powerful and rich that it didn't match her body. Everyone in the audience was in total astonishment and very well pleased with Yvette's performance, giving her a standing ovation as she concluded her showcase. Mario, who was seated with Benji and Mecca, joined Yvette on stage as she humbly took her bows.

"Come on, I want to introduce you to some folks," Mario said, taking Yvette by the hand. In attendance were A&R executives from Arista, Sony, and Interscope Records. They were all eager to meet Yvette and put their offers on the table as soon as possible. Mario introduced Yvette to each of them, doing the majority of the talking. He agreed to a later meeting with each executive. It was happening for both Yvette and Mario. He had worked with and produced many artists, but he had never broken a new big artist.

Where the hell is E-Way? He didn't want E-Way's being Yvette's manager to prevent them from inking a deal in the event that E-Way didn't turn up.

The festivities began to dwindle. Mario saw Yvette and Mecca to their car, prepping Yvette on tomorrow's events.

"Make sure you have E-Way call me as soon as you hear from him," Mario said as he closed Yvette's car door. He wanted to say something other than just good night to Mecca, but the words wouldn't form in time. Mecca had said goodbye and closed the door, then started the car.

Mario stood there and watched as Mecca backed out of her parking spot, feeling as if he had missed his only chance in the world. Benji's horn broke his trance as he drove by Mario and waved goodbye.

Mecca was buzzing good, compliments of the free bubbly, and the drive home was rather quick. She and Yvette entered the house and raided the fridge in search of some leftover chicken and fried cabbage Yvette had prepared the day before. Mecca, after putting her plate in the microwave, noticed that the answering machine was blinking, indicating unheard messages.

She walked over to the answering machine and pushed the talk button. Her food was ready, so she retrieved her plate from the microwave and began doctoring her chicken with Sal's Sassy Sauce. The voice of Momma came across the machine first.

"Mecca, please give me a call when you get in." There was a short pause in Momma's words. Mecca had begun demolishing her food when Momma continued, "They found Matt. Please give me a call." Momma hung up. Mecca could hear Momma's voice trembling as if she had been crying all day.

Mecca spat her food out and raced over to the phone and dialed Momma's number. It was pretty late, so Mecca didn't know whether Momma had turned in already. Momma answered after one and a half rings.

"Hello!" she said, sounding like something out of a horror flick.

"Momma, it's Mecca. Where's E-Way?"

"Chile, he's with God," Momma said.

Mecca dropped the phone down to her chest. It had been confirmed, her worst fear, that E-Way was dead. The details surrounding his death didn't matter to Mecca. It wouldn't bring him back to life. Mecca could hear Momma still talking in the distance, but her words weren't registering. Yvette looked up from her food and noticed Mecca. She had turned white and her eyes were bucked.

"Mecca, what's wrong?" asked Yvette as she got up and took the telephone from Mecca. "Hello."

Momma ran down the story to Yvette. She said that the police found E-Way in the trunk of his car behind the bar, after receiving a phone call tipping them off about the murder and location of the body. Momma had been to the morgue but was unable to identify E-Way because the white mice had eaten away at the flesh of E-Way's face, among other body parts. E-Way was carrying his driver's license. That was how they were able to contact Momma. E-Way's most recent dental records confirmed his identity. His body was then released to Swanson Funeral Home for the preparation of his burial. Just like that it was over and done with. One minute you're riding in a Bentley enjoying life and the fruits of your labor, then the next thing you know death comes and snatches your ass. Life is funny like that.

Mecca knew she had to find the strength to somehow be strong or otherwise risk the chance of having a nervous breakdown. After wrapping up her conversation with Momma, Yvette comforted Mecca, letting her cry her eyes out on her shoulder. Everything was happening too fast: the record deal, losing Mecca's father, getting to know Mecca, and now E-Way's death. Yvette somehow felt responsible for it all. She wanted to feel guilty. Anything, as long as it lifted the burden from Mecca.

Chapter 24

Since the discovery of E-Way's death, Mecca hadn't done but two things: cry and lie in bed. Benji, of course, being the friend he was, sat by Mecca's bedside, consoling her. Benji also helped Momma with arrangements for E-Way's funeral, which was set for today. The weather reflected today's occasion. It was pouring. From the look of the sky, you would think it was midnight. That's how dark and gloomy it was.

Mecca lay spread-eagle across her enormous bed with two pillows covering her face. She was dreading the funeral service and all the fake smiles that came with it. Benji's feminine voice could be heard in the distance. "Come on, Miss Thang, time to get that ass up," Benji said, coming from inside of Mecca's walk-in closet. He laid an outfit of Mecca's across the bed, then returned to the closet.

Moments later he returned to the room, carrying a pair of shoes and a few accessories to match Mecca's clothes. "Did you not hear me? I said it's time to get that ass up!" Benji said, snatching the two pillows from Mecca's face.

"Leave me alone," Mecca moaned, then rolled over.

Benji wasn't letting up one bit. He grabbed Mecca by the legs and dragged her out of bed. Mecca landed on her butt. "I'm not going," Mecca said, trying to sound serious.

"The hell you ain't. Come on," Benji said, reaching down to pick Mecca up. He picked her up and threw her over his shoulder, then carried her into the shower.

"Ten minutes and I'll be back," Benji said, looking at his watch before leaving the bathroom.

Mecca reluctantly undressed and climbed into the shower. She began to relax as the water ran down her face and body. Her thoughts were starting to clear. For the first time in four days, she realized that she hadn't seen Yvette since E-Way's death. She began to panic at the thought of something being wrong with Yvette. Was she hurt? Was she alive? All kinds of questions filled Mecca's mind. Her thoughts began to cloud themselves again. She turned the water off and reached for a towel. She needed Yvette, especially right now. It seemed like everyone around her was dying, and she needed to know that Yvette wasn't one of them.

While Mecca took her shower, Benji was downstairs in the kitchen cooking himself and Mecca a quick breakfast. He prepared for each three scrambled eggs with cheese, onion, and bell peppers, sausage links, wheat toast, and orange juice. As he fixed the plates and laid them on the counter, he found a note from Yvette addressed to Mecca. For the first time in four days Benji, too, had just realized that Yvette was missing. As he read the contents of the note, Mecca's footsteps could be heard coming down the stairs.

Benji quickly balled the piece of paper up, then shoved it inside his back pocket. Seconds later, Mecca entered the kitchen wearing only her robe.

"Why aren't you dressed?" Benji asked. "We have to be leaving here shortly."

"Have you seen Yvette?" asked Mecca.

"No, I haven't. But I'm sure she isn't far. Come on and have breakfast before your food gets cold," Benji said, motioning Mecca to a stool at the counter. Benji hated lying, especially when it came to Mecca, but today had to be an exception.

Mecca couldn't stop thinking about Yvette and her whereabouts. She barely touched her food, picking over it until it became cold.

"You don't have much of an appetite, huh?" asked Benji, gathering the dishes.

"Nah," Mecca answered dryly.

"Well, g'on and get dressed so we can get going. We're going to have to drive slow because of the weather."

Mecca slid down off her stool with her head hung low and proceeded up the stairs to her bedroom. She slowly dressed, not really caring how the clothes looked on her. She didn't pose for her floor mirror as usual, just grabbed her belongings and headed back down the stairs. Benji fluffed Mecca's hair out and straightened her attire before leaving.

They drove in relative silence with the exception of the radio, which was at a very low volume. Neither of them was actually listening to the music. Each was lost in their own thoughts. Benji was thinking once again how he could be a super friend and possibly find Yvette. Mecca was thinking about E-Way and what he'd look like in his casket.

The drive was long and quiet but seemed short to both Benji and Mecca. They looked on in awe at the number of cars that outlined Word of Faith Church and the number of people ducked low under umbrellas scattering for the entrance. It was jam-packed.

Benji managed to find a parking spot. He double-parked right outside the front door and threw his hazards on. He and Mecca ducked low under a Louis Vuitton umbrella and scurried inside. They were escorted to the front row of the church like celebrities. It felt more like a Bobby Johnson gospel concert than a funeral. People were dressed to impress with minks, 'chillas, gators, and the whole nine.

Mecca and Benji were seated next to Momma and the rest of the family. Folks were approaching and offering their condolences to Momma as they passed E-Way's casket. The majority of the people in attendance were there because of Momma, not because they knew E-Way himself.

"Come on, let's go say goodbye to E," said Benji, grabbing Mecca by the hand. Mecca didn't budge one bit. She had made her mind up that she would not be walking past E's casket. She knew she'd break down. Benji didn't press the issue. He excused himself and went up to pay his last respects to E-Way.

Mecca watched from the pew as people inched past E-Way's casket, some kissing him while others laid single roses on him. She noticed a few familiar faces in the line, that of Kev, Big Whitney, Chuck, and Chuckie Bom's, all wearing white tees bearing "KFB-4 Life" and a picture of E-Way, reading "RIP" underneath. The sight of them angered Mecca. It just came off as corny and fake shit to her. "Where were they when E-Way needed them?" Mecca asked herself. She didn't rule out the possibility that they may be responsible. Everybody bore watching.

Another familiar face appeared in the line. It was Mario. The sight of him lightened Mecca's mood a bit. For sure he had heard from Yvette. *Bing, that's where she's been, in the studio with Mario.* She looked farther into the crowd in hopes of seeing Yvette. Yvette was nowhere in sight.

"Excuse me, excuse me," Benji said as he climbed over the many legs on his way back to his seat. He flopped down next to Mecca, then grabbed her hand and held it for support. "They did a wonderful job on E-Way. He looks as if he's sleeping," said Benji.

Mecca didn't respond to Benji's comment. She was too focused on Mario, who was making his way over toward Mecca after making eye contact while standing in line. After kissing Momma and offering his condolences, Mario approached Mecca and did the same, offering support. "Mecca, if there's anything I can do, I mean anything, please don't hesitate to ask. Okay?" Mario said, leaning down over Mecca. Mecca nodded. Before Mario could turn on his heels, Mecca pulled him close to her and then asked about Yvette.

"I haven't seen her in almost a week. We were supposed to meet at the studio yesterday, but I figured she was helping out with the funeral and whatnot," said Mario.

From the look on Mecca's face, Mario could see that something had come over her. "Why? When was the last time you spoke to your mother?" he asked, realizing Yvette was missing.

"It's been about the same time frame. But I'm sure everything's all right," Benji said in an attempt to convince Mario, Mecca, and himself.

"Well, I'll call you probably in a couple of days. She should have turned up by then. See y'all at the reception," Mario said before heading for a seat.

The service lasted well over two hours. Members from Momma's church, Word of Faith, sang solos, the choir did several numbers, and Pastor Keith Butler put on a show as well. Everybody and they momma gave a eulogy with the exception of Mecca. She was too weak and too angered by all the fakeness going on to give a proper eulogy. *E-Way would understand,* she told herself. E-Way was like Mecca in a sense. He hated phony shit.

After the funeral, everyone piled into their cars and followed E-Way's hearse to the cemetery. It was still pouring, so everyone stood under an enormous shed. Those who were unable to fit under the shed stood under umbrellas. Pastor Keith Butler said a few words, and then folks said their final goodbyes. Mecca still couldn't manage to pull herself together enough to approach E's casket but knew she had to. It was only proper. So, she waited against the back wall alongside Benji until everyone was out of sight.

Together Benji and Mecca approached E-Way, slowly inching toward him. Mecca began crying, instantly realizing that it was for real. That there was no sequel to life, and this was it.

She first stood over E-Way sniffling, until her sniffles turned into screams. "Why?" she yelled, looking up at God as if she expected an immediate answer. "Why? Why?" Mecca continued to ask between sobs as she leaned over E-Way's casket, nearly climbing in. Benji held her up from falling while she went through the motions, letting it all out. After Mecca calmed down, Benji gently pulled her away from E-Way's casket. "Come on, say goodbye," Benji said, still pulling Mecca away from the casket.

Mecca was drained, frustrated, and mad at the world. She ordered Benji to take her home. There was no way she was about to sit up and deal with a thousand phony, hungry mothafuckas in her face who didn't even know E-way let alone care about him. They were there to eat and be seen, point blank and simple!

"Are you sure you don't want me to take you to the reception?" Benji asked as he pulled in front of Mecca's house.

"I'm fine. That's the last thing I need right now is to be in a room surrounded by a bunch of fake mothafuckers. But you go ahead without me. Call me when it's over," Mecca said, then leaned over and gave Benji a kiss on the cheek. "Thank you," she said, looking Benji in the eye, then reached for the door handle.

"Poor thang," Benji said to himself as he watched Mecca walk to the door before pulling off.

Chapter 25

The morning after Mecca buried E-Way, she fell right back into her routine, starting her day with her morning exercise, shower, and then off to the shop. She made up her mind that she wasn't about to continue to grieve for a long period of time. She told herself that death was a part of life, and there was only one way to deal with it, which was to move on. That's exactly what Mecca intended on doing.

All eyes were fixed on her as she walked through the salon door. Mouths dropped, and all gossip ceased as Mecca walked toward her office in the back with her head held high. It was apparent that she had her swagger back. Either that or she was putting up one hell of a front.

"Morning to all," Mecca said, continuing toward her office.

Benji excused himself from his customer so he could go check up on Mecca. He found her getting situated at her desk when he entered. "Mecca, what are you doing here?" asked Benji.

"Last time I checked I was half owner of this juke joint. Unless something has changed? I would suspect that I'm free to come and go as I please," Mecca said sarcastically.

"That's not what I meant, and you better know it. It's just that you're supposed to be home—"

Mecca cut Benji off before he could finish. "Home doing what? Grieving? Crying my eyes out over some shit that's done and over with? Life don't stop, so I gotta keep on keepin' on."

"Are you sure? Because the worst thing you can do is avoid the grieving process. It'll come out eventually," offered Benji.

"I'm good."

"Okay. Well, let me get back out here and finish this skank's hair. Holla if you need me," said Benji, taking one last look at Mecca to ensure that she was really all right. Satisfied with the vibe, he turned and left.

Before Benji could close the door, Mecca shouted for him.

"Yes, Miss Thang?"

"Have you heard from Yvette?" asked Mecca.

Benji hesitated before answering. He hated lying but wanted to spare Mecca the pain. "Nah, I haven't. I was going to ask you the same thing."

"Hmm, maybe I should call Mario and see if he's seen her. I'll do that in a little while."

"A'ight, call me if you need me," said Benji. He felt bogus for concealing the contents of Yvette's note he found on the kitchen counter.

Mecca sat at her computer, surfing the internet, looking at designer handbags for a few hours as she did on any given day. Her stomach began rumbling from hunger pains. She looked at her watch, and it was close to eleven and she had yet to eat breakfast or lunch. She turned the computer off, grabbed her purse, and headed out front.

The gossip that filled the air ceased as she emerged from the back office. Once again, all eyes were on her. Tory's silly ass broke the tension.

"Y'all some of the nosiest bitches in all of Detroit," she said while doing a customer's nails. No one wanted to snatch the statement out of the air and ask Tory just who in the hell she was talking to, so everyone started back up their conversations.

"I see ain't much changed," laughed Mecca, looking at Tory.

"Just the date. But how are you?"

"I'm good, you know," Mecca said sincerely.

"Good, because I ain't been to Henry's Palace in a minute. You game?" asked Tory.

"When, tonight?"

"Yeah. Tonight is jumbo dick night. Ten inches of better."

"You's a mess," laughed Mecca.

"So, is it a date?" Tory asked, waiting patiently.

"It's a date."

"What y'all over there chuckling about?" asked Benji.

"None ya," said Tory.

"None ya?" Benji repeated before realizing Tory had just got him. It was too late.

"None ya damn business," Tory said.

"Anyway, Mecca, what's up?" asked Benji.

"We gon' hit Henry's tonight. You wanna come?"

"Do I wanna cum?" Benji said, joking. "Of course I wanna cum."

Everyone in the shop fell out laughing. For Mecca it felt good to be back at the shop. Being around all the gossip and flashy bitches put her at ease. "Shit I wanna cum too," said Marie.

"Shit, we all can cum. All y'all gots to do is bring ya asses to the club tonight. It's going to be dumb dick in the place," Tory said in a high-pitched voice.

"Girl, you are crazy," one customer said in between laughs.

All the laughter and chatter ceased when the front door opened and a fine gentleman entered. Mecca, whose back was turned, spun on her heels to see why everyone had grown silent. It was an event. Mario's fine ass had come through the door. Women were making subtle comments among themselves as they watched him intently.

Mario broke the ice, speaking to everyone. He spoke to Benji while heading directly toward Mecca. Mecca began to feel butterflies in her stomach. Mario was just that fine. He had an aura about himself that demanded a woman's attention. Mecca couldn't remember the last time she had been nervous in front of a man, other than the first time she laid eyes on Mario. "Looking for me?" she managed to ask in an attempt to disguise her nervousness.

"Actually, I was. Is there somewhere we can go and talk?" asked Mario.

"How about Red Lobster?"

"Red Lobster?" Mario repeated in confusion.

"Yeah, your treat."

"All right, what the hell? Are you ready now?" asked Mario.

"Yep, let's go," said Mecca, heading for the door.

"Details, bitch!" shouted Benji as the door began to close behind Mecca and Mario.

"So, what is it that you wanted to talk to me about?" asked Mecca. She and Mario had just placed their orders and were both feeling a bit uneasy. Neither of them said much the entire drive.

"It's about your mother. I'm beginning to worry about her whereabouts. I haven't heard from her since, well, since E-Way passed. Have you seen your mother?"

"Nah, I haven't. I don't know what's the deal with Yvette. I've got my own shit I'm dealing with right now."

"Yeah, you and me both," Mario said, sounding down on his luck.

"Are you okay?" Mecca asked sincerely. She could see the dismay in Mario's eyes.

"I'm good, I guess. It's just . . . forget about it."

"You can talk to me. Tell me what's going on with you. You seem so gloomy. That's not like you."

Mario took a few moments to answer Mecca. He looked away to avoid eye contact and then took a deep breath. Out of nowhere he said, "I think my wife's having an affair."

Mecca was at a loss for words. Her mouth dropped in awe. "Mario, are you sure? How do you know that?" Mecca didn't know Mario's wife. She had never laid eyes on her before.

"I just know. The love ain't the same no more. At times I feel like I'm living a lie, only sticking it out for the sake of my daughter."

Mecca remembered seeing Mario with his daughter at Burger King a while back. His face and mood lit up as he talked about his little girl.

"If it weren't for my daughter, I often wonder where my wife and I would stand."

Mecca really didn't want to say anything because she didn't know Mario's wife and didn't want to be throwing salt on his marriage. Still in all, she wanted to be of some help. "Have you approached your wife with your feelings?"

"Nah, not yet. Like I said, I'm certain she's stepping out on me, but I don't have any proof as of yet. And I don't want to scare her off her true intentions by jumping the gun and accusing her of cheating."

"So, what are you going to do?"

"I really don't know. But I know I can't go on living like this."

The waiter returned with their food and drinks. Mecca couldn't help but feel sorry for Mario. He came off as one of the few good men left in the world, and here some bitch was dogging him out.

After lunch Mario dropped Mecca back off at the salon. He tried to appear normal, but Mecca could see the hurt in his eyes. She wondered just how long he'd been suspecting his wife of cheating on him. Being in the music business and constantly on the road, Mario didn't see it at first. He often blamed himself for not being there enough.

"Here we are," Mario said, pulling in front of the salon. "I want to thank you for being an ear."

"Anytime. If you ever need to talk to someone, don't hesitate to call me or stop by the shop," Mecca offered.

"Thank you," Mario said. "I just might take you up on that offer."

"No, thank you for lunch. Well, let me get on in here. Today's booth rent, and these hoes be trying to duck paying."

"A'ight," Mario said, laughing. He watched Mecca walk to the door before pulling away from the curb.

"Details, bitch!" Benji said as soon as Mecca walked through the door. "Excuse me. I'll be right back," Benji said to the woman whose hair he was doing. He hustled behind Mecca into the back office, slamming the door behind him.

"The sign out front should say 'Ghetto,'" said the woman whom Benji excused himself from. "Moth'fackas just walk off in the middle of doing ya hair," the woman continued to complain. Other folks in the shop were snickering at the woman's remarks. She was an older woman who wasn't used to this day and age.

"Preach," Tory added.

"What happened with Mr. Mario?" teased Benji, waiting for Mecca to dish.

"Ain't nothing happen. What was supposed to happen?" Mecca asked in confusion.

"Bitch, please. I see the way you look at that nigga like you wanna just rip his clothes off and take the dick."

"Are you high? 'Cause you trippin'."

"Whatever, ya ass can't fool me. Neither can his ass. Just watch and I'll tell you. Y'all gon' be fucking before it's all said and done."

"He's going through some changes with wifey. He suspects that his wife is having an affair."

"This is the perfect time."

"Perfect time for what?" asked Mecca.

"To get some of that pipe. His ass is vulnerable right now."

"You is outta control," laughed Mecca, taking her seat at the computer.

"Let me get back out here and finish this ho's head. We still on for tonight, right?"

"Oh, hell yes! I ain't seen Drew's sexy ass in a minute. So you know I'm in the spot."

"A'ight, holla if you need me."

Benji reentered the front of the shop. The woman's face was all balled up as Benji approached her chair. "I apologize for taking so long," Benji offered.

"Just hurry up and finish my shit," said the woman in a heated tone.

Benji walked behind the old hag and looked at the back of her head with an expression on his face that said, "Bitch, who is you talking to?" Benji caught himself, took a deep breath, and exhaled. Out of respect for the business he didn't flash. That and the fact the woman was old enough to be his grandmother.

Tory's silly ass as usual wasn't letting it go that easy. "You heard what she said. Finish her shit."

Benji took his curlers and pretended to throw them at Tory. Just another day at the shop.

It was almost closing, and all the women and Benji were anticipating ladies' night out at Henry's. They all rushed to finish their customers, even putting the CLOSED sign up to prevent any further traffic. Tory, who had already finished up for the evening, sat across from Mecca, separating all her singles from larger bills.

"Shit, I'ma need at least two hun'd singles for the night. All that dick that's gon' be up in there," Tory said. "You got some singles?" she asked, talking to Mecca.

"Nah, but we can get some on the way."

"These slow-ass bitches. Y'all needs to hurry y'all asses up. I want to get a good seat." Tory looked at her watch.

"Shit, why don't you and Mecca head out and get us a booth right in front of the stage?" suggested Benji.

"You ain't said nothing but the truth. Come on, Mecca," Tory said, gathering up her money.

"See y'all there," said Marie as Mecca and Tory headed out the front door.

Chapter 26

It was close to nine o'clock. The club had begun to fill with its regulars, and parking space was scarce. Mecca scanned the lot for a spot. She found one and quickly parked. Before Mecca could cut the engine, Tory was out the door, hustling toward the entrance.

"Come on so we can get a good seat," she said, looking back toward Mecca. They made it inside and paid the door fee. They noticed that all the center-stage seats were taken with the exception of one. Tory raced toward the table in effort to claim it, but a group of four women beat her to the table. Tory and Mecca came to a disappointing stop. The women had beaten them by a mere second. They pulled their chairs out and parked their asses firmly. One of the women looked back at Mecca and Tory who were standing over the woman's shoulder.

"May I help you?" asked the woman in a funky tone, which really meant, "Bitch, why is you standing all over me?"

Mecca snarled down at the woman, then replied, "Yeah, y'all sitting in our seats."

"And what's your name?" the woman asked.

"Mecca. Why, what difference does it make?"

"Because I don't see 'Mecca' written on this chair nowhere." The woman looked at the back of the chair. "Nevaeh, look at the back of your chair and tell me if you see 'Mecca' on it."

The woman looked at her chair, then back at her friend. "Nope."

"Look, we come here every Thursday, and this is our table. You can ask anybody up in here," said Tory. "We don't want no trouble."

"And I'm sure you don't, so why don't y'all do yourselves a favor and find somewhere else to sit for tonight?" the woman said.

"Bitch, what?" Tory said, getting super ghetto. She slid out of her heels and squared off with the woman who had been doing all the talking.

Before the woman or her friends could react, two muscle-neck bouncers were on the scene. One of the bouncers stepped between Tory and the woman. The other bouncer, playing diplomatic, asked, "Is there a problem, ladies?"

"Yeah, these bitches are in our seats," said Tory.

"I ain't gon' be too many more bitches."

"Shit, if you see a bitch, slap a bitch," one woman said.

The four women stood up, taking off earrings and other jewelry. The music stopped, and the entire club's attention focused on the bunch. Just when things couldn't get any worse, who shows up? Benji's gay blade ass along with Marie and Tae. Noticing a situation on hand, Benji pushed himself into the midst of things. "What's going on, Mecca?" he asked.

"Yeah, what's going on, Mecca?" asked a familiar sexy, deep voice, which sent a chill down Mecca's spine.

She turned around, ignoring Benji all together. She was all smiles. It was Drew. He was lookin' good as ever. Mecca's pussy moistened instantly.

Drew returned Mecca's smile while looking deep into her eyes. "Mark, I got this," Drew said, grabbing Mecca by the hand and escorting her to a booth toward the back.

Benji, Tory, Tae, and Marie reluctantly followed. Well, all with the exception of Tory. She wasn't looking to get into it with nobody. Her ass was scared straight. Tae's old ass was down to scrap though.

"I was beginning to think you quit me," Drew said. He and Mecca stood while Benji and the rest of the gang took a seat.

"You know I could never quit all this," Mecca said, almost whispering while rubbing Drew's six-pack with her index finger.

"You lookin' good as usual. Tell me something, can I see you tonight after the club?"

"Why? Are you going to perform for me?"

"Don't I always?"

Mecca laughed. "Why, yes, you do, baby."

"So is it a date?"

"We'll see," Mecca said, teasing. More like lying. She knew damn well she was coming up off that pussy. Her panties were already soaking wet. Just Drew's presence had that effect on her.

"Work that mothafucka! Work that mothafucka!" The club's anthem had begun playing, and the women were going crazy. Several horse-dick niggas took to the stage and were doing exactly what the song said. They were working that mothafucka.

"That's my cue. I'll see you after I come off the stage," Drew said. He kissed Mecca on the forehead and then headed for the stage. Mecca joined the gang at the booth. She was all smiles from ear to ear.

"Damn, bitch, you cheezin' hard as hell. Details. What, you got some dick lined up after the club?" asked Benji.

Tae and Marie had rushed toward the stage with their fists full of singles. Tory was seated right next to Benji, gettin' her swerve on with one of the dancers. He was grinding his piece all in Tory's face. "Can I touch it?" she asked.

"Look at this bitch," laughed Mecca, pointing at Tory's freaky ass.

"Back to you. Dish, bitch, details. Are you leaving here tonight with thunder dick?"

"And you know it. Shit, I need my pussy ate."

"I know what cha' mean. Me too," said Benji.

Mecca and Benji both had to laugh at that one.

"Yo' ass is too crazy," laughed Mecca.

"I'm serious. Soon as I get home I'ma sit right on Devin's face."

The club continued to crank. Everyone was buzzin' nicely, perhaps too nice. The liquor had for sure taken its effect on Mecca. She was hella horny. As she watched Drew perform his set, she imagined everything he would do to her later. She got so worked up that she couldn't wait until after the club. She had to have Drew now!

Drew's set ended, and he made his way over to Mecca's booth. Several women grabbed at his hand as he walked by. They wanted him to perform a lap dance, but he declined and kept on toward Mecca.

"I see your fan club is in the building," said Mecca.

"Yeah, so I guess that makes you the president," Drew said jokingly.

Mecca couldn't argue with that. He was looking entirely too good to argue with. The lights from the club beamed across his sweaty chest, making him glisten all over.

"Damn, Pretty Ricky," said Tory's silly ass. "I like the way the sweat is dripping all over yo' body," she said, teasing. She was pissy drunk. Drew and Mecca couldn't help but laugh.

"Come on," Mecca said, excusing herself. She led Drew by the hand toward the rear of the club. "Hold on," she said, stopping in front of the ladies' room. She stepped inside and inspected each stall. Seeing that all the stalls were empty, she opened the door and snatched Drew inside. Before the door could close she was on Drew's ass like a bitch in heat. She stepped back while kissing Drew all over, and while jacking his dick.

They ended up in the last stall. Mecca pushed Drew back onto the seat. He jacked his dick while watching Mecca half undress. He grabbed her by the waist and lifted her up on top of his dick. Mecca fit Drew like a glove. She wrapped her arms around Drew's neck and bounced up and down. Drew palmed both of Mecca's ass cheeks, spreading them wide so he could dig as deep as possible.

"Fuck me! Fuck me," Mecca squealed as she reached her first climax. Her head was leaned back with her eyes rolled to the back of her head.

Drew wasn't missing a beat. Every stroke was consistent, hitting the bottom of Mecca's ass every time.

"Oh, my God," she continued. She was cumming so intent, it felt like she was pissin'. Both Drew and Mecca were so caught up in the moment, neither one of them heard the bathroom door open. A woman and one of the dancers ended up in the stall beside Mecca and Drew.

"Get this pussy," Mecca encouraged, trying to help Drew reach his peak.

"Ah, shit. Fuck!" Drew yelled, still slamming Mecca down onto his dick. He slammed Mecca down onto him one final time and then held her tightly by the waist as he shot an ounce of semen into her. Mecca leaned forward and grabbed Drew's face. She kissed him passionately, sucking on his tongue as if she were going to swallow it.

"Fuck me, oh, baby."

Mecca stopped kissing Drew. "You hear that?" she asked Drew.

"Hear what?" Drew asked. He hadn't heard a thing. He was too focused on Mecca.

"Shh, listen."

"Ah. Oh."

"Somebody's in the stall next to us," Mecca said. She climbed off of Drew and started fixing her clothes.

"So what? They doing them just like we doing us. Come here," said Drew.

"We've got all night. How do I look?" asked Mecca, still straightening her clothes.

"Good enough to eat."

"We'll see," said Mecca, blushing. "Come on, let's get outta here."

"I once got busy in a Burger King bathroom," Tory's simple ass said loudly as Mecca approached the table.

"I don't know what you're talking about."

"You know what they say—guilty tongues always speak. Now dish, bitch," said Tory.

"Yes, do please. Details," demanded Benji.

"Was he hittin' it like this?" Tory joked. She pretended as if she were Drew fucking Mecca from the back.

Everybody fell out laughing.

"I'm not tellin' y'all ass nothin'," said Mecca.

"You got your glow back, baby," Benji said, smiling. "Shit, soon as I leave I'm going to get my shit off too."

"Amen, praise the Lord," said Tory.

The grand finale had gotten underway. It was a half hour to closing, which meant last call for alcohol and all dancers to the stage. The DJ spun the club's anthem one last time.

"Work that mothafucka," all the women demanded.

The woman whom Tory had words with at their table emerged from the ladies' room with one of the club's dancers, Darius. Ole girl had that glow, the same glow Mecca was wearing. Mecca witnessed the entire scandal.

She thought that she must have been who was in the stall next to her. She wasn't hating or being at all judgmental because she, too, had just gotten her shit off.

"Skank bitch," Tory said while the woman walked past and to her seat.

The woman hadn't heard Tory because of the loud music and women screaming.

"Work that mothafucka," the women continued chanting until closing.

Chapter 27

Mecca tailed Drew back to his condo after leaving Henry's. Her pussy was throbbing and soaking wet from anticipation, and she and Drew started going at it as soon as they hit the front door. They kissed each other's body intently, while shedding articles of clothing until they both stood naked. Drew swooped Mecca up into his arms and carried her into the bedroom.

Drew was a freak down to the core, a Rick James superfreak. The nigga had swings and gadgets hanging from the ceiling, body position pillows, and every toy ever made. He took Mecca and placed her inside one of the swings, then got down on his knees, positioning himself between Mecca's legs. Mecca grabbed Drew's head and gripped it violently. She squirmed in satisfaction as Drew mouthed her entire pussy.

Mecca leaned backward and seductively wrapped her legs around the chains of the swing so Drew could have full access. Drew vigorously ate at Mecca's pussy, making his mouth vibrate by humming in between sucks. "I can't, oh, shit, I can't take it," Mecca moaned.

"Umm," Drew continued.

"I can't take it," Mecca said, pulling Drew up. Mecca was damn near in tears. She was hot and bothered. Her pussy was beating like a heart, literally.

Drew wasn't about to stop. He got his rocks off by watching women get off. He jacked his dick until it was fully erect while looking down at Mecca, who was still cumming. Cum was running down her thighs like milk. Drew inserted the head of his dick, making Mecca jerk. She dug her nails into his strong back and slowly pulled him inside. Drew found his rhythm taking long deep strokes. He looked downward. Watching his dick slide in and out of Mecca's pussy turned him on. He pumped faster and harder, making the swing rock back and forth.

Feeling himself about to cum, Drew pulled himself out and inserted his long, thick yellow dick in Mecca's asshole using the pussy juice as lubrication. Drew grabbed hold of the chains of the swing and began pushing them, pulling Mecca into his stiff dick. Mecca was in so much pain and cumming so hard, she couldn't even scream. She had never before in life been fucked like that. Drew began mumbling something as he reached his peak. "Oh, my God, this is the best pussy I've ever had," he said, as he stood over Mecca jacking his dick, landing large clots of semen on Mecca's chest and stomach. Drew grabbed the back of Mecca's head, and she stuck his half limp dick in her mouth. Mecca sat up in the swing and sucked Drew back to life. They fucked for hours until the sun started rising and the birds could be heard chirping.

They lay in bed, both exhausted. Mecca was lying across Drew's chest, playing with his nipples. Drew had enjoyed the night and what took place, but he started wondering why Mecca hadn't left last night like she usually did.

"Say, um, Mecca, you know it's morning?" Drew said.

"I know what time it is. What, you putting me out?" Mecca replied jokingly as she yawned.

"Nah, I'm just making sure you're on point. I don't want you falling out with ole boy because you fell asleep."

"We don't have to worry about that anymore," Mecca said, smiling, and then she gave Drew a kiss.

Drew didn't kiss Mecca back. *What the fuck does she mean we won't have to worry about that?* Drew asked himself. The last thing he was looking for was a relationship. He was content doing him. "A'ight, now, I don't wanna see you mess up a good thing," Drew said. He didn't know that E-Way had passed away.

"And who's to say it's a good thing?" asked Mecca, sitting up to face Drew.

"Is it?"

"You know what? This is corny. I'm not about to get particular with mines," Mecca said, obviously growing agitated by the conversation.

"I'm just saying."

"You don't have to say anything. What's already understood need not be said. Drew, you ain't gotta be acting all concerned. I know you're not looking for a commitment, and that's cool because neither am I." Mecca rolled off the bed and grabbed a shirt off the dresser, then headed for the bathroom. After washing up, she gathered her clothes from the living room and quickly dressed.

"You ain't gotta leave," Drew said as he stood in the living room watching Mecca dress.

"I have to be going anyway," Mecca said dryly. "But thanks for last night," she said, trying to get Drew to realize that he was to her what she was to him: a piece of ass and that's it.

"I hope you're not in your feelings about anything, Mecca."

"Baby, I don't deal with feelings," Mecca said, then kissed Drew before leaving.

Chapter 28

After leaving Drew's, Mecca drove home so she could shower, change clothes, then head off to the shop. Before leaving the house, she checked her voicemail, and it was full. All the messages were from Mario. He hadn't said what it was he wanted but stressed that it was urgent. Mecca started thinking the worst, that maybe it was concerning Yvette. Mecca picked up the kitchen phone and dialed Mario's cell.

"Hello!" answered Mario on the first ring as if he'd been waiting by the phone all night. His voice sounded frustrated.

"Mario, it's Mecca. Is everything okay?"

"Do you think we can meet for lunch?"

"Uh, sure, what time?" asked Mecca.

"Say eleven at Floods?"

"Okay. But what's going on? You're making me nervous. It's not about Yvette, is it?"

"No. Have you heard from her yet?"

"Nah, I was hoping maybe you had," Mecca said, sounding a little down. "Well, I'll see you at eleven."

Just as Mecca was about to leave, the phone rang. She paused, not really wanting to go back and answer it, but something told her to go and answer it. "Hello."

"Mecca, how are you? It's Momma," E-Way's grandmother said.

"Oh, I'm fine. How about you? How are you holding up?"

"I'm toughing it out. Listen, when you get a chance, swing by the house. We really need to talk."

"I'll try to make it over there a little later, Momma. You need anything?"

"No, thank you, but thanks anyway. See you afterwhile."

"All right," Mecca said, ending the conversation.

"Details, bitch," Benji said as Mecca walked into the shop. "Excuse me, I'll be right back," Benji said, excusing himself from his customer. "Dick," Benji said, closing the door behind them. Mecca was getting settled at her desk, turning the computer on and whatnot. "Come on, I need details. I ain't got all day," Benji said jokingly.

"I'm not feeling Drew's ass like that no more. Let me stop lying. I can't stop feeling him," Mecca said, smiling. "But he pulled some bitch shit this morning."

"Like what? I'm not gon' have to fuck him straight up, am I? 'Cause you know I'll beat the yellow off of his ass."

"Boy, calm down. You always ready to fight. Nah, he just called himself making it clear that he wasn't looking for no baggage. Neither am I. It's just how he did the shit that got me upset. I spent the night over at his house, and this morning he started asking me what my guy was going to say. Tryin' to sound all concerned, but really he was just picking for information."

"Um, so what are you gon' do?"

"I'm gon' continue to get my pussy ate and whatnot. He fucked the dog shit out of me last night."

"Amen, praise the Lord. Yeah, Devin fucked me something vicious last night. And like I told you, I got my pussy ate too," laughed Benji.

"Yo' ass is too nasty," laughed Mecca. "Can you touch me up after you finish with ole girl? I gotta meet Mario at Floods at eleven."

"You've been spending an awful lot of time with that booshy nigga lately. It's just a matter of time."

"Matter of time for what?"

"Until you'll be like, 'Oh, Mario, oh, oh, fuck me,'" Benji said jokingly.

"Boy, forget you. You gon' do my hair?"

"Yeah, I got you."

Mecca had Tory do her nails while she waited on Benji to finish with his client. Gossip filled the air of the shop, hoes talking about other hoes, who was the best.

"Hold on," said Mecca, jumping up from Tory's nail station. She ran toward the plasma mounted in the waiting area and turned the volume up. Everyone ceased conversation, not wanting to miss the low-down. There was a breaking story on Channel 7 News. Mecca recognized Big Whitney's mug shot, which was what caused her to rush to the television. The news anchor showed pictures of E-Way's Bentley and the scene where his body was found. The anchor said that fingerprints from Big Whit, real name Whitney Rolland, were found on the steering wheel and driver's side of the Bentley. When questioned by detectives, Big Whit broke down and started crying, admitting his guilt and involvement. The anchor then went on to say that the police were now looking for Kev, Chuck, and Chuckie Bom's. Their mug shots were flashed as well.

Mecca's stomach dropped and she became furious. Her intuition all the while had told her that those grimy niggas had something to do with E-Way's death. Tears began to well up and stream down Mecca's cheeks. Folks in the shop didn't know what was going on, with the exception of those who knew E-Way and Mecca to be a couple. Benji walked up behind Mecca and put his hands on her shoulders so as to console her, then escorted Mecca into the back.

"Why would they do something like that?" Mecca cried out, falling into Benji's arms and crying her heart out on his silk shirt.

"Envy, baby. Envy! Jealous bastards," Benji said heatedly. "It's going to be all right, Mecca."

"They didn't have to do him like that," Mecca cried as she pictured E-Way lying in the trunk of his car with white mice.

Mecca was imagining how E-Way felt at the time of his death. Questions started racing through her mind, like, did E-Way see it coming? Did he beg for his life? Who actually pulled the trigger? The more Mecca thought about it, the harder she cried. It was just total betrayal on those niggas' parts. She thought about the time their house had been broken into. *Them bitch-ass niggas did it,* she told herself. She vowed that if the law didn't get they ass, she would.

Chapter 29

After gaining her composure, Mecca drove over to Momma's house. She wanted to see what Momma had wanted and wanted to break the news about the latest discovery regarding E-Way's murder if Momma didn't already know. Like any other given day, Momma's house was filled with visitors and relatives. Mecca parked on the street across from the house and then walked through the huge front yard up to the porch. She was eyed by the many old men sitting on the front porch drinking beer and watching the traffic.

"And who might you be?" one of the older gentlemen asked as if he still had his mojo.

"Leave this girl alone, you old freak," Momma snapped. "This is Mecca, Matt's girlfriend."

"Hello, Momma, how are you?" asked Mecca.

"I'm okay, baby. Come on in outta this heat," Momma said while holding the screen open for Mecca.

"Shit, Matt can't do nothing with all that now," the old gentleman said after the screen closed.

"That's right, that's right," laughed the other men.

"You hungry, baby?" asked Momma, leading Mecca into the kitchen where a spread of food lay across the table and countertops.

"I really don't have much of an appetite. Did you see the news?"

"Yeah, them hoodlums killed my boy. They gon' get what's coming to them soon enough."

"Is that what you wanted to see me about?"

"Not quite. Are you sure you don't want anything to eat? I made your favorites, fried catfish and greens. G'on and fix yourself a plate, and I'll be right back," Momma said and then disappeared into her bedroom.

The food smelled good, and Mecca's stomach was touching her back from hunger pains. She fixed a healthy plate and poured herself a glass of Momma's famous iced tea. Momma returned to the kitchen to find Mecca pigging out. She smiled to herself as she often did from knowing that folks were enjoying her cooking.

"I have some papers I need for you to sign," Momma said, opening a manila envelope and then spreading its contents across the table.

"What are they?" Mecca asked in between bites.

"Oh, just Matt's estate papers. I need for you to sign right here so Matt's attorney will release his will to us."

Mecca stopped eating and picked up one of the documents that Momma wanted her to sign. It was drawn up in big, ambiguous words designed to confuse its reader so they would just hopefully sign it verses getting a migraine headache trying to decipher its meaning. Mecca, however, wasn't your average bear. She peeped what the document was saying. Momma was asking Mecca to release E-Way's will to her in its entirety.

"I can't sign this," Mecca said, then pushed the document across the table back to Momma.

Momma was looking screw-faced. "They won't release Matt's will to us without these papers."

"I didn't know Matt even had a will. What's all in it?"

"I'm not certain as of yet. I have to get with his attorney. But before we do that, we have to get these documents signed. All this is saying is that we acknowledge we're the beneficiaries."

"Momma, with all due respect, that's not what that form is asking. It's saying that I'm releasing whatever's in Matt's will for me to you. Why would I do that?"

"Because I'm his grandmother."

"So what are you saying?"

"You and Matt were not married. I know he loved you, and I'm certain he would want to see you with something, but that something has to be determined."

"Determined by whom?"

"By me. I will see to it that you get your just dues," Momma said, then pushed the documents back across the table and placed a pen on top. "Mecca, if you will, please sign these."

"I'm afraid I can't do that. Maybe Matt has already determined what he wants me and everyone else to have. Where can I get a copy of his will at?"

"That won't be necessary if you sign the papers."

"I think I should be leaving now," Mecca said, standing.

"Mecca, I didn't mean to upset you. I'm just trying to save us the hassle of going through the courts and the whole nine."

"Patience is a virtue," Mecca said. "Thank you for the meal." She then headed for the front door. She pushed the front door open violently, slamming the screen against the front of the house.

"I like 'em rough," the old gentleman said as Mecca stormed out.

She stomped down the porch steps with as many "umps" as she could, pretending each step was Momma's face. *The nerve of that old bitch,* Mecca thought as she got in her BMW, slamming the door. If it weren't for E-Way being dead and Momma being his grandmother, Mecca would have flashed up in that house. It took all she had and then some to hold back.

"Who did that bitch think she was talking to?" Mecca asked no one in particular as she sped down Mt. Elliott Street, driving nowhere special. Mecca never really liked Momma's mush-mouth ass anyway. The only reason she tolerated her shit was because of E-Way. The bitch was just too nosy, always had to put her unwanted two cents in everybody else's mix. It seemed like the nosy mothafuckas always outlived everybody else. *Like they're afraid if they die, they nosy ass is gon' miss something*.

She was steaming. She was so mad that she hadn't even noticed the yellow caution traffic light. She just blew right through the intersection of 7 Mile and Mt. Elliott.

"Crazy bitch!" yelled a passing driver. It was a woman driving an SUV with her son seated in the back in his car seat.

"Bitch, fuck you!" Mecca yelled back at the woman, flipping her off.

A traffic cop who was tucked away in the cut witnessed the scene and pulled out into traffic behind Mecca, then flicked his lights on, signaling her to pull over.

"Ain't this about a bitch," Mecca said, pulling over to the curb. She sat for what seemed an eternity waiting for the cop to get out of his squad car and do whatever it was he planned on doing. Growing impatient, Mecca slammed down on her horn. "Come on," she yelled, looking into the rearview mirror at the cop. The cop didn't budge for another five minutes or so, taking his sweet time. In the midst of Mecca's waiting, her cell rang. It was Mario. Mecca looked at the clock on the dashboard and remembered for the first time that she was supposed to meet Mario for lunch. It was five minutes to twelve, and she was late.

"Hello."

"Mecca, is everything all right?"

"Not quite. I'm sitting here on 7 Mile and Mt. Elliott, pulled over by Detroit's finest."

"Are you going to be able to make it to lunch?"

"Hold on, Mario, this dick sucker is knocking on my window. Could you please not bang on my window with that heavy-ass flashlight?"

"License and registration," the cop ordered, disregarding Mecca's request.

Mecca reached over and got her credentials out of her purse, then cracked the window enough to pass the paperwork out, then rolled it back up in disdain so as to dismiss the cop. The fat, short, bald cop waddled back to his cruiser unfazed.

"Mario, yeah, I'll be able to make it. I really need to speak with you about something anyway."

"A'ight, well, I'm here already. I'll be waiting."

"Okay, bye-bye."

The cop took another ten minutes writing Mecca several citations and probably having a doughnut break, Mecca thought. His fat, musty ass finally emerged from the squad car. He was carrying several tickets in one hand and Mecca's license and registration in the other hand. Mecca cracked the window and snatched the papers stanky.

"You have a ticket for speeding."

"I'll see you in court," Mecca said, cutting the cop off, then shifting her car into drive before peeling off and leaving the cop standing there looking stupid.

He had his nerve. "Mothafucka gon' write me a ticket, then wanna talk about it afterwards, shit," Mecca said while punching it down 7 Mile.

Mario was seated in a booth near the entrance. His table was next to a bay window decorated nicely with flowers and plants. He was enjoying a beer and the soft jazz that filled the bar and grill when he saw Mecca's Beemer pull up and park. Mecca hopped out, looking like a cool million. Even with the current events the girl still had her swagger. She walked through the front door as if she owned the place. Mario waved her over to their table, then pulled her seat out for her.

"Thank you much. So sorry I'm late."

"Oh, no, it's all right. I was just enjoying the jazz and a few beers. Can I get you something to drink before we order?"

"Apple martini, please. As a matter of fact, make that two," Mecca said, getting herself situated.

Mario motioned the waitress over and ordered more drinks. The waitress filled their order and left two menus on the table. Mecca and Mario browsed through their menus while making small talk. "This pepper steak looks good," Mecca said. She was still hungry. She hadn't finished her plate at Momma's.

"That sure does. With some potatoes with some melted butter and sour cream. Yeah, that's what I'll have," said Mario.

"Make those two orders of the same."

The waitress returned with their drinks, and Mario placed their order.

"So what was it you wanted to see me about?" Mecca asked.

"You said that you had something you needed to share with me as well. Mine can wait. You first."

"I just left E-Way's grandmother's house. She tried to get me to sign a bunch of documents to relinquish all of E-Way's will to her."

"And why would you do something like that?"

"Amen. That's what I'm saying. I read over the papers. Now I'm no lawyer, but I know what they were hitting on. She thinks I'm just a young fool."

"Did you sign them? Please tell me you didn't sign them." Mario sat up in his chair.

"I didn't sign nothing, and I'm not signing nothing."

"Good, good. Listen, I got somebody. He's a good friend of mine, an estate attorney. He'll take good care of you. I'll give him a call sometime tomorrow. Is that it?" asked Mario.

"Yeah, that's it. Will he be able to tell me what's all in E-Way's will and whom he left what to?"

"Trust me, not to worry. My guy is official."

With that Mecca began to lighten up. There was something about Mario that the average man didn't possess. His level of confidence was so high one couldn't help but to believe in him.

"Okay, enough about me. Now what's going on with you?"

Mario's enthusiasm disappeared. He dropped his head and stared at the tablecloth.

"Mario, what's wrong? Talk to me," Mecca said, reaching across the table to hold Mario's hand.

Mario didn't speak. He reached down beside him and grabbed a white envelope, then set it on the table. Mario cleared his throat before speaking. “I hired a private investigator to follow my wife. Here she is out at some male strip club,” Mario said, opening the envelope and spreading several pictures of his wife across the table. The woman was hugged up with a cock-strong brotha, one of the dancers at the infamous Henry’s Palace. The woman pictured was the woman Mecca and Tory had gotten into it with the other night while arguing over their VIP table.

“Oh, my God,” Mecca said, putting her hand over her mouth.

“What? What’s wrong?” Mario asked.

Mecca hadn’t realized she had said that aloud. “I just can’t believe she’s cheating on you,” she said, trying to clean up her stuff.

“Yeah, well, I haven’t caught her in the actual act as of yet, but I’m working on it.”

“So what is it exactly you want me to do?” Mecca asked, at a loss.

“I guess there’s nothing you can do, except be an ear. Thank you, Mecca.”

“You’re more than welcome. I just feel so bad.”

“Yeah, well, it is what it is.”

The waitress interrupted the odd moment, laying their food out in front of them. They didn’t really have much of an appetite after looking at those pictures. They were only pictures. They didn’t show Mario’s wife out actually fucking nobody, but Mecca knew the real deal. She has witnessed her come out of the restroom with ole boy in the picture a few nights ago. Mecca couldn’t figure out why she was feeling so damn bad on the inside. Shit, she was at the same club doing the exact same thing. She tried justifying to herself though that she wasn’t a married woman. Usually, Mecca would applaud a bitch on being ahead of the game, but for some reason she felt sorry for Mario. Maybe because she knew deep down that Mario was a good, hardworking, faithful man. The kind of man every woman claims to want, but when she gets him, she dogs him out.

Oh, well, that's the way the cookie crumbles, Mecca tried telling herself. *Just what am I supposed to do, rat the bitch out?* It wasn't Mecca's style. Besides, she wouldn't want no nosy-ass bitch all up in her situation, kind of how Olivia's bitch ass was all in hers. *He'll learn and eventually get over it.*

Chapter 30

Mario was a man of his word. The following morning, he called Mecca to inform her that he'd spoken with his lawyer friend and that they were to meet with him at ten o'clock at his office. It was almost eight when Mario called. Mecca was finishing her morning workout when the phone rang. She happily agreed to the meeting and thanked Mario a dozen times before hanging up. Mario would swing by the house and pick her up, then carry her downtown to see the attorney. He wanted to stand in to make sure Mecca felt as comfortable as possible while dealing with such a touchy subject: money.

Mecca cut her workout short and raced to the shower. Money, money, money, money was all she could think about. "How much you leave me, baby?" she asked while looking up at the shower ceiling as if she were talking to E-Way face-to-face. "A million, two million?" Her pussy got wet just thinking about how much E-Way had left her. She turned the shower off, then reached for a towel. She dried quickly, then raced through the house naked. She stopped at her dresser and recovered a matching bra and panty set, then raced over to her walk-in closet. "What to wear, what to wear? So much to wear," she said in a rhythm. "Here we go," she said, snatching down a brand-new Al Wissam shorts set. She pampered herself with Gucci perfume and strawberry Bath & Body Works lotion. Then she dressed to perfection, matching her jewels to her attire. She was about to go see about some money. *Might as well look like money,* Mecca told herself, modeling in front of her floor mirror inside her closet.

Mario arrived about nine thirty. He rang the doorbell twice and stood on the front porch examining the quiet street. It wasn't much different from his except his house cost several million dollars. Mecca looked in the mirror one last time to inspect every detail and then blew herself a kiss. She walked down the stairs into the front vestibule. Before opening the door, she peeped out, then stood back and fluffed her hair a bit. Mario was at a loss for words as he looked Mecca over. She got the hint like always that she was killing shit. Her legs were pretty as ever. They were gleaming and fresh looking. She wore a pair of Maury gator sandals, exposing her picture-perfect feet.

"You like?" Mecca said, cheesing while twisting from side to side.

"You look absolutely beautiful," Mario said, looking into Mecca's deep, sensual eyes.

"Thank you. Are you ready?"

"Ready whenever you are."

"Okay, just let me grab my purse and I'll be right out."

Mecca locked up the house and jumped in Mario's Audi A8. "This is nice. I never knew Audi made such nice cars. How much does this run for? No, never mind, that was inappropriate," Mecca said, catching herself.

"It's okay. It starts at a hundred and twenty thousand, this model anyway. I just got tired of the Benzes and Beemers everyone seems to have nowadays. My wife drives a Benz still," Mario said. His voice sounded faint at the mention of his wife. *Poor thing,* Mecca thought.

It was a rather short drive. Mario's Audi breezed through the morning traffic like a spaceship. That's what the interior and drive put Mecca in the mind of: a spaceship. They parked on Hubbard Street. Mario fed the parking meter and ushered Mecca into Wilkins, Haskins, & James: Attorneys at Law. Mecca recognized the name from commercials on television and ads in the newspaper. Mario approached the receptionist and told her that they had a ten o'clock meeting with Mr. Haskins. The woman picked up her desk phone and said a few words, then hung up.

"Mr. Haskins will see you now. Right through the door," the woman said, pointing.

"Thank you," Mario said, leading Mecca into Mr. Haskins's office.

"Mario, good to see you," Mr. Haskins said, embracing Mario with a huge hug and a firm handshake.

"How's it going, Dre? Excuse my rudeness, Dre. This is Mecca, and, Mecca, this is Dre. Dre and I went to school together."

"Nice to meet you," Mecca said.

"Mario, you didn't tell me she was this beautiful. Please, have a seat," Dre said, ushering Mecca to a leather seat facing his desk. "Can I get you all anything?"

"No, thank you," said Mecca.

"How about you, Rio? You can help yourself to a drink."

"I think I just might do that," Mario said, walking over toward the bar.

"Okay, so, Mecca, Mario tells me that you're having trouble with your spouse's estate. Please tell me what's wrong."

"Well, I didn't even know Matt had an estate or will until the other day. His grandmother tried getting me to sign some documents saying that I wished to release all assets to her."

"And tell me you didn't sign them."

"Of course not."

"Good. Well, what I can do is find out who's holding Matt's estate, such as his lawyer, or who has power of attorney. I then would need your permission of course to have Matt's will disclosed to me."

"You mean tell you what's in it for me?"

"Exactly."

"And how soon can you find this out?"

"In a day or so. I'm going to have you sign a freedom of information release form, and I'll be able to get what we need."

"You're in good hands. Dre's the best. I'm going to have him handle my divorce just as soon as I get the rest of the dirt I need," Mario said.

Mario was a different kind of brotha, cut from an entirely different cloth than the men Mecca was used to dealing with. He was smart, legally rich, and tied in with important people who made shit happen. Mecca felt at ease around him because he knew what he was doing.

"Well, if that's all, I should be calling you in a couple of days. I have to get ready for trial."

"Okay, thank you, Mr. Haskins," Mecca said, standing and extending her hand.

"Oh, nah, please call me Dre. And thank you. See my receptionist before you leave so you can sign those forms."

Mecca and Mario stopped at the receptionist's desk as instructed by Dre. The documents were already waiting on her desk with a neat fountain pen laid across them. Everything just seemed to be going right. Mecca examined the forms quickly, then signed them and handed them back to the receptionist before leaving. She was on top of the world, and couldn't nobody tell her nothing right then. She knew that if E-Way had left a will, she was all up in it, and she was about to be paid for the rest of her life.

She thanked Mario a hundred times during their drive back to her house. She said that after she got the news from Dre, she'd treat him to lunch. Mario happily agreed.

He was just happy seeing someone else happy despite his marital problems.

Mecca had Mario drop her off at home, and she was so geeked up that she didn't bother going inside. She jumped right in her Beemer and was out. Within five minutes she was pulling up at the shop. She had to share the news with Benji like she couldn't just call him from home and tell him. She had to be up close and personal so they could jump up and down with greed in their eyes.

"Afternoon, people," Mecca said with an extra aura of confidence as she strutted into the shop heading for her office.

Benji saw that glow and knew instantly something was up. "Excuse me," he said to his client, then followed Mecca into the back. "I want full details. Dish. What's going on?"

"Where did I tell you I was going this morning?"

Benji tried remembering. "I don't know, Drew's?"

"Nah, but I'm on my way over to his house as soon as I leave here. Anyway, I went to see that attorney I was telling you about regarding E-Way's estate."

"Oh, my God," Benji said as gay as possible, covering his mouth. "Let me take a seat. Okay, how much?" He awaited Mecca's answer.

"I don't know yet, but Dre Haskins said that I'm 'bouts to get my issue. He had me sign some forms so he could find out exactly what my issue is. Bitch, we 'bouts to be paid!" Mecca said, jumping up and down with Benji joining her.

The women out front could hear the loud chatter and snickering. Marie, not wanting to miss the details, excused herself from her client so she could see what was going on. Mecca and Benji froze as she walked in.

"Un-huh, don't stop talking because I stepped in the room. Details, y'all know the drill. What's going on?"

“Mecca was just telling me about another one of her episodes with Drew,” Benji answered as casually as he could.

“You ain’t tired of Drew ass by now? Girl, you gots to upgrade.”

“Trust me, I’m about to,” Mecca said with a grin.

After leaving the shop, Mecca called Drew while driving in the direction of his condo. It was still considered to be morning in Drew’s world, dancing all night until the sun came up. He was still in bed with his cell phone off and his house phone off the hook. That didn’t stop Mecca. She tried a few times, then kept on her way.

She knocked and knocked on Drew’s front door, then rang the doorbell, lying on it, but to no avail. Drew was knocked out stone-cold in his room with the radio playing. Mecca walked around back to Drew’s bedroom window, which was cracked. She peeped in and saw Drew spread-eagle across the bed. She decided to surprise him by playing Catwoman and climbing through the window. She made it in without awakening Drew. She stripped down naked, then climbed in bed with him. She gently pulled Drew’s large limp dick through the hole of his boxers and started giving him head.

Drew came alive, both he and his penis. He awoke, baffled, not knowing how Mecca got there. He had to ask himself, did he go to bed with her last night? Anyhow, the head was far too magnificent to be worrying about such frivolous matters. Mecca continued to suck Drew off until he was about to cum, and she could feel his leg twitching, so she stopped. She wanted to get hers off before he exploded, so she climbed on top of Drew and went for hers. She gripped his chest with both hands while working her hips and throwing her soft yellow ass every which way.

She and Drew came right after each other. Mecca continued riding Drew until he went limp. She lay across his chest tonguing him with his dick inside her. “You miss me?” Mecca asked in a whisper while kissing around Drew’s ear and neck.

“You know I miss you. I don’t know why you be tripping going into your little spells and whatnot.”

“It won’t happen again. Forgive me?”

“I wasn’t never mad at you. I was just making sure you were on top of your shit, that’s all.”

“Thank you,” Mecca said.

She was just happy to be laid up with her thang-thang, and nothing or no one in the world could ruin how she was feeling right then. She was about to be a paid bitch, and she was fucking arguably the finest nigga in all of Detroit. She had a nice home, the best clothes money could buy, jewelry out the ass, and a few European whips. Hell, she was doing a hellava lot better than most drug dealers, and she ain’t never sold one piece of nothing. She was winning.

Chapter 31

Less than twenty-four hours ago, Mecca was on top of the world, and a bitch couldn't tell her she wasn't. It's funny though what can change in the course of just one day. Mr. Haskins called Mecca and told her to meet him downtown at his office. He said that he had a copy of E-Way's estate. Mecca got all dolled up, then raced down to Mr. Haskins's office. From the moment she stepped foot in his office, she could sense that there was some shit in the game. She just had that feeling. It didn't feel the same as yesterday. Mr. Haskins even seemed a bit agitated, like he was wasting his time or something.

"Mecca, I've read over Matt's estate, and I must say that the young man had done quite well for himself. There's one thing that does concern me though."

"What's that?" Mecca asked, dreading the answer.

"He doesn't have a will. Just like many young millionaire black men, he didn't leave a will. He didn't think he would die at such an early age, so he didn't prepare one."

"So what does all that mean, and where does that leave me at?"

"According to the law, you and Matt were not considered to be husband and wife. Your relationship was all of six years long. That's one year short of seven, which is what the law deems to be substantial to justify a common-law marriage."

"So what are you saying?"

"Seeing as how Matt didn't leave a will, all of his assets will be released to his next of kin."

Mr. Haskins continued talking, but Mecca had zoned out. *Next of kin.* Momma's mush-mouth ass would get everything. Mecca's heart rate increased severely. *Oh, my God.* "What about my house?" she blurted and then waited for Mr. Haskins to respond.

He looked up with conviction in his eyes. "The house was in Matt's name also."

"They can't take my house. What am I going to do?"

"I suggest trying to reach a settlement with his next of kin before they decide to take everything."

Mecca thought for a moment. "Momma did offer to give me something. Can you set it up?"

"Yeah, I can give Matt's attorney a call and see what can work. If not, I'm afraid there isn't much else I can do."

"Well, call me just as soon as you get the word," Mecca said, standing and ending the meeting.

"Will do."

"Fuck! Fuck! Fuck!" Mecca screamed while slapping the steering wheel. She was sitting outside Mr. Haskins's office doing what she wanted to do when he broke the news to her. "You ain't leave me shit?" she asked, looking up at the sky. She quickly gathered her composure and thought about how she got her slice of the pie. She took a deep breath, then exhaled and started the car.

Within minutes, she was pulling in front of Momma's house. She told herself, *be nice, Mecca.*

The scene at Momma's was about the same as a few days ago, with the same drunk old men lining the porch, spectating.

"If it ain't my got damn birthday, what day is it?" the old man said as Mecca climbed the porch steps. "You missed me, uh? I knew you'd come back. They always do. Um huh, um hum."

Mecca paid the old bastards no mind. She rang the doorbell and looked through the front door, which was open. Momma's front door was always open. She believed that if you had to lock up your house, then you were in the wrong neighborhood. Soul food could be smelled burning in the kitchen. Momma was at work on her latest addition to the menu at her restaurant Mom Dukes. Mecca continued ringing the bell until Momma appeared.

"Just who in the hell is it?" Momma yelled while walking from the kitchen into the living room.

"It's me, Mecca."

"George, how come you ain't let the girl in?"

"Ain't my company," the old man said.

"Well, yo' ass can sleep out here on the porch tonight, how about that? Come on in, baby."

Mecca immediately started apologizing for the other day. She said that she was going through a lot, losing E-Way and all. She told Momma that she thought about it and wanted to just sign the forms so they could move forward.

Momma watched Mecca spill her guts. She knew it took everything Mecca had in her to come to her so humble, but Momma didn't care about that not one bit.

"Mecca, have you ever known me to BS anyone?"

"No."

"Well, I'm not going to start here today. Mecca, I know that you don't care for me, I do. But the feeling is mutual. I know you've been snooping around trying to figure out what's in Matt's will, because my attorney told me that you had signed some information release forms and hired an attorney. Furthermore, you know just as well as I do that Matt didn't leave a will and that you're pretty much out of the picture unless I say otherwise. The fact that you took me for a fool, as if you could walk into my house, sit across from me, and shoot a lie at me, doesn't sit well with me. And me knowing deep down the only reason you're here now is because you're assed out doesn't sit well with me either, so what I'm going to do is ask you to leave and never return to my house. You no longer welcome."

Mecca sat puzzled for a moment. She couldn't believe how real Momma had come at her. Mecca had to say something. *What about me? What am I going to get?* She wanted to ask it but couldn't find the words. Mecca had gotten the picture. In so many words, Momma had already answered her question. The answer was simple. Mecca wasn't getting shit if Momma had something to do with it.

Mecca got up from the chair and tried to casually walk out. Her world was crushed. Right now she hated E-Way. She hated him for not taking care of his business and leaving her fucked up. She hated herself for not taking care of her own business, for not making sure that E-Way put a will together with her name all over it.

Mecca drove home and climbed in bed. She didn't want to go to the shop, be with Drew, or nothing else. She just wanted to cry.

Chapter 32

"Can you zoom in any closer?"

"Yeah, hold on. It's harder to see at night than during the day. How about now, can you see?"

Mario was camped outside of Henry's in the parking lot with a private investigator he hired to follow his wife. So far, all the PI had been able to get were photographs but nothing solid. Mario was looking at the monitor of a video camera pointed at his wife, who was seated in her car with one of the dancers. Mario could see movement in the car but couldn't make out any details. "I can't believe this bitch," he said, watching from the distance.

"You wouldn't believe how many women I catch cheating on their husbands," the PI offered.

"What is she doing?" Mario asked, looking closer at the monitor. Mario's wife's head had disappeared.

"Looks like a blowjob to me. Come on, this is what we've been waiting for," the PI said, then grabbed the camera.

Together he and Mario crept out of the van they had been watching from and inched toward Mario's wife's car. The PI got all what he needed on tape. Mario's wife's head was going up and down on ole boy's dick.

"Tammy, what the fuck is you doing?" Mario yelled, banging on the driver's side window. Tammy was startled and caught red-handed. The dancer got out of the car and casually disappeared, not wanting to be there when shit got ugly.

"Baby, let me explain," Tammy pleaded.

"This ought to be good," the PI said, still recording the episode.

Mario wasn't the type of man to put his hands on a woman. It took everything he had in him to just walk away. His wife was crying and pulling on him, trying to get him to listen. But it was over and she knew it.

Mario wanted to kill something. He was steaming. He had the PI drop him off at his car. He drove with the music up full blast while crying. All he could think about was his daughter. Words couldn't describe the feelings that were going through him. He needed someone he could talk to, someone who would listen and would understand. He didn't call none of his partners because he knew that he'd break down in front of them, so he called Mecca.

Mecca's cell and house phone were off. She didn't feel like being bothered. She had been in the house ever since she learned that she wasn't getting anything from E-Way's estate.

Mario tried and tried again but got no answer. That didn't stop him though. He drove over to Mecca's house and rang the doorbell frantically.

"Who the hell?" Mecca said, getting up pissed. She thought about Benji. Maybe he was worried and was coming to check on her. Mecca peeped out to see Mario standing there looking distraught.

"Mario," she said, opening the door with surprise.

"Mecca, I know it's late, but I really need to talk to someone. Can I please come in?"

Mecca really didn't feel like being bothered, especially with Mario, seeing as how he hooked her up with that good-for-nothing attorney. But the look on Mario's face was so pitiful Mecca couldn't refuse him.

"Sure, come on in. Can I get you something to drink?" Mecca asked, leading Mario into the living room where she had been chillin'. She had the fireplace lit, a bottle of bubbly popped, and her theme song playing: "Love Don't Live Here" by Faith Evans.

"Sure," Mario said, flopping down on the sofa.

Mecca poured him a glass of champagne and filled her glass up. "So, what's going on?" asked Mecca, taking a seat next to Mario. She tucked her legs underneath her behind and faced him, ready to listen.

"I caught my wife cheating tonight. She was parked up at the damn Henry's Palace, giving some guy a head job."

"Are you serious?"

"Yeah, and I got it all on tape."

"Mario, I'm so sorry," Mecca said, setting her glass on the coffee table, then scooting closer to Mario so she could console him.

"I gave her everything. I never cheated on that woman one time. How could she do this?" Mario asked as he began breaking down.

Mecca could hear it in his voice. "It's okay, let it out. I'm here for you," she said, pulling Mario close to her breast, rubbing his head affectionately. Mario cried his eyes out on Mecca's shoulder. She couldn't help but feel sorry for him.

"You're a good man. Don't let this change who you are. You deserve better than that, you hear me? Look at me," Mecca said, sitting him up to face her. "You dry your eyes now. You'll get through this. I'll be right there for you." The bubbly was talking now.

The sight of a man crying just did something to Mecca. It lit her inside up with passion and desire. She and Mario looked eyes. They both saw something they wanted.

Mario leaned in for a kiss, and Mecca received him without refusal. His kiss was so sincere, and the way he held the side of her face with masculinity drove Mecca wild. They slid down from the sofa and lay spread out in front of the fireplace. They continued to kiss passionately, both forgetting about their current situations. Everything just seemed right. It wasn't love, or lust, it was just meant to be.

Chapter 33

Mecca woke up the following morning to find Mario lying closely behind her. His arm was wrapped around Mecca at the waist, pulling her close to his chest. Mecca yawned and stretched, then smiled down at Mario, who was still asleep. She thought about their passionate kiss. Nothing else happened. They both were still fully dressed with the exception of their shoes. Mecca couldn't remember the last time her G-spot had been hit just by kissing. She imagined just how the real thing would be.

Mario looked so peaceful that Mecca didn't want to wake him just yet. He looked like he hadn't had a good night's sleep in a while anyway. *Poor thing,* Mecca thought as she slowly got up, trying to be careful not to wake him. She showered, then cooked herself and Mario a big breakfast. The aroma from the sausage links and scrambled eggs woke Mario up. He stretched his arms out, then sat up, trying to gather his senses and figure out where he was. He could hear the sound of the links frying and Mecca moving about in the kitchen. Mario got up and went to the bathroom to wash his face, then entered the kitchen.

"Hey, sleepyhead. You hungry?" asked Mecca. She had a spread of everything: pancakes, eggs, links, orange juice, milk, doughnuts. It looked like a huge breakfast.

"You got somebody coming over?" asked Mario, looking at all the food.

"No, why you ask that?"

"'Cause I know just me and you aren't gon' eat all this."

"Variety is the spice of life. Come on and have a seat," Mecca said, fixing Mario a healthy plate. They pigged out, going for seconds and thirds. Mario was enjoying his food so much that he barely looked up from his plate.

"How's your food?" asked Mecca.

"Um," Mario moaned while chewing a mouthful of food. "I didn't know you could burn like this."

"Yeah, well. You know I does what I can do when I can," Mecca said, cheesing. "So what are you going to do with regard to your wife?"

"It's over," Mario answered dryly. "I can't forgive her for something like that. I can't."

"Well, if you need a place to stay until you can sort things out, you're more than welcome to the guest house."

"Thank you, but I can't impose on you like that."

"It's not a problem at all. Like I said, if you need me, I'm here."

"Thank you," Mario said sincerely as if he was now in debt to Mecca for her generosity.

Mecca cleaned up the dishes while Mario sat in the living room watching the morning news. She got dressed so she could go to the shop. She was in desperate need of a touch-up. And she missed Benji. She was a little upset that he hadn't checked up on her. Mecca stopped in the living room before leaving and handed Mario an extra set of house keys. "Use them if you need to."

"Thank you."

"Well, I'm getting ready to go get my hair and nails done, so call me if you need anything."

Neither she nor Mario had made mention of their romantic kiss last night. Mecca knew that it was probably best to try to forget about the kiss for right now and let Mario gather himself. But she told herself that it wasn't over.

She drove to the shop with the top down on her Beemer, listening to her theme song by Faith Evans. She pulled into her parking spot, then got out. The shop didn't feel the same as Mecca entered. Nobody was gossiping about others, and Tory wasn't being silly. There was something wrong. Something was missing.

"Where Benji, in the back?" Mecca asked, stopping in front of Marie's station.

Marie didn't say anything. She dropped her head so as not to make eye contact with Mecca. Marie didn't want to be the one to have to break the news to Mecca.

"Marie, you didn't hear me. Where's Benji?"

Again, Marie ignored Mecca. Mecca could tell by the look on Marie's face that there was something wrong. She turned toward Tory, who also didn't answer. Tae excused herself from her client and escorted Mecca into the back.

"What's wrong with everybody today? Tae, where is Benji?" Mecca demanded with fear in her voice.

"Have a seat," instructed Tae. "Benji is in the hospital. He's been in the hospital for two days now."

"Hospital! For what?"

"He's really sick."

"How come ain't nobody call me and let me know?"

"We tried calling, but your phone was off, and we kept getting your voicemail. You didn't check your messages?"

Mecca dug down into her purse and checked her phone. It was full with back-to-back messages. She felt horrible for going through her little stunt of saying "fuck the world." Here Benji was sick and needed her, and nobody couldn't get in touch with her because she had turned off her phones.

"Where is he?"

"Detroit Receiving Hospital."

"Can I go see him?"

"Yeah, visiting hours are in about a half an hour."

Mecca broke down at the sight of Benji laid up in that hospital bed with tubes up his nose and an IV running through his veins. Benji had been sleeping when Mecca entered his room. He woke up at the sound of Mecca sniffling and crying. She was holding his hand gently while looking down at his pale face.

"Hey, Mecca," Benji said, opening his eyes. The sight of Mecca brought a smile to his face. "I thought you weren't going to come and see me. I know how much you hate these places."

"Benji, what's wrong? What's all these tubes and stuff for?" Mecca asked, still crying.

"Chile, that sin drum is catching up with me."

"Sin drum?" Mecca repeated, confused.

"That sin drum as in syndrome that checks you the fuck out of here. AIDS, girl," laughed Benji. Despite his condition, he still had a sense of humor. He figured what's done was done.

"You're going to make it though, right?" Mecca asked.

"Mecca, I'm tired. I can't go on living like this."

"So what are you saying, you're just going to give up?"

"I'm not giving up. I'm just tired. I'm tired of taking all these different medications, losing weight then gaining weight. Look at me. I look like a got damn crackhead," Benji said, pointing to his arms and how skinny they had gotten. He started coughing real bad, sounding like he was about to cough up a lung or something.

Mecca patted him on the back and helped him sit up. "I didn't mean to upset you, Benji," Mecca said.

"I'm not upset. I'm just tired."

Mecca rubbed Benji's forehead and held his hand tightly until he drifted off to sleep. Mecca felt helpless seeing Benji laid up like that. She would have rather been the one lying in that bed verses Benji. That was how much love she had for him. He had to make it. He was all she had left. To hear Benji talk like that sent chills of fear down Mecca's spine. He just sounded defeated. That wasn't the Benji Mecca knew though. She knew a man a lot stronger than the one lying in that bed.

"You gotta make it," she whispered to Benji as he slept. "Bitch, we got shit to do, tags to pop, you hear me? You better not check out on me."

Mecca slept by Benji's bedside that night. She was awakened by a loud ruckus. Nurses and doctors were everywhere.

"What's going on?" she demanded.

"Get her out of here," one of the doctors ordered.

Benji gave Mecca a scare. He had to be hooked up to a respirator so that he could breathe properly. His immune system had started breaking down, and he couldn't breathe because his lungs weren't taking in enough oxygen. Benji looked like Christopher Reeve lying in that hospital bed with all that shit hooked up to him. The doctors made Mecca wash her hands and feet and then put on some scrubs before she was allowed back in, to prevent any germs from getting into Benji's system. They were afraid he was too far gone to fight any viruses off.

Mecca wanted to buy everything inside the gift shop. That still couldn't have expressed how much love she had for Benji though. Besides, them damn doctors wouldn't allow anything exposed to the air inside of Benji's room. All the restrictions just made Mecca think about how serious the matter was. She looked at Benji and cried, wondering how long it would be until she would be able to take Benji home so they could hit Henry's, talk about folks, go shopping, stunt on bitches, all the stuff they enjoyed doing together.

Everybody from the shop came to the hospital to show their love and support. Benji was loved by so many people. Visiting hours around the hospital lately looked more like a prison visiting hall. That was how many folks stopped by to see about ole Benji. No one minded having to wear the scrubs and all the restrictions because it was all love. Mario had called Mecca's cell, and she told him the news. He raced down to the hospital so he could support Mecca and Benji both.

"Mecca, you look exhausted," Mario said after coming out from seeing Benji.

"I am. I've been here since yesterday when I left you."

"Maybe you should go home and get some rest."

"I can't leave Benji here by himself."

"He's going to be fine, trust me. There are a hundred doctors and a thousand nurses running around here. Benji's going to be just fine. Let me drive you home so you can freshen up and catch a few z's, and then I'll bring you back."

Mario had a way of making things better or at least making them feel better. Mecca kissed Benji's hand and told him that she'd be back later that day to check on him. Benji was sound asleep. Even if he had been awake, he wouldn't have been able to talk with that respirator hooked to his mouth. On the way out, Mecca stopped one of the many doctors who were constantly checking on Benji. She asked the doctor just how long it would be before Benji was released. The doctor had been asked that question at least several hundred times, and yet it still seemed like the first. There was no set way to tell someone's loved one that he or she wasn't going to make it, and the truth of the matter was that Benji probably would never be released, unless it was to the morgue. So to save her the heartache, the doctor lied.

"It shouldn't be that long. We just want to make sure everything's in check before we release him. Not to worry."

"Thank you," Mecca said, smiling.

The doctor thought, *at times I guess it's best to just tell folks what they want to hear and just deal with reality when the time comes.*

Mario drove Mecca home and cooked breakfast while she showered and got herself together. He hadn't been home or talked to his wife since he caught her up at Henry's with ole boy. Being there for Mecca helped him block out what he was going through himself. His wife had been blowing up his cell phone and his phone at the studio, leaving three-minute messages about how sorry she was and that they needed to talk. Mario had listened to them all while at Mecca's house. He made his mind up that it was over, that there was nothing to talk about.

Mecca didn't have much of an appetite. She picked over her food, taking small bites. Mario sat across from her, chowing down on his meal. He looked up from his plate and could see that Mecca was stressing.

"When was the last time you had a massage?" asked Mario.

It had been a good while. The last massage Mecca had was from E-Way. "Why you ask that?"

"Because I can see you've got a lot on your mind, and one of the best stress relievers is a massage. Come on, I give a mean back and neck massage."

"I'm really not in the mood."

"Nah, I insist," Mario said, getting up to scrape the dishes. He grabbed Mecca by the hand and then led her into the living room. He instructed her to lie flat on her stomach. Mecca lay spread-eagle across her deep plush carpet. She tried to relax as Mario began working his magic. Mecca closed her eyes and sighed deeply when

Mario cracked her neck all the way down to her back. "Oh, my God," Mecca said.

"Hold on, I'm not finished. I'm just getting started." Mario lifted Mecca's arms with one hand, guiding them in certain directions, while he applied pressure to her back with the other hand. Mecca's back cracked in a hundred different places. She felt like she was visiting a professional chiropractor. Mario worked his way down to Mecca's feet, sending chills back up to her skull. His touch was so authentic, so strong and demanding, she had to stop him. Mario's hands were sensual. He knew his way around the woman's body and how to touch it.

"Your feet are so pretty I could massage them all day," Mario said, still rubbing Mecca's feet.

Mecca blushed and pulled her feet back. "You're just saying that to make me feel better."

Mario inched closer to Mecca, looking her dead in the eyes, then said, "I'm serious. Mecca, the first day I laid eyes on you I wanted to get up with you, but I was happily married at the time and you, of course, were with E-Way. I just saw it as inappropriate to try to cross those boundaries."

Mecca didn't say anything. She listened with a shocked look on her face.

"Mecca, have you ever met someone and from the moment you saw that person, somehow you knew you two would be together?"

"I don't know. I never thought about it."

Mario reached for Mecca's face, pulling her to him, then kissed her. He kissed her for all of five minutes. Mecca enjoyed every second of it. Mario suddenly stopped, then asked, "Does it feel right?"

"Yeah," Mecca answered, sounding like a little girl.

"Well, kiss me," Mario said.

Mecca did as she was told. She leaned in, kissing Mario like she had never kissed any man before. She lay stretched out on top of Mario, kissing him all over his neck and face. She unbuttoned his shirt, exposing his hairy, masculine chest. She kissed his chest and sucked his nipples seductively, working her way down to Mario's Johnson. She unbuttoned his pants and then helped him out of them. She watched in awe as his big, thick dick plopped out of his boxers. Mecca grabbed hold of Mario's manhood and kissed it all over while using Mario's precum as lubrication, jacking him softly.

Mecca inhaled the head of Mario's dick, taking small portions of him in and out of her mouth. She teased the head of his dick, flicking her tongue at it, then licking it all around and suddenly putting it back in her mouth. She sucked him while lying across his stomach with her eyes closed. Mario was gripping the carpet, trying to hold back his nut, but Mecca sucked it out of him. She looked up into Mario's eyes as he began cumming in her mouth. She jacked him while drinking all that came out until Mario was drained.

"Get it back up," Mecca said seductively, still jacking Mario's dick. Mecca put Mario's dick back in her mouth and sucked it back to life. She stripped out of her nightgown and then climbed on top of Mario, reaching for his dick. She slowly put the head of his dick inside her and then sighed. Mario grabbed Mecca by the waist and pulled her down onto his dick, ripping Mecca's pussy walls open. "Oh," Mecca sighed. Mario slid Mecca up and down on his dick violently. Mecca was leaning forward over Mario with her titties in his face, and she gripped the carpet and bit her bottom lip while looking up at the ceiling. Mecca was throwing her ass everywhere in a rhythm trying to work Mario out of another nut and get hers off at the same time.

"Oh, my God. Oh, fuck, shit," Mario babbled as he shot an ounce of semen all over Mecca's ass crack and up her back. Mecca reached down and put Mario back inside of her after he finished ejaculating. She lay across his chest, exhausted, while Mario rubbed her hair. They lay there in silence. The moment felt so right but still seemed awkward and inappropriate.

"Mario," Mecca said, sitting up to face him.

"Yeah, Mecca."

"Do you feel . . ."

"Awkward?"

"Yes, that's the word I'm looking for."

"A little, probably because of the circumstances surrounding the whole matter. I kind of feel just as guilty as my wife now."

"Well, what are we going to do, pretend as if this never existed?"

"Not at all," Mario said, sitting up, looking Mecca in the eyes. "I think that we should definitely consider our feelings, because although it's seeming awkward right now, what about tomorrow and the next day? I'm certain that you'll be all I can think about."

Mecca blushed, then leaned forward and gave Mario a kiss. *The hell with his wife. And E-Way is dead and gone. Life goes on.*

Chapter 34

Every day Mecca went to visit Benji at the hospital. She would be right there as soon as visiting hours began and would stay until the doctors put her out. It had been two weeks since Benji was first admitted into Detroit Receiving Hospital, and about a week and a half since being hooked up to the respirator. The doctors still hadn't removed the respirator from Benji's mouth. It limited his speech severely and it caused him to be drowsy all day long. Mecca would read to him from *Jet* magazine, *Sister 2 Sister, Ebony, Vogue,* and every other publication that was gossiping about folks. Benji would smile and point as Mecca read. Hearing the latest dirt seemed to keep him alive.

After reading, Mecca would inform Benji of all of her latest affairs with Mario and the ordeal with E-Way's estate planning.

"What about donkey dick?" Benji joked.

"Who?" Mecca laughed.

"Drew."

"Oh, I haven't been to see him lately. It's been up here to see you, to the shop, and home to fuck Mario's fine ass. I got that nigga right where I want him, too, with his nose wide open."

"What about his wife?"

"Shit, what about her? Mario put the rush on his divorce papers, and just as soon as that's finalized, we're going public."

"You sound like you're involved in a Hollywood scandal. 'We're going public.'"

Mecca and Benji both laughed. They would go on gossiping all day until visiting hours were over or Benji's medication kicked in, whichever came first. Mecca would kiss Benji on the forehead before leaving, promising she'd be the first one he'd see when he opened his eyes tomorrow. On her way out, Mecca was stopped by Benji's doctor. He said that he had a concern that needed to be addressed.

"Oh, my God, is Benji going to be all right?" she asked frantically.

"As of right now, he's stable, but that's not my concern." The doctor went on telling Mecca how Benji's insurance had run out and basically that money was needed. For the around-the-clock intensive care Benji was receiving to all the medications, the doctor estimated a few hundred thousand dollars was needed. He looked at Mecca as if to say, "We need our damn money or else."

Mecca was studding what that pale-face devil was talkin' about. She politely excused herself. *The nerve of the Yankee. Use some type of government funding or some of those kickbacks y'all receive every year for undertreating mothafuckas,* Mecca thought. She knew that they couldn't just kick Benji out of the hospital in his condition, at least that's what she was hoping. Mecca felt sorry. She wanted Benji to receive the best damn medical treatment money could buy, but as of right now she didn't have any money. Momma was trying to take it all.

Mecca had a late meeting scheduled with Mr. Haskins. She sat impatiently in Mr. Haskins's office, tapping her feet a mile a second. Butterflies and anxiety filled the depths of her stomach as she waited for Mr. Haskins to end the conversation he had been having when she walked in.

"Okay, bye now," Mr. Haskins said, hanging up the phone. "Mecca, Mecca, Mecca. It doesn't look good." Mr. Haskins shuffled through some papers on his desk. He didn't spare Mecca the heartache one bit. He just gave her the news.

"As we both know, Matt didn't leave a will. I talked to his grandmother's attorney regarding a settlement, and she's not budging. She wants all that she has coming, which is everything."

"What about my house?"

"Oh, you mean Matt's old house, which is now Grandma's house. She's willing to sell it to you at fair market price."

"She can't take my fuckin' house."

"You do mean her house, of course. Anyhow, she has given you ninety days to enter into a contract. Otherwise, she'll put it up for sale to the general public."

"So that's just it?" Mecca asked, baffled.

"Yep, unless we have something else to discuss, that's about it," Mr. Haskins said, tapping his fingers across his desk. There wasn't really no sweat off his back, except his commission, but he'd live. He hadn't just lost his livelihood like Mecca.

Mecca wanted to reach across that desk and strangle his bitch ass. Somebody! She felt defeated in every sense of the word. How could this be happening? She got up and shot Mr. Haskins a look of death, then stormed out of his office.

"Over my dead body. Ain't nobody taking my damn house," Mecca cried while driving home.

Chapter 35

Mecca was so stressed out from the latest news regarding E-Way's estate that she overslept. She woke up to the sound of her house phone ringing. She rolled over, looking at the clock before answering the phone. It was eleven o'clock in the morning. Where was Mario?

It was the hospital calling. They said that it was an emergency regarding Benji and that she needed to come to the hospital immediately.

"Is everything all right?" Mecca asked nervously.

The hospital wouldn't give any details over the phone. They were calling because Mecca was listed as the emergency contact. Mecca slammed the phone down in whoever's ear who was only trying to help, but Mecca wasn't impressed. She rolled out of bed, scrambling toward her closet, grabbing at anything to wear. She washed her face and was out the door.

"Please let Benji be all right," Mecca repeated while driving like a bat out of hell and while on the elevator on her way up to Benji's hospital room.

It was too late. Nothing but sad faces and deep cries could be seen and heard outside of Benji's room. His visitors each learned the news as they tried to visit their friend Benji. Tory and Tae rushed over to Mecca and gave her a hug, both crying their eyes out.

"What's wrong with Benji?" asked Mecca, dreading the answer.

"He's gone, Mecca. He passed away this morning," Tae informed her.

Mecca broke away from Tae and Tory, charging toward Benji's room, but was stopped at the door by a nurse and two doctors.

"Get the fuck out of my way," Mecca yelled and tried pushing past them but was unable.

"Miss, please calm down," one of the doctors said. Mecca was going berserk. One of the doctors took Mecca into his arms, hugging her while she let it all out.

"No! No!" Mecca screamed as she cried her lungs out on the doctor's shoulder. "Where is he?" Mecca demanded.

"And you are?" asked one of the nurses.

"Mecca Tobias."

"You'll have to identify the body down at the morgue before it's released to the family. I'm afraid you won't be able to see the body until then," said the nurse, then walked away.

Just like that, Benji was gone. Mecca continued to scream and cry not wanting to believe it. She knew she'd wake up at any moment. This had to be a bad dream. Benji couldn't be dead.

"No," Mecca screamed through the halls of the hospital and on the elevator as Tae and Tory dragged her by the arm. They drove Mecca downtown to the morgue so that she could identify Benji's body. Benji had beaten them there. It seemed as though the hospital had a teleport machine inside of it, because once a person died, they wasted no time getting them to the morgue. Mecca thought, *I guess death is nothing to the doctors and nurses. They've seen so many pass that it's like, oh, well, back to work.*

Mecca felt like the hospital purposely killed Benji because he couldn't afford the medical bills. Maybe they poisoned him or cut his respirator off. She wanted to believe anything except the fact that Benji was gone.

The morgue was ice cold on the inside. The smell that emerged in the air was that of death. It sent chills down Tae's, Tory's, and Mecca's backs as they entered. They were buzzed in by a security guard after Mecca gave the guard her name and who she was there to identify. The guard let them through the dimly lit freezer, passing lots of unidentified bodies that had been there for anywhere from a day to a few weeks. The guard looked at each toe tag as he passed the corpses in search of Benji. Mecca, Tae, and Tory walked close to one another, holding on to each other's hands and shoulders.

"Here we are," the guard said, stopping in front of a body covered with a large white sheet.

Mecca immediately broke down. She knew Benji like the back of her hand. She could identify him just by looking at his feet. She cried and cried some more when the guard snatched back the sheet, revealing Benji's feminine face. The moans and deep cries confirmed Benji's identity. The guard pulled the sheet back over Benji's face, then approached Mecca, clipboard in hand. He didn't even give the sista a chance to recover and gather her composure.

"Ma'am, I'm going to need for you to sign here, here, and here. All this is saying is that you are who you say you are, you've identified the body, and the body is to be released to whatever funeral home you desire."

Tory snarled at the guard, then snatched the clipboard from him. She scribbled Mecca's initials down and then slapped the clipboard into the guard's chest. "Come on, Mecca," Tae said, ushering Mecca out to the car.

Mecca still couldn't believe that Benji was dead. "What am I going to do?" Mecca cried, asking Tae.

"Baby, you've got to be strong and keep on keepin' on. I know that's what Benji would want you to do. It's going to take some time, but we'll get through this. I promise," Tae said, holding Mecca's hand while driving.

Just when it seemed matters couldn't get any worse, there was a crew of workers on Mecca's front lawn staking a Century 21 FOR SALE sign in the ground as they pulled up.

"Mecca, I didn't know that you were selling your house," Tory said from the back seat.

Mecca hadn't seen the crew because she had her head down while listening to Tae. She looked up at the workers and felt defeated. "It's a long story," she said, thanking Tae and Tory for their support and concern. Mecca gave her car keys to Tory and asked her to please bring her car over when she got a chance.

Grams didn't waste any time selling the house. Once Mr. Haskins contacted her attorney with the news that Mecca wasn't interested in buying the home, Momma contacted a real estate agent to represent the sale. Mecca didn't even acknowledge the workers on her way in. She told herself she'd let the insurance lapse and then mysteriously burn the son of a bitch down. All Momma would be able to sell were some damn ashes.

Chapter 36

The following day, the trial for E-Way's murder was set to start. Big Whitney was the State's star witness against Chuck and Chuckie Bom's and of course himself. The State offered Big Whitney twenty-five years to life with a chance of parole for his testimony. Kev was killed during a standoff with the SWAT team and Detroit Police. He vowed not to be taken alive, because he knew with Whit telling, they'd never walk the streets again.

It was ten minutes after ten, and jury selection had just been completed. On today's agenda were opening statements by both the State and Chuck and Chuckie Bom's court-appointed mouthpieces. Then the jury would hear testimony from the fat rat, Big Whitney.

The trial was to be a short one, straight down to the nitty-gritty. It was expected to last only two days. Everyone was present: Momma, all of her church folks, E-Way's family, everyone with the exception of Mecca. She knew what today was and what it entailed. Hell, it was marked on her calendar on the refrigerator. She wasn't going because she felt betrayed by Momma and by E-Way. *How could he leave me fucked up in the game like this?* Mecca tried rationalizing to herself. She figured she had far more to worry about right now than to be downtown in somebody's courthouse.

"Come on, the trial has already started," Mario said, pulling the sheets off Mecca. He had been up early taking care of some business. He just knew that by the time he got back, Mecca would be long gone.

"I'm not going," Mecca said, yanking back the sheets.

"And give me one good reason, and it better be a hellava good one," Mario demanded.

Mecca didn't want to tell Mario the real reason, her being selfish, only thinking about herself.

"Well, I'm waiting."

"I'm just not going. I don't feel like it."

"Correct me if I'm wrong, but you did love E-Way, didn't you?"

"Of course."

"So what's the difference?"

Mecca couldn't answer the question, but she got the point. "You make me sick always being right."

"G'on and get ready. I'll be downstairs waiting."

Big Whitney had just taken the stand when Mecca and Mario busted into the courtroom. All eyes turned in their direction, and whispers were all that could be heard. "She got some nerve bringing that nigga up in here," E-Way's cousin Felicia said loud enough for Mecca to hear as she walked past. Their entrance had taken away the focus of the trial.

"Order in the court!" yelled the judge.

The courtroom quieted down like a roomful of third graders.

"Now if everyone is finished, I'd like to get back to the issue at hand. Please resume, Mr. Jenkins."

Mr. Jenkins was the prosecuting attorney for the State. "Mr. Jones, please describe for the court and jury the night of the murder. And please talk into the microphone."

"Well, we all went to Pretty Woman strip club that night. Me, Chuck, Kev, E-Way, and Chuckie Bom's. E-Way had picked all us up earlier that day in his new Bentley. We rode around for a while and then went to the club. While

E-Way got up to use the restroom, Kev said that we were going to do it tonight."

"Could you please be more specific? When you say, 'We were going to do it tonight,' what do you mean by 'do it'?" asked the prosecutor.

"Kill him."

"Why that night?"

"We had been plotting to rob and kill Matt for a while. We just never could catch him at the right time with the money. We broke into his house, but we didn't find any money or drugs. It was pure jealousy on all our parts, and when Matt pulled in that new Bentley, we couldn't stand it. It went from robbing to killing him. Just wanting him dead."

Big Whitney broke down the entire ordeal behind E-Way's murder, along with Bubbles's murder. People were in awe as they continued listening to the senseless plot. The State showed pictures of E-Way when his body was discovered. White mice could be seen still alive in the graphic photos. Chuck's and Chucky Boom's court-appointed lawyers put up minimum arguments. They knew it was over. It was just a matter of going through the motions, and then off to Jackson State Penitentiary.

Big Whitney broke out into tears, offering apologies to everyone, Momma in particular. "Momma, I'm sorry," he said.

"I am not your momma!" Grams shouted in anger, then broke down into tears. "Why would you do that to my boy?" she yelled, demanding an answer.

There was no logical explanation in the world either one of them could have given Momma. Chuck and Chuckie Bom's sat at the defense table as if nothing were said.

"You bastards," Momma shot in their direction as she headed out of the courtroom. She had more than she could stand. She'd be back on sentencing day, best believe, so she could watch them receive their sentences of eternity.

Mecca couldn't help but share the same emotions as Momma. She mean mugged all three of them. If only she had a gun. There would be a scene from *A Time to Kill* up in that courtroom. Mecca snarled at them until her anger rose and she began breathing heavily. Tears fell from her eyes as she looked at the photos of E-Way lying dead in the trunk of his car. *If E-Way had left them niggas in the ghetto where they belong, he'd still be alive.*

She got up and grabbed her purse, then stormed out of the courtroom. That was some closure, Mecca thought. *They asses need to be killed and tortured just like they did E-Way.* That was the only closure she was interested in, because them getting life sentences didn't mean shit. They would still be able to walk around, talk to family, eat, work out, and occasionally smile. *What they asses need is to die.*

Chapter 37

Folks from all ends of Detroit and other major cities were in attendance to pay their last respects to ole Benji at his funeral. He didn't have a family. He and Mecca were the only family he knew. But like he used to always say, "Sometimes you gotta make your own family." Everyone loved Benji. You could sense that people were there in his best interest and not just to be seen in their new outfits. If you met Benji just once, he'd left a lasting impression on you forever, and you wouldn't mind being in his company again. People filled the pews of New Missionary Baptist Church, some standing in aisles, and those who couldn't fit inside the church watched the service from outside on a large projector and surround-sound system. There were so many people you'd have thought a celebrity had passed.

Benji went out in style. Mecca couldn't see him going out no other way but in class. He was dressed in all white, white slacks with a white silk and velvet blazer, and of course his signature necktie. Two diamond studs were placed in Benji's ear, and he wore a sparkling gold necklace and cross. Mecca would do her best to make sure Benji went in the ground wearing it. His hair was freshly groomed in its usual style, short perm-brushed waves, and his face was nicely done with a bit of foundation. Benji looked so peaceful lying inside his cherry-oakwood casket with eighteen-karat gold trimmings. He looked as if he were just taking a nap.

Mecca looked down at her friend and remembered him telling her how tired he was. He appeared to be finally at rest. There was so much Mecca wanted to say, but she couldn't find the words. People stood back and let Mecca have her last moment with Benji. She held his hand while softly crying, trying to hold herself together. She knew Benji would want her to be the strongest one in the room, and even with him lying dead in the casket, Mecca could still feel his strong presence. She could still hear his authentic high-pitched voice.

"'Details, bitch,'" Mecca laughed to herself. "I promise to always keep you posted on the details," Mecca said, smiling. "Benji, I'ma miss you."

The tears were flowing. Mecca couldn't hold them back any longer. To stay strong, she had to end her talk with Benji. She leaned forward and kissed Benji on the cheek, rubbed his hair, took one final look at him, then took her seat.

It's like people don't know just when to give a motha-fucka they space and whatnot. Mecca knew deep down that everyone offering condolences was only trying to help. But Mecca didn't care for their support. No one shared in that pain. She just wanted to scream and tell everybody to get the fuck out of her face! Mario was the only comfort Mecca felt. He held her close to his shoulder while they listened to the many eulogies. Everybody had at least ten stories about Benji, all good times. The folks telling the stories lit up as they relived the unforgettable, once-in-a-lifetime experiences. They all left the podium still smiling with tears in their eyes. It's not too often in life you'd meet a person such as Benji. He had that effect on people.

Mecca was set to be the last speaker. Mario helped her to the stage and to the podium. Mecca knew she'd only be able to get a few words out, maybe even a paragraph, before she broke down into tears. She took a look at the enormous crowd before her and then took a deep breath.

"You know, as I stand here today, I feel like I'm the one lying in a casket. I can't begin to explain what Benji was to me. He was my best friend, confidant, shopping buddy, business partner, my backbone," Mecca said, as the tears welled up in her eyes.

She wiped them before they could stream down her face. She was determined to finish her speech. "Benji was my brother. All who know us knew we did everything together. My big brother," Mecca said, looking down into Benji's casket. "He taught me everything: how to cook, how to pay bills, how to take care of myself as a woman. I don't know what I'll do without him. I remember him telling me a while back that love will only let you down! At the time I really didn't grasp what he was saying. But today, I know that to be the truth. And as selfish as it may sound, he let me down."

Mecca hadn't prepared a speech. She just said what was in her heart. She concluded her eulogy by saying that she would always keep Benji in her heart, and that he would be forever missed.

A reception was held for close friends at the VFW hall. Mecca and Mario went to just thank everyone for their support in such a time of need. Mecca paid for all the food, drinks, and entertainment. Yet and still, she didn't stay to enjoy the festivities. She ordered Mario to drive her home because she wasn't feeling well. On their way home, Mario stopped at the gas station on 7 Mile and Syracuse to pick up some Tylenol for Mecca's headache.

"Oh, my God," Mario said as he pulled into the gas station. He looked over at Mecca to see if she had seen what he had. He tried to turn back out of the gas station, but Mecca stopped him. It was too late.

"Nah, it's okay," Mecca said.

"Are you sure? We can stop somewhere else," said Mario.

"Yeah, I'm sure. I need to get this off my chest anyway," Mecca said, opening the car door.

It was her mother, Yvette. She was standing next to the entrance of the gas station, panhandling. She looked like her old self again, the way Mecca had grown to know and hate her. Yvette hadn't seen Mecca get out of the car. She was too busy begging so she could get a fix.

Mecca walked right up to her and looked her up and down in disgust. "Look at you," Mecca said harshly, breaking Yvette's crack concentration.

"Baby girl. How you doing? I knew you'd come check up on yo' momma."

"You're not my mother," Mecca said as if she wanted to kill Yvette. "You couldn't even be there for me when I needed you most. When E-Way passed, you left me like you always do when things get tough. You don't have the right to call yourself my mother, so stop saying it."

Mecca was going off. People were stopping and looking on, but she didn't give a damn. She just needed to vent. "Do you know where I'm coming from right now? Take one guess. Benji's funeral!"

Yvette's eyes bucked at the news. She looked like she'd just smoked a rock.

"That's right, Yvette, Benji's dead. And you missed his funeral because you out here doing God knows what to get some damn crack. The same person who helped you at one point get off crack, and you couldn't even be there for him. You know why, Yvette? 'Cause you don't love nobody. Not even yourself. I hate you. Move," Mecca said, stepping inside the service station. She stood at the counter and watched as Yvette climbed into the passenger side of some white guy's pickup. A few words were exchanged, and then they disappeared into traffic.

Mecca watched the taillights of the pickup and wondered if she'd ever see Yvette again.

Epilogue

One Year Later

Mecca frequently visited Benji's grave and gave him all the "details" and goings-on in her life and others. She would sometime sit out there for hours as if she were having a real conversation. She really missed Benji.

The shop was still booming with gossip on top of more gossip, but it was still missing Benji. Mecca hung a large photo of Benji in the shop's entrance in memory of him.

Mecca had stopped messing around with ole Drew. His ass and Henry's Palace were played out. They had a new spot jumping called Swerve. It was nothing but Henry's on steroids.

Nowadays though, Mecca had to be careful if she didn't want to come up short in the game. Momma sold the house and took the cars, everything except the shop, which was in Benji's name. It didn't take Mecca long to bounce back though. She had sunken her claws into Mario.

One day they were dining out when two of Mario's ex-wife Tammy's best friends spotted them. They called Tammy, who raced down to Floods, blowing up the scene.

"So, this bitch you call yourself leaving me for?" Tammy asked boldly as she stood over Mecca, looking her up and down. She immediately recognized Mecca from the night at Henry's when they had words. "Bitch, you tryin' to be me?" she spat. Tammy thought Mecca had maybe been responsible for her divorce.

"Tammy, what do you want?" Mario asked.

It was quite clear what she wanted. She wanted blood, Mecca's blood. But Mecca sat unfazed by the slight situation. She sat back and let Mario defuse the matter. She figured there was no sense in her fighting and carrying on. She had already won. Mecca grabbed her glass of bubbly and smiled as she raised it slowly to her mouth so the three bitches could get a full view of the five-carat rock Mario had recently put on her finger. The lighting in the place caused the diamond to flicker then sparkle all in their faces.

Not being able to withstand the torment, one of Tammy's girls said, "Beat that bitch ass!" Tammy lunged toward Mecca, but Mario and the bar's owner intervened. Mecca continued sipping her champagne while quietly laughing at the women as they were dragged outside. Mario returned and apologized. He felt so embarrassed.

"It's okay, baby. Come on, let's go home," Mecca said.

After Mecca and Mario tied the knot, Mecca made him buy a house twice the size as the one he lived in with his wife. And this time she made sure that "Mecca Tobias" was written on the deed of trust. Her name was on everything: the cars, life insurance policies, bank accounts, credit cards, and yes, the will.

Mecca had learned her lesson about putting her faith in others. She vowed never to love again. Because every time she played that silly game called love, she lost horribly.

She didn't even love Mario. The only reason she married him was because it was convenient for her. Because in the end a bitch still needed Prada, Gucci, Fendi . . .